CAR CRASH

T.GEPHART

Car Crash
Published by T Gephart
Copyright 2019 T Gephart

ISBN-13: 978–0-6483959–1-1
ISBN-10: 0–6483959–1-X

Discover other titles by T Gephart on
Facebook, Twitter, Goodreads, or *tgephart.com*

Cover by Hang Le

Editing by Insight Editing Services

Formatting by Type A Formatting

DEDICATION

To Christine, it's been a pleasure and an honour.
Thanks for the love.

DALLAS

JESUS. FUCKING. CHRIST.

She was crying.

Not just a little bit, but full-blown bawling.

Fuck.

I wasn't good with tears, especially not after sex.

"Umm, baby?" I was freaking confused, wondering if I hadn't pounded her so hard I'd shaken something loose.

Her shoulders shook, wrapping the sheet around her body as she blubbered into her hands while I looked on in panic.

"Oh, Dallas." Her voice warbled as she peeked through her fingers. "That was my first time."

First time?

"Your first orgasm, baby?" Sure, I'd given her three, but I wasn't going to get hung up on semantics. Hard to believe I was the first guy to ring her bell in twenty-three years, but some assholes had no idea what they were doing down there. I, on the other hand, was a master.

A clit whisperer.

Lots of guys made all sorts of claims but weren't up to the

job. They got tired, impatient, or even worse, selfish. It wasn't easy, but when you got that toe-curling scream and the wide-eyed surprise of a really good earthshattering O, it made you feel like Superman. And let me tell you that I prided myself in giving her two or three before I'd chase down my own.

That's the type of guy I was.

Such a giver.

I could make a girl come with any part of my body; I was just that good. So if I, the Master, was able to achieve what other men hadn't been able to, I was pretty fucking stoked.

"No," she whispered, her eyes stained red from the waterworks. "I mean, *yes* it was my first orgasm with a man, but I meant it was . . . that was my first time having sex."

Hold.

The.

Fucking.

Phone.

A virgin.

I'd just had sex with a . . . *virgin?*

I might have been the clit whisperer, but actor I was not. So there was no chance I was able to hide the fucking shock and surprise that tackled me like a linebacker as I tried to get my head around what she was saying.

A virgin.

Shit.

"Babe, why didn't you tell me?"

Not to say that I still wouldn't have fucked her—she was five different kinds of hot and had been giving me the "look" for close to an hour at the bar earlier that night—but I'd have liked to have had that knowledge before I'd done the deed.

Lots of aftercare with virgins, and not that I didn't like to plant my flag where no other man had been—it was actually pretty freaking sweet—I just didn't have the time to dedicate to the cause considering I hadn't planned to spend the night.

If I left, I was an asshole, and if I stayed, I was giving her false hope that we were more than just the one-night stand I'd assumed we were. It wasn't personal, I mean, I could barely remember her name.

Kelly?

Kate?

Kara?

Pretty sure it started with K, but I went with babe all the same just to make sure she didn't knee me in the nuts for calling her something else.

She flicked her red hair out of her eyes as her gaze shifted to me. "I thought you would turn me down, and I really wanted to have sex with you."

I ran my hand along her chin, trying to reassure her we were all good even though I was slightly freaking out. "Babe, I wouldn't have turned you down, just would have been more careful with you. Did I hurt you?"

"No, it was perfect. You were perfect." She sniffed, turning to snuggle into my arms.

Ah.

Crap.

When it came to commitment, I wanted none of it. Girlfriends were a complication I didn't need or want, especially since I was enjoying the many choices I had available. Not to say that eventually I wouldn't settle down with one woman, probably like when I was George Clooney's age or something like that. But for now, the idea of being tied down when I was in my prime gave me a rash just thinking about it.

Surely I owed it to myself to play the field while I was able to, right? Share myself with the many rather than confine myself to one person. Besides, I'd never met a woman I could even contemplate long-term with, so why waste their time and my own for something that would only end up with both of us resenting each other. So yeah, what I was doing was definitely better.

When I'd met her earlier in the night I thought we were on the same page. I always made it clear that I'm not boyfriend material and for the most part, everyone is A-Okay with the hook-up scenario. I always made sure they were well and truly taken care of before I blew my load, and never did shady shit like say I'm in love with them.

But, every once in a while, I will stumble headfirst into a *Fixer Upper*. They see me—the tats, the hair, the piercings and the attitude—and think I'm playing a bad boy for Halloween. Suddenly, the mind-blowing sex—nothing more—we all agreed on is no longer enough and I become a fucking project. Like I can be trained like a border collie with some treats and enough "good boys."

Not to say I don't like treats and praise, and when given in the right context, I will sit up and bark if that's what a girl was into. But, being tricked into a relationship was definitely not cool, and while I might have fallen for it a few times in the past, my eyes were wide open now.

And fucking a virgin was a game changer with an added degree of danger.

Fuck.

"So . . . I guess I should go."

Asshole it was.

Honestly, I didn't like being a prick. I got no joy out of it and it didn't make me feel warm and fuzzy. But confronted with the reality, I was in over my head. Better for her to hate me now before she got even more attached; it was a price I had to pay for being a sex god.

Her head snapped up, her tits bouncing a little as she sucked in a few quick breaths. "You're leaving? But I just told you—"

"I know, babydoll." I stopped, not needing the repeat. "And I'm glad I was your first. At least now you know what it should feel like." I moved out of the bed knowing my window to get out of Dodge was getting smaller by the second. "So if the next dude pumps you twice and then blows his load, you know to kick him to the curb. You deserve the best."

The men in her future were most likely going to be a disappointment but that wasn't my problem to solve. Nope, that was between her and whoever came after, all of which were none of my business. I'd fulfilled my end of the bargain and that was to blow her mind.

Which I did.

Three freaking times.

Reaching down, I pulled on my jeans, opting to go commando than waste time with boxers. My departure was time sensitive, and the longer I lingered the more chance there was of shit going bad.

She watched me with interest, her eyes narrowed like she wasn't hearing my words right. But I wasn't about to give her a repeat—either with my words or my dick—so I ignored the staring competition and continued to get dressed.

"Okay, sweet stuff." I was no closer to remembering her name. "Tonight was great." I gave her a quick wink, shoved my feet into my boots and my boxers into my pocket. "I'll see you around."

And with a quick wave, I turned and headed toward the door, counting the steps until I was finally free.

"You're an asshole, Dallas," she screamed, a shoe hitting the wall beside me before I'd made it safely outside.

I didn't stop.

Couldn't.

I wasn't sure if she was going to continue to be happy tossing shoes or if something else would come flying. Maybe her aim would improve, needing a throw or two before she was warmed up. Not a risk I was willing to take as I slammed the door behind me and jogged down her street in the dark.

It wasn't ideal, and not how I'd planned the rest of my night. I'd have preferred to have banged her a few more times, had breakfast in the morning and then weaseled a ride to the shop. My house was out of the question for obvious reasons—I didn't want a woman I barely knew knowing where I lived—but considering she'd already been to where I worked, there was no harm in her taking me back there. Not that it mattered now, a man had to do what a man had to do, and currently that man was double-timing it away from her house as I pulled out my phone and made a call.

"You in trouble again?" Josh's voice was surprisingly chipper considering it was close to midnight. Not that my best friend wasn't the best wingman of all time, but since he'd shacked up with his smoking-hot woman, he was less enthusiastic about nighttime bailouts.

"Dude, I need you to come get me. I left my car at the shop and I'm in the city." I glanced over my shoulder, checking I didn't have a tail. "Shit got complicated and my night didn't pan out as expected."

The bastard laughed, his throaty voice exploding into my ear as I rounded the corner and hit the main street. "Really?" he asked, but not sounding surprised. "Tell me where you are, dipshit, and I'll come get your sorry ass."

Out of the corner of my eye, I spied an all-night diner and made my way over. I gave Josh my location and decided to chill until he arrived. Besides, I could always eat, and pie was one of my favorite things. Pun totally intended.

The bells on the door of the diner jingled as I pushed it open. There were a few people inside but none of them paid me any mind as I slipped into a booth and breathed a sigh of relief.

Clean getaway.

Now all I had to do was sit tight and wait for my ride to get here.

Nothing to worry about at all.

Josh was the real deal.

I'd known the dude since junior high and we were tight. Not only was he like a brother to me—considering I had none of my own—but I also spent almost every day with the guy. Well, technically he was my boss, but neither of us really bought into that bullshit. Nope, Art Addiction might have Josh's name on the door but I was just as important.

Not only was I talented between the sheets, but I was also the number one tattooist in Queens.

Fine, Josh was number one—not that I'd ever tell him that, my buddy able to ink skin like no one I'd ever seen—but I was an incredibly close second. So close, it almost made no difference, which was why I'd agreed to let him take most of the limelight.

Generous of me.

He could do all the interviews, let them hail him as the *Tattoo King of NYC* in *Ink Magazine* and I could get my adulation from the female population.

Besides, the girls were wasted on him, even before he hooked up with Eve—his woman—he was never into them like I was. So it seemed it was all for the best.

"Coffee?" The waitress looked bored as she hovered beside me with her hip cocked and her coffee pot idle.

I'd met dozens of Ms. Do-You-Want-Coffee in my time. Bored women working shitty jobs, hoping to get a decent tip because their men didn't know how to fuck them. And while I couldn't help all of them, it was this lovely lady's lucky night.

I nodded, flashing her a smile as I leaned back and let her get a decent look at my goods. "I'll take some pie too, sweetness. *Cherry* pie."

Her eyes dropped down to my crotch, a smile making its way up her lips.

Yeah, that's right, baby. I'm packing heat.

She was still going to get a regular tip—I wasn't cheap—but I figured I'd do what I could to make her night a little better. A little flirting didn't hurt anyone, and my dick liked the attention.

"Hi." She smiled and pushed her hair behind her ear like she was seeing me for the first time. "I'm Gemma."

"Dallas." I gave her a wink. "Rough night?"

"Like you wouldn't believe." Gemma shot me a grin as she turned over my cup and poured right to the brim. "Nightshift is always the worst."

"I bet. Pretty girl like you shouldn't be cooped up in a shithole diner like this."

She wasn't the hottest girl I'd seen, but she definitely had potential. Probably didn't see the point in making herself look good when a quick glance around the diner could see the effort would have been wasted anyway.

Her cheeks pinked, her eyes widening as she dropped her voice to almost a whisper. "You think I'm pretty?"

Yeah, it had definitely been a while since she'd been told.

"Come on, gorgeous." I laughed, leaning forward as I looked her up and down. "You know how hot you are, don't pretend like this is a revelation. I thought I was supposed to be the player?"

See, always honest.

"I-I'll go get your pie," she stammered, her eyes so wide I thought they were going to drop from her head. "Stay right there. Right there. I'll be back."

Lucky for her, I wasn't going anywhere, happy to provide the public service and doing what I could to help improve her self-esteem.

Sure, I was a player just like I claimed, but I'd been upfront about it and as long as no one got hurt then what was the harm.

Maybe my aversion to relationships was from growing up with two older sisters and watching them get married, pop out kids and then both get divorced before they'd turned thirty. Maybe it was because I loved fucking too damn much and the idea of doing it with just one woman made me worried I'd get bored. Who cared?

All I knew was that I was happy and it helped pass the time.

My phone buzzed from inside my pocket, but I didn't need to see the screen to know it was probably some girl. I mean, it was close to midnight and Josh was already on his way. Other than a family emergency there was no one else calling me that late. Even my parents knew to text me first, the parental units not fully understanding my lifestyle, but supporting it nonetheless.

I couldn't help but smile as I checked out the name of my latest booty call.

"Kitty." The smile was automatic as her name lingered on my tongue.

Mmmmm.

When it came to fond memories, she was at the top of my list, the tingle in my dick confirming it in case my brain wasn't sure.

"Hey, is Josh with you?" she asked without even so much as a hello.

"Why do you want Josh, sweetness? I'm sure whatever you need I'm more than able to provide."

I'd only had the pleasure of sleeping with Kitty one time, but it had been one of the best nights of my life. She was off-the-scale hot, blond hair and green eyes with an insane body no man with a pulse could ignore. She was tiny—maybe five-two—petite except for the most amazing set of tits I'd ever seen. And had I not felt those babies with my own two hands, I'd have thought they were fake for sure. Not only was everything about her the real deal, but she had flexibility that would make a Romanian gymnast jealous. If there was ever a woman I was dying for a repeat with, it was the one on the other end of the line.

She laughed, her voice sending a shiver right to my balls. "Well, considering Eve told me you're stuck at a diner in Manhattan, not sure you're in a position to help me."

Kitty and Eve weren't the kind of girls you'd think would even be friends. Eve had more dead presidents in her bank account than all of us put together and knew which fork to use when it came to a fancy dinner. She'd loosened up some, but for the most part, she was straight down the line. Kitty, on the other hand, was a free spirit. Didn't follow anyone's bullshit rules, preferring to dabble on the wrong side of the tracks. To be fair, that's where most of the fun was.

Other than both being ridiculously hot, they had nothing in common. Unless you counted Eve's asshole ex-boyfriend who decided it would be a good idea to have Kitty as his sidepiece. Bastard didn't count on them channeling their inner girl power and both of them kicking the loser to the curb.

And if not for the freaking sweet back piece my buddy had inked on the very sexy Kitty a few months before, Eve and Josh might not have gotten their fairytale ending. It was *that* tattoo that had sent Eve on a quest to find the artist, Kitty the connection that hooked those two up. Still, not that any of that mattered now, their situation not helping me any.

"She was mistaken, I was bored and wanted to hang out," I lied, not knowing how much of the story Eve had given Kitty and not wanting to admit more than was necessary. "So, tell me, what did you need?"

"Well." She took a pause, taking a breath before continuing. "I called Eve looking to borrow Josh and she said he was on his way to get you. I tried to call him, but he's not answering his phone."

I didn't give a shit if Josh had his phone on silent or he'd been carjacked by a gang of thugs. Okay, maybe that was a lie. I hoped for both our sakes he hadn't been carjacked because he was my best friend and I'd miss the fuck out of him. But the important thing was, he hadn't picked up and had given Kitty a reason to talk to me.

"What do you need Josh for?" I asked, curious why she was looking, and why Eve would be willing to lend out her man.

She huffed out a breath, seeming to be annoyed. "Fine, I've handcuffed myself to my bedpost and I can't reach the key."

That slight tingle I'd felt in my balls earlier was now a full-blown hard-on.

"Oh really?" I asked, watching as Gemma, the friendly waitress, returned with my pie. "That's a story I want to hear."

"Yeah, well maybe you will. But right now I'm not telling you anything until you promise to get Josh to come over and bring something to cut them off. Or search my apartment, whichever will get me out of these things faster."

My eyes flicked to Gemma, the plate lowered in front of me. She lingered, seeing I was on the phone and waiting like she had more to say. Sadly though, my original flirting game with her no longer interested me.

Not when I had Kitty in handcuffs.

"Thanks doll, the pie looks great." I shot her a wink, trying to do my best to put the sexy eyes on ice while I returned to my call. "Sit tight and the minute Josh gets here we'll come break you out."

"Wait, you have pie?" Kitty asked, stopping me from killing the call. "What kind?"

I smiled as my eyes dropped to my plate. "Cherry."

"Bring me some apple." She ended the call without a goodbye, the whole exchange making me so hard I had to shift in my seat.

"Your friend in trouble?" Gemma twirled her hair around her finger, the lack of customers meant she had more time to spend with me. And while I usually liked the attention, I had bigger plans brewing.

"Yeah, unfortunately I'm going to have to bail the minute my pickup gets here." I tried to look disappointed even though I wasn't feeling it. "Can I grab this and a slice of apple pie to go and the check?"

The look of disappointment I hadn't shown was plastered all over her face. "Oh. Okay. Sure. Let me go get that for you." She waved awkwardly and then headed back to the counter.

Poor girl, I was probably the highlight to her shitty night and there I was, pulling the pin early. Not something I liked to do, especially with a woman.

"So who is it this time?" Josh shuffled into the booth, rolling his eyes. "Please tell me you didn't bang the brunette from this afternoon."

"Dude, have a little faith," I shot back indignantly. "I know she's booked in for another sesh, I'm not an idiot." While I didn't necessarily agree with Josh's *hands off the customers* policy, I respected it. Figured he was my buddy so I'd throw him a bone. But the minute the work was done, I was in the clear to partake in all the spoils. And partake I did.

He shook his head, checking his watch. "Lucky for you Eve was working late in the Gallery, or you, my friend, would have been shit out of luck."

He said it like he meant it, but I knew better. No matter how many times he'd told me that he'd leave my sorry ass in whatever trouble I found myself in, we had too much history.

"Yeah, yeah. Whatever," I laughed, shuffling out of the booth. "And as much as I know you want to hear about my love life, we have a mercy mission."

Gemma came back with a box for my pie, another box, which hopefully contained the apple, and the check. "Here you go." She placed her bounty of goods on the table while sizing up Josh, her eyes going wide at the sight of him.

Typical.

Women took one look at the asshole and lost their freaking minds. And sure, if you liked tall dudes who were built like brick walls, he was pretty impressive. But I'd gained twenty pounds recently—all freaking muscle—and didn't have his surly disposition. And more importantly, I was available.

"Thanks, Gemma." I peeled off a bill as I shot her a smile. "You've been amazing."

Josh leveled me with a look, moving slowly out of the booth

as Gemma got my pie into the to-go box. "We're in a hurry?" he asked, not being in the loop on the 9-1-1 we needed to assist.

"Yeah, I'll tell you all about it in the car." I grabbed the pies—I mean, no point abandoning dessert, especially when Kitty had asked for it—and moved to the door.

Josh followed close behind cursing under his breath. "Why do I have the feeling I'm going to regret this?"

I didn't think my grin could get any wider as I tossed over my shoulder, "Come on, man. When have I ever led you astray?"

KITTY

SO, WHEN IT CAME TO choices, I didn't always make the best ones.

I wasn't stupid despite what people believed, but I was an excellent example of book smarts not translating into the real world in any practical way.

In my professional life, I was an executive assistant to the CEO of a huge logistics company. I could juggle his calendar, snap up a Power Point display, work circles around an Excel spreadsheet, all while planning a seven-course gala for his fiftieth birthday. There was nothing I couldn't do or work out when it came to the office. And while my petite feminine looks had me on the receiving end of lot of dumb-blond jokes, my annual salary begged to differ. I mean, I wasn't pulling six-figures just yet, but mark my words, I was well on the way to becoming the highest paid and most irreplaceable assistant in the company.

But.

When it came to other things—like in general, in life—I was a walking, talking disaster.

I *always* picked the worst guy in the world. It was like I had an internal compass guiding me to the shittiest, most unreliable guy in the whole universe, and then became totally attracted to him. Cheaters, liars, criminals—I had dated them all, and every single time I was somehow surprised that my gut hadn't found me Mr. Right.

Ha.

What a joke!

Mr. Right could have taken out a billboard in Times Square and I would have missed it. Too busy falling over myself to get the hot—but questionable—guy who probably had a body stuffed in the trunk of his car.

And as much as I wished my horrible gut intuition was only restricted to my dating life, it wasn't my terrible taste in men that was to blame for my latest dilemma.

I yanked on the handcuffs as the metal bit into my skin. I knew I should have gotten the ones with the fluffy bits around the wrist, not that my hindsight would do me any good. Oh, and side note, trying them out while I was alone and leaving the key somewhere in the living room was an incredibly bad idea.

At least I wasn't naked and shackled to my bathroom sink. It was a small concession but one I was happily taking.

"Kitty."

I heard Josh's voice outside the front door and breathed a sigh of relief. It was the one time I was glad my apartment was basically a shoebox, able to hear him through the wood even though I was in my room. Square footage *wouldn't* have been my friend.

When I'd discovered I was in over my head—literally—and needed help, I decided to call the one guy who wasn't the biggest douchebag of all mankind. Ironically, we'd never dated which is how I knew he was a good guy. But sadly Josh hadn't answered his phone which forced me to call his girlfriend and my gal pal, Eve.

And yes, I may have told a tiny little white lie when I asked if she could send Josh over to check a leak under my sink. Sure, a probable leak *might* have been able to wait until morning, but I knew Eve wouldn't ask questions. She was too busy with her new art exhibit to even notice how late it was or notice my tiny untruth. Besides, it was either lie or risk her calling the fire department. I figured she'd end up forgiving me once she knew the truth and that it was the leak in my brain that was responsible for the emergency rather than my plumbing.

"The spare key is above the door inside the owl," I yelled hoping that my voice carried enough for him to hear me.

My dad was mortified I kept a spare key above the door of my apartment, but to be fair there was a greater chance of me locking myself outside—something I'd done at least five times—than a burglar finding it and robbing me blind.

I heard the click of my lock disengaging and the sweet, sweet sound of footsteps. *Thank God.* My body sagged against the headboard. He would find the key, set me free and we would never speak of it again. Except to his girlfriend, of course, because I trusted Eve wouldn't hold it over my head for leverage.

"You know, when Dallas told me, I thought he was kidding." Josh's huge body filled the open doorway to my bedroom. "I really hope you're leveling with me and some asshole didn't do this to you and bail?"

Ah Josh, ever the nice guy with a heart of gold. And it didn't hurt that he was gorgeous too.

"Yeah, playing is fine but leaving before packing up your toys is a big no-no." Dallas came up beside him looking serious.

While Josh was gorgeous, Dallas was downright hot. Standing a little under six-foot and a body that screamed athletic, he'd been working out recently and added some really, *really* nice muscles. His edgier side was aided by two full arm sleeves and a torso covered in tattoos, multiple piercings—especially where it counted—and hair that would be more at home on stage in a rock band than in a tattoo shop. Jet-black that hung just below his ears and buzzed down on one side, it was rail straight and glossier than any man's should be. It served as the perfect backdrop to his stunning, luminescent hazel eyes.

"As much as I'd love to pretend I wasn't the idiot who did this to myself, there is no one else to blame," I laughed. "I think the key is somewhere in the living room. Either that or we're going to need to saw it off."

"Let's try to find the key first. I'll go check the living room," Josh offered, hiding a grin.

Dallas moved closer, inspecting the cuffs. "Lucky you only restrained one hand." His fingers trailed along the red line forming on my skin as he leaned in.

I nodded, breathing in his heady scent of shampoo and soap that smelled so good I forgot my hand hurt. "I wanted to give them a dry run."

He smirked, his eyes blazing with mischief. "Well, when you're ready for the *wet* run, make sure you call me."

Sure he was crude, and flirted like it was his life's mission, but he one hundred percent had the goods to back it up.

We'd slept together once, and it was by far some of the best sex I'd ever had. Dallas had made me come so hard I almost blacked out with just the right amount of freaky and seductive. He didn't treat me like a china doll or a whore, exploring my body like I was a gift designed for his unwrapping. And unwrap me he did, over and over again until we were nothing more than a sweaty heap on the floor. But as much as I would have loved the repeat, I decided it was a one-time deal. Not only because we'd *been there and done that*, but I was relationship napalm. If we dated, there would inevitably be *something* wrong with him and we'd become decent friends lately. Besides, he thought *monogamy* was a type of wood, so it was best we kept the fireworks in the past.

"Maybe I will," I teased back, only half joking.

At least if I slept with Dallas I would be guaranteed orgasms.

I'd had to fake it with the last guy I'd slept with. It was either that or he'd keep poking me like I was mound of Play-Doh, and trust me, no woman wants to be tongued for an hour and feel nothing but chafing.

"Dallas," Josh warned, returning with the tiny silver key between his fingers. "You want to wait until we get Kitty unlocked before you try humping her leg?"

"At least he's house trained." I smiled, relieved the key had been found.

Josh moved closer and with a quick twist, the metal unlocked and my wrist was finally free.

I cheered, throwing my arms around Josh and giving him a huge hug. "Yay, you guys are my heroes."

Josh blushed, giving me a quick squeeze before releasing me. "Just try and be more careful next time." He put the key on my bedside table.

"What about my hug?" Dallas grinned, edging Josh out of the way as he watched me stand. "I not only aided this operation, but I also brought you dessert."

"You brought me pie?" I asked, remembering when I'd called him he'd been at a diner.

He nodded, opening his arms and waiting for me to fill the space. "Sure did, babe. Apple, just like you asked. I put it on your kitchen counter on the way to the bedroom."

I didn't even think, wrapping my arms around Dallas and nuzzling against his beautiful firm chest. Pie definitely deserved hugs. "You are the greatest."

"Please don't, Kitty." Josh laughed from behind us. "He already has an ego the size of the Grand Canyon, positive reinforcement is not the way to go."

Dallas pulled me close, taking my body and holding it against his. "Don't be jealous she's giving me the better hug, J. You didn't bring her pie."

Giving Dallas another squeeze, I allowed my hands to drop and pull away. Hugging him was great, but since he'd mentioned food, I had my mind on other things.

Midnight snacking was one of my favorite things, and I'd been restrained for the better part of two hours before I'd finally admitted defeat.

"I have vanilla ice cream in the freezer," I called out, walking to my kitchen. "We can reheat them in the microwave."

Josh and Dallas followed me, with Josh hesitating at the door. "We should probably get going. Eve should be finished working soon and I need to drop Dallas off at his car."

I whipped around, the tub of ice cream still in my hand. "Oh, well okay. Thanks for helping me out. Oh, and ummmm." I did some hesitating of my own. "You want me to tell Eve about the handcuffs or do you want to do it? She thinks I needed you to check a leak under my sink."

Josh laughed shaking his head. "I'll take care of it. Ready Dallas?" He turned to his sexy sidekick, his keys already in his hand.

"Nah, Dude, I think I'm going to stay for a while." He waved off Josh, not breaking eye contact with me.

Josh blew out a frustrated breath probably annoyed. "D, it's late and I'm not coming back."

"So I'll take a cab or an Uber." Dallas shrugged, not interested in Josh's annoyance as he moved closer. "Besides, I want to hear how Kitty ended up in handcuffs all by herself."

Josh rolled his eyes, tossing his hands in the air. "Just both of you try and stay out of trouble. I'm going home." We watched as he walked out of the kitchen and let himself out.

"He's annoyed I didn't get him pie." Dallas grinned. "Now, tell me the story."

I let out a sigh, figuring it was probably easier just to tell him. After all, if there was one person in the world who wouldn't judge me, it was the guy standing in front of me. Besides, he'd brought me dessert and we'd already established that I loved midnight snacking. I figured it was the least I could do.

"I was doing this online quiz and read a lot about bondage and how it heightens sexual arousal." I opened the two pie boxes sitting on my counter.

Dallas nodded, listening intently as I transferred the pie to plates and then put them into the microwave to warm. "I'd have gone with rope, but continue."

"So . . . I wanted to know what being cuffed felt like before I tried it with someone. I'm all for some excitement in the bedroom, and will try anything once, but handcuffs are a big commitment."

To be honest, there wasn't anyone in particular I had in mind when I purchased them off a website. As far as boyfriends went, I was in-between bad decisions so was enjoying some time of self-exploration. And I was a curious person by nature.

"Makes total sense." Dallas watched as I pulled the pies out of the microwave and scooped on the ice cream. "In fact, more women should try stuff out. Then you know exactly what you like and what you don't like."

"See, I knew you'd understand." I smiled, licking the ice cream off my spoon.

While most guys would have questioned the sanity of restraining myself, Dallas just got it. It was one of the things—besides his extremely hot body—that attracted me to him in the first place. It was also why we were still friends even *after* we'd had sex. There weren't too many men I kept around after we'd sealed the deal, probably best for everyone involved too considering most ended up being degenerates.

"Of course I do. Got anything else you're curious about?" He smiled, his eyes dropping down to my boobs.

It didn't matter that I was wearing a T-shirt, and probably the most boring pair of leggings I had in my wardrobe, Dallas's eyes were always on a discovery mission.

I shoved him playfully and laughed. "You're such a perv."

"You say that like it's a bad thing," he countered, carrying our pies to my kitchen table.

It wasn't how I thought I'd be spending my night but as far as backup plans, it was a pretty decent one. And it sure as hell beat being shackled to my headboard; those handcuffs were definitely not my thing.

"Enough about me." I took a spoonful of pie and brought it closer to my mouth. "What were *you* doing that required Josh's assistance?"

Even though it was only a Wednesday night, I could almost guarantee Dallas had been involved in some kind of crazy antic. Because, for all the bad decisions I had made, he had a stack of his own from what I'd heard.

"I was with a woman, things got complicated," he answered, not even trying to hide the fact he'd been on a date.

I savored the pie, the spice of the apple and creaminess of the vanilla inducing a pleasured moan. "This is soooooo good." I loaded up my spoon before continuing my questioning. "What got so complicated? It was just sex, right?"

It was probably none of my business, but I was curious. As someone who had slept with Dallas, there wasn't *a lot* to be confused about. He had an ego on him sure, but he knew what he was doing when it came to pleasing a woman.

Dallas stopped, his spoon halfway to his mouth. "Are we allowed to talk about this?" he asked, cautiously looking around the room like someone was going to burst in at any moment.

"What do you mean?" I leaned in closer, wondering if he knew something I didn't. I was well aware that my iPhone microphone was being misused, targeted ads showing up in my web searches after only a casual mention. But I didn't think I was important enough for full-scale surveillance.

His voice dropped to a whisper, his face turning serious. "I don't think I'm supposed to be talking to you about other women."

I started to laugh, throwing my head back as the sound bubbled up my throat. "Oh my God." My hand clasped against my chest in relief. "I thought you meant my place was bugged or something like that. Phew! Of course you are allowed to talk to me about other women. Why the hell wouldn't you be?"

"Because . . ." He paused, looking like a deer in headlights as he gestured to me. *"You're* a woman."

I laughed again, his expression so adorable I couldn't help it. "Ahhh, yeah I am, thanks for noticing. Which makes me the perfect person to speak to."

"I don't know." He rubbed his neck nervously, hesitating. "Something about this feels . . . like a bad idea."

"Trust me, we're good. Talk," I prompted. I knew bad ideas, and talking to Dallas about some girl he'd been with didn't seem to fit the brief.

He blew out a breath, looking around cautiously again. "Fine, but I want you to remember that I was trying to be a gentleman."

"Noted." I nodded, returning my attention to my pie. "Now, tell me what happened."

He raised his head, leveling me with a stare. "She cried."

"Huh?"

"Like really *crying*," he emphasized. "Not the kind from when you come hard either, because I've seen that. I'm talking like some-one died kind of tears."

I shook my head, not any more enlightened with the clari-fication. And as much as I hated to ask, I did anyway. "Did you hurt her?"

"No!" he shot back almost immediately. "It was completely consensual and not even that interesting. I mean, I made sure she got off before I did, but that was it."

There usually were two kinds of tears during consensual sex.

Good ones, when it felt *oooh sooooo good.*

And bad ones, when the guy you were with either didn't know what he was doing *or* was trying to jam something in without proper preparation.

I'd experienced both and knew the difference. And boy, was there a difference.

Having first-hand knowledge that Dallas absolutely knew what he was doing; his account of the tears was perplexing.

"Was she wet?"

He snorted. "Of course she was, she was the Hoover Dam down there. That was so *not* the issue." He stopped, leaning in closer as his eyes widened. "She said she was a *virgin*." The word said so cautiously it was as if he'd discovered a unicorn.

I bit the inside of my cheek, trying not to laugh.

I really, really tried.

But I couldn't resist.

My mouth opened to talk and a giggle escaped before I could stop it.

"Don't laugh, this is serious. Between the crying and taking her virginity, I was starting to freak the hell out. I know it was good for her, but I'm not exactly small . . . maybe I was too much for her to take for her first time."

"I'm sorry, I don't mean to laugh. It's not funny." I tried to contain my laughter, not wanting to hurt his feelings. "Let's back up here for a second. Did she *feel* like a virgin?"

"Fuck, are you sure we're supposed to be talking about this? This isn't some kind of test and then you yell at me for doing something I shouldn't have." His brow rose with suspicion.

"Okay." I set aside my plate, the pie all but forgotten given our current dilemma. "You are not bragging about it like it is some conquest, we're trying to work out where things went wrong. Trouble shooting. Like when you get the blue screen of death on your computer."

Besides, I wasn't jealous. I'd already been *there* and done *that*.

And while our night together had been A-mazing, that's all it was. A one-time deal. Dallas and I were friends now; sure we flirted a little, but friends nonetheless. And I liked helping my friends.

"So tell me, did she *feel* like a virgin?" I repeated the question, trying to sound as clinical as I could.

He shrugged as if weighing his reply. "She was tight but I didn't feel like my dick was in a vice if that's what you're asking."

"Come on, Dallas. You have to know that is *not* a sign of a virgin." I rolled my eyes. "Did she seem like she knew what she was doing? Or was she uncoordinated and awkward?"

His hand scrubbed his face in frustration like he wasn't sure if he should answer. "I didn't think so. She sucked my dick like a champ."

"Then I'm going to go out on a limb and say chances are she's done it before."

He screwed up his face in horror, like the thought hadn't even occurred to him. "So she was lying?"

"Dallas," I crooned, the smile automatic. "Surely you've been lied to before? Especially in bed."

As much as I hated to admit it, lying during sex was often necessary. Sometimes for your own sanity, and sometimes because you didn't want to hurt the other person's feelings. But always as a means to an end.

If he'd looked horrified before, he'd reached a new level of disbelief. He shook his head, the conviction ringing in his voice. "No, they don't. Not with me."

He was so adorable, almost innocent in his naivety.

"*Oh Dallas, I've never seen anything that huge.*" I brought my hand to my mouth feigning shock. "*Baby, no man has ever made me feel like that. I think I might actually die.*" My voice was breathy, my hand sliding down my throat. "*I'm coming, baby. Oh. My. God. I'm going to explode. Hold me, I just can't take it anymore.*"

"What the fuck?" He rose out of his chair, shuffling back. "Are you telling me you did that to *me*?"

I shook my head, reaching out for him. "Me? God, no. Any screams you got from me were well earned, but I have in the past with other guys. Babe, trust me. If she wasn't hurt and they weren't tears of ecstasy, then she was probably feeding you a line. Maybe she was hoping to guilt you into a relationship or get you to spend the night? We aren't frail creatures like some people might have you think."

His eyes widened, like he hadn't even considered the possibility. "Fuck," the one word cursing out his mouth. "*She* was playing *me*."

I pointed at him with a smile. "Says you, the biggest player of all."

"I never do mind games, Kitty." He looked at me seriously. "But thanks for the head's up, I never would have seen it."

"You're welcome." I grinned at him, feeling like I'd done a good deed. "Now, let's get back to the pie."

"Wait a minute." He stopped suddenly, reaching out and grabbing my arm. "That's exactly what I need."

"Pie?" I asked, wondering if that was the case, why we weren't eating it already.

He shook his head, his voice turning serious. "No, don't you see. You gave me a peek over the fence and now I want another look."

Wait a minute.

Was he asking me for *sex*?

There were no surprises when it came to Dallas Rodgers. He was interested in sex probably during every waking moment of every day. I had no problem with that.

But I *wasn't* about to jump into bed a few hours after he'd been with someone else. That was the ultimate in bad decisions, and if I—Miss Queen of Dumbassary when it came to men—could see that, then it was definitely stupid.

"Dallas, we've slept together, you've seen everything already.

But thanks for the offer."

"No." He waved his hands in the air. "That's not what I meant. Although, I wouldn't say no if you were asking, because you're fucking hot." His grin widened with appreciation. "But what I *do* want is for you to be my in. Decipher the lady code and help me be able to pick the non-crazy ones." Eyes wide, with his face completely serious like he was asking me to lend him an iPhone charger.

"You want me to help you get women?" I asked, clarifying if he was suggesting I moonlight as a pimp.

He reached out, a finger trailing across my forearm seductively, "Babe, I do *not* need help getting women. I can hunt and gather all by myself, it's weeding them out that's the problem. Which is why I need *you*. You give me the keys to the kingdom, the insider info."

I'll admit, his idea did have some merit. How good would it be to have a guide, someone whispering in your ear, cracking the code of what all those bullshit lines meant? Of course, I was talking about myself, because I sure as hell could use some insider info—help me avoid the deadbeats and the losers.

"Oh my God!" I jumped out of my chair, my mind brimming with the possibilities. "I help *you* and you help *me*. Between the two of us, we're bound to have seen everything. This is freaking perfect."

He nodded, the smile brimming off his face as he joined me on his feet. "We'll be unstoppable."

"Like superheroes!" I agreed, jumping excitedly in place.

It really was the perfect solution.

Neither of us wanted a serious relationship, but enjoyed the company of members of the opposite sex. And both of us seemed to be afflicted with the attraction to crazies. *Virgin girl* was nothing, he'd told me once some woman had robbed him after sex and left him stranded at a beach. And we didn't even need to go into my track record.

Maybe this was the key, the answer to the madness, because it surely couldn't get any worse.

"Okay." I clapped my hands figuring out of the two of us I was probably the one who was most organized. "If we're going to do this, then we need some guidelines. Things to help us out and get to know each other a little better too."

Dallas nodded looking so pleased with himself you'd think I'd told him we were going to Disneyland. "Agreed. And if one of us sees the other making a wrong turn, they have to call it. I don't want you letting me get involved with a stage-five clinger just because I didn't see all the signs."

"I will one hundred percent do that." I made possibly the easiest promise I'd ever made. "Now, let's finish our pie and get to work."

DALLAS

I'LL BE HONEST, THE ORIGINAL plan when Kitty called me was find out how she got herself chained up and then offer to keep playing if that was what she was into. Yes, I had just been with another woman, which technically made me a whore, but I had not hidden that fact from anyone. So, I needed to ditch Josh, put the moves on Kitty, and try to salvage the night so I could look back on it with fond memories.

But plans don't always work out like you think they will.

It was obvious the minute we started talking about me and my *evening*, sex wasn't going to happen. It was a disappointment, but I was still going to get to eat pie with a beautiful woman and hopefully score a kiss or—if I was lucky—touch her boobs before I went home alone.

Who knew I'd end up getting to look behind the curtain.

You see, I could make a woman come so hard she'd forget her own name. I needed no help with that. But what I had a little difficulty with was finding women who didn't want to feed me my balls after the fact.

Not all of them of course, some were regular girls who took

what I gave them and we parted as friends. But I figured that was more the law of averages rather than anything else.

After we chowed down on some pretty awesome pie in the kitchen, Kitty got serious as we settled onto her couch. She was so fucking smart, brainstorming scenarios and asking all kinds of questions, and I very much enjoyed being her star student. I had productive shit to contribute too, tossing in suggestions on when she should zig instead of zag with a dude, something that she seemed to appreciate immensely.

It was late when I finally got back home, well into the morning, but thankfully the Uber ride wasn't long because we lived close by.

Shit, who would have thought it?

I had an amazing time with Kitty and we'd both had our clothes on the entire time. I hadn't even thought about sleeping with her once we'd move to the living room, too busy trying to learn how to speak chick-ese so I could know what to avoid.

"You want to tell me what last night was all about?" Josh knocked on my door as I dumped my headphones on my desk. He'd no doubt been at the shop since some ungodly hour like nine, which made sense since it was his ride and he was making the big bucks. But I preferred a more fluid working schedule, not wanting my art to suffer due to lack of Zs.

I smiled, unable to wipe the freaking grin off my face since I'd left Kitty's. "Dude, she is amazing. I swear to God, I think it was three in the morning before I got home."

"Well, considering it's almost noon now, I'm not surprised." He raised an eyebrow, pretending he was displeased. "And I don't want to hear about whatever the two of you got up to. In fact, the less I know, the better. But I'm warning you, D, don't be a dick. It will piss Eve off if you mess with her friend, which will in turn piss me off. And we don't want me pissed off, do we?" he warned, folding his arms across his chest like the badass he was.

If I hadn't known the guy since forever, I'd have probably

been worried. Even with my recent bulking up thanks to a gym regime, he still had me beat by twenty pounds or so. And those pounds weren't hanging around his gut courtesy of tossing back beers and pizza either.

"Relax, I didn't fuck her." I tipped my chin to him, hoping he might chill on the bodyguard routine.

His eyebrow rose, looking skeptical as he took a seat opposite me. "D, you know I love you like a brother. And I'm not going to tell you how to live your life. But most guys don't need their buddies to pick them up from a diner after they've run from a woman's house like a fugitive."

"Whoa, hold up a minute." I raised my hands, annoyed at the suggestion. "Like I told you last night in the car, there was something not right about her and any man would have bailed. Even you, Superman. She was crying. And on top of that, she was probably lying as well. So I had no choice."

The one thing I loved about Josh was that he never gave me the *"why don't you find a nice girl and settle down"* speech. Occasionally I got the *"stop being such a cock"* or the *"your dick is going to fall off if you keep putting it in places like that,"* but other than that he kept his nose out of my biz.

But I could tell something was eating at him, and I wasn't sure if it was me and my love life that was the issue. "Things okay with you and Eve?" I asked, wondering if his involvement last night landed him in the doghouse.

"Yeah, things are great actually." He laughed, his eyes landing on me. "I asked her to marry me, and she said yes."

"Jesus, Josh." I jumped up from my seat and patted him on the back. "That's freaking awesome. For a minute there you had me worried."

While getting hitched wasn't my box of doughnuts, I had never seen him happier than he'd been recently. And just like he supported my lifestyle, I was waving my own pom-poms for his.

Marriage, babies . . . whatever he wanted.

Josh finally smiled, cracking the mask of doom he'd been wearing since he'd gotten in. "Thanks, man, it means a lot. Which brings me to my other point of business."

"Of course I'll be your best man, I mean, who else is there?" I laughed, slapping him across the back. It was a done deal, firstly because I was his best friend and secondly because I literally was the job title—the best man.

He nodded, smile widening as he grabbed my shoulders. "Good, and since you're going to be my *best man*, I have a favor to ask."

Bachelor party, like it even needed to be said.

"And no, it's not about the bachelor party." He threw water on my thoughts of body shots off hot strippers. "With Eve running the gallery, and me here, we aren't going to have a lot of time to plan the wedding. Which is why I'm hiring a new artist, take the load off a little."

It seemed like Christmas had come, with all the good news being tossed out at once. I'd been up his ass to hire someone for over a year, and finally he'd decided to listen. "Dude, that is the best news I've heard all day. And I swear, you can count on me to be a team player. I won't even haze him that badly."

"Dallas," he warned, the vein in his neck starting to pop out. "*Please* don't screw this up. He's a great artist and a nice guy, and you said it yourself, we need the help. Just be the dude I know and don't get into a pissing contest with him."

I tossed my head back and laughed, shaking off whatever concern he had about me. "Dude, I know I can be a pain in the ass but I swear, you can trust me. I'll be a model citizen, show him the ropes. I'll even take him under my wing and show him the nightlife. Now you know I don't do that for just anyone."

"Thanks, man. Honestly, between the ring burning a hole in my pocket and talking to you about the new artist, I feel like I haven't taken a full breath in a week." His shoulders relaxed, the tension easing out of his face.

"I've got you." I tipped my chin at him, thankful after all the times he'd helped me out, I was finally able to reciprocate.

And I meant it too. While there was nothing I would have loved more than to mess with the new guy, having my buddy's back was more important. Besides, it would be much more fun to mess with him when he *wasn't* expecting it.

He blew out a breath, looking more like the old Josh I knew as he leaned in. "So everything is cool?"

"Rock solid. And since you shared your good news, I think it's fair I share mine," I announced proudly, puffing out my chest as I met his eye. "Kitty and I have a project of our own we're working on."

His brow scrunched in confusion as he tilted his head to the side. "Come again?"

"Last night's predicament didn't need to have happened."

He laughed, the asshole finding it amusing. "Of course it didn't, you can get to know the woman *before* you put your dick inside her."

"Very funny, but no." I rolled my eyes. "Instead, Kitty and I are going to coach each other, giving each other the in so we don't end up with the crazies."

Josh laughed, his body shaking as he shook his head. "You two are going to join forces and coach each other?"

"Yep." I nodded proudly.

"D, you really think *that* is a good idea?" Josh raised an eyebrow, the grin still on his face. "Isn't it a little like the blind leading the blind?"

I scratched my head, failing to see where he was going with the analogy. "What are you talking about? Blind people get led all the time with no issue, what do you think the dog is for?"

"The dog can fucking SEE, Dallas!" He cursed out a laugh. "I'm not sure which one of the two of you is worse, but even a *blind* person would see what a hot mess this is going to end up as. Lord, help us all."

I got his concern—even if it was misguided—but I was more than confident we were going to prove him wrong. "Trust me, we've got this. Seriously, what is the worst that can go wrong?"

He shook his head, slowly backing toward the doorway. "Dude, stop talking. I can't even reason with you when you're in this mood. Let's get some work done, I've got Mason coming later to check out the shop."

"Whatever." I flipped him off and watched him leave.

I wasn't sure when he'd found the new guy or why he hadn't mentioned it before. And had I been a pussy, I might have gotten my feelings bent out of shape. But honestly, I didn't care. As long as this dude was a decent artist and not a serial killer, I was happy to have him on the team. Besides, there was the very real possibility that Josh *had* mentioned it and I hadn't been paying attention. Business shit bored the hell out of me, so anytime we had a "meeting" I had a tendency to zone out. Not like I had a say in the matter anyway, it was his business and he was going to do what he wanted, so it was really just a waste of brain activity.

And I had more important stuff to fill my brain.

Trish, the chick who was scheduled for a hip piece rapped at my open doorway. "You ready for me, Dallas?"

And even if I hadn't been ready, I sure as shit would be. Super-hot, nice tits and a pair of bright pink lips that were begging for a blowjob—she wasn't the kind of woman I could ignore.

Besides, it was our last appointment which meant all that heat she'd been tossing my way no longer had to be ignored. I needed to play a lottery ticket or something because surely the day couldn't get any better.

"Sure thing, sweetheart. Take a seat and give me a few minutes to set up." I tipped my chin to my tattoo chair, my machines not ready.

She nodded, swaying her hips with intent as she moved across my room and planting her ass as directed, relaxing into the chair. "No stress, I'm not in any hurry."

Good thing too, because I wasn't a man who liked to be rushed, especially when it came to beautiful women or my work.

She watched with interest as I went through the motions, covering my machines and setting up my colors. Her lip biting didn't go unnoticed as I snapped on a pair of black nitrile gloves.

"Now." I slowly took my seat in my stool beside her, unable to hide my beaming grin. "Let's get your pants off so I can get started."

ⅇⅇⅇ

"HEY, YOU GOT A MINUTE? Mason is here." Josh appeared at my door like he did whenever he needed something, watching me clean off my latest work. I'd just finished an armband for a frat boy named Brendon who talked a good game until he'd sat down and then had to grit his teeth so he didn't cry. And had I not had such a stellar morning, I might have been annoyed. But I had Trish's number tucked into my pocket and all kinds of positivity swimming around in my head, so a whiny twenty-year-old wearing a popped-up collar polo shirt wasn't half bad.

"Just finishing up, big guy." I smirked at Josh before turning to frat boy and giving him the rundown on after care.

He nodded, the silent understanding passing between us that I wanted to wrap up as soon as possible. "Awesome, meet me in my room."

Josh disappeared and I rang up Brendon out front. We still hadn't gotten a permanent front desk person, needing us both to multi task. But I was hoping with the addition of a new artist, someone to answer our phones and help out would be soon to follow.

Small steps.

Or, I could just hire someone myself when Josh inevitably went on his honeymoon. See, there was always a work around.

As I left the front reception area and got closer to Josh's room, I heard the laughing. Two male voices chuckling like they'd shared the funniest thing ever, and I was anxious to hear what was so hilarious. After all, Josh was the more serious of the two of us so if the new guy thought *he* was funny, he was going to piss his pants when he finally met me. Either that or he was one of those eager-to-please lapdogs. God, I really hoped not.

"What's so funny?" I walked into the room, not bothering with an intro.

"Nothing important." Josh shrugged, the grin still on his face. "Mason was just telling me about a friend we have in common. Reliving some history."

Mason was sitting down, but I could tell the dude was well over six-foot. Big in the shoulders, which probably meant he wasn't a lightweight, and a set of blue eyes that I was positive were contact lenses. Paired together with blond hair that hung down to his shoulders, the dude looked like he was trying to be Brad Pitt from that movie *Troy*.

Awesome.

A fucking pretty boy.

So much for my excellent morning.

At least he had ink, the exposed skin on his arms covered in decent art was a small consolation.

"Oh really?" I asked with interest, wondering which old *friend* they were discussing considering I'd known Josh more than half of our lives. "And who would that be?"

Okay, so I had already decided I didn't like him. Partly because he looked like he would be more suited for tanning in Venice Beach than doing ink work in Queens, and partly because the bastard had come into *my* house and was acting so familiar.

"Joe Langston," asshole responded wearing the same stupid smirk he'd had on when I'd walked in. "Joe was my old boss back in San Diego."

Yeah, so I was right about the douchebag liking to tan, just needed to go a little further south on the west coast.

Josh tipped his chin to the untaken chair beside dumbass. "Take a seat, Dallas. We both have an hour before our next clients."

"Nah, I'm good." I nodded, preferring to stand so I could get a better read on the situation. "I'm Dallas." I held out my hand, being a man and shaking the dick's hand.

He reciprocated, giving it a decent shake before dropping it. "Mason. Heard a lot about both of you actually, it's great to finally meet you."

Yeah, well we'd see how his *great-to-finally-meet-you* stood later. "Joe's a lying piece of shit, I wouldn't believe anything he said." I folded my arms across my chest and added a smirk of my own. "The dude's only successful because he's all the way over there. No way he'd hack it out here in New York."

"D, you know Joe's a solid artist." Josh laughed, rolling his eyes.

"Whatever." I shrugged, not giving a shit about Joe Langston or his abilities. "So you're the *new* guy." I hoped the dumbass was sharp enough to catch the emphasis on new. "What brings you all the way across the country?"

Working for Josh was as good a reason as any—there were guys who'd give up their left nut for the chance to work in our shop—but I was curious if there wasn't some other motivation.

He could easily be a plant, infiltrating our set-up so he could go back to Joe and tell him what we did. While Joe might be a decent—and I used that term lightly—artist, he wasn't even in the same realm as Josh and me.

The bastard eased back into his chair, not at all bothered by my question. "Well, my sister and brother-in-law just had a baby and they live out in Brooklyn. And since I'm the only family she has, I wanted my niece to grow up knowing her uncle. I mentioned it to Joe that I was looking to make the move and he hooked me up with Josh, seemed like fate."

"The timing couldn't have been more perfect," Josh added. "And while Joe is awesome, we're going to really put you through your paces."

The dumbass—Mason, not Josh who seemed to have a serious lovefest for the douchebag—continued to tell us how he and his sister were both orphaned in their teens. And blah, blah, blah, he'd had a hard life, finding his way back through tattooing.

Great, because it wasn't enough I disliked the guy, now he'd told me his fucking life story I was going to feel bad about it. And I hated to feel bad about anything.

"So Mason is going to come in for the rest of the week, do some consults and help at the front desk, and then start working on his own clients next week," Josh announced, tipping his chin to the man in question. "If you have any questions let us know, but you can set up the third room however you want it and just make yourself feel at home."

"Yeah, all the stuff Josh said. Happy to have you on board. " I gave him a smile even though I wasn't really feeling it.

"Thanks, I'm going to go take a look around." Mason rose from his chair, confirming as he stood that he was a tall bastard. He nodded to me on his way out, heading down the hall to the empty room toward the back.

"What was *that* about?" Josh asked, getting to his feet and shutting the door to his room. If I assumed our little meeting was over, I'd have been mistaken.

I shrugged, pretending like I didn't know what he was talking about. "Huh?"

"Come on, Dallas. How long have I known you?" He chuckled,

retaking his chair and giving me a look as he kept his voice low. "Usually I can't get you to shut up, and yet you barely said two words to the guy."

"Didn't realize I needed to," I answered. Besides, anything I was going to say wouldn't have been complimentary, and I'd already given Josh my word I'd be nice to the guy.

But if I was trying to be slick, Josh wasn't buying it. "Be nice."

"Yeah, yeah. We done, or do you want a commitment I'm going to let him sit with us at lunch and be his best friend?" I laughed, because Josh cared waaaaaay too much about people's feelings.

"Get out of here, moron." He shook his head with a grin. "And for the record, it wouldn't kill you to show him around. Maybe even take him out for a drink to meet some people considering he's new in town. I would do it myself but . . ."

He didn't need to finish, his lack of time pretty fucking obvious since he had a woman at home he was intending to give his last name to. Besides, even when he *was* single, he was never as good at the social interactions as I was. I was a legend, able to make almost anything turn into a good time. And when it came to meeting people, they flocked to me like I was Jesus turning water into wine. Guess that was just my cross to bear.

"I'll take care of it," I offered, hoping it wouldn't come back to bite me in the ass. "See how awesome a wingman I am? You should give me a raise."

He laughed, whatever concern he had easing out of his face. "I already pay you more than I should. Let's just say you're doing this out of the kindness of your heart."

"Well that doesn't sound like me at all." I screwed up my face in disgust. "Let's just agree it's an early wedding present instead."

Josh gave me a nod and a smile. "Whatever it takes. And for what it's worth, thanks."

"Stop with the gratitude. It's making me feel weird." I shivered, not used to being on the receiving end of Josh's thank yous.

And with another laugh he smacked me across the shoulder and then started to get ready for his next client. He was good like that, stopping before it got weird. It was my cue too, stepping out of his room and heading back to my own.

Guess the week was going to be more interesting than I'd anticipated. Not necessarily a bad thing. I still hadn't worked out what Mason's angle was, but getting close to him would serve a dual purpose. No better way to get to know his intentions than to be all up in his business, and I could keep an eye on him too.

Besides, not even babysitting the new guy was going to ruin what had been an unbelievable strike of luck. When it came to living the best life, I was the number one contender.

KITTY

"SO YOU JUST CALLED JOSH? And he came?" Lani's eyes widened, her mouth dropping open in case she wasn't conveying enough shock.

"Well, I called him but he didn't answer, so I had to call Dallas. But they ended up being together." I shrugged, our lunchtime session used to explain why I was sporting faint bruising around one of my wrists. It had definitely been a poor choice not getting handcuffs with padding, but yanking at them when I realized I was stuck hadn't done me any favors either.

Unlike me, Lani had a regular boyfriend. He was decent looking and seemed smitten, but when I saw them together I couldn't help but yawn. I wasn't even sure either of them were attracted to one another anymore—their relationship, the definition of boring. But she didn't judge my lifestyle and consequent bad choices, so I thought it was fair I didn't judge her ordinary ones. Some people got off on routine and stability, it was just a shame I wasn't one of them.

"Eve isn't weird about having her boyfriend around you . . . you know . . ." Her eyebrows rose as she whispered, *"Alone?"*

It had been one of my prior lapses in judgment that had brought Eve into my life. Or was it me into hers? Either way, our introduction had been far from conventional. Hard for anything to be *conventional* when you're blowing what you thought was a cute, single guy from the office and he ends up being the boyfriend of someone else. I'd like to say it had been an isolated incident but unfortunately it wasn't. At least it *had* been the first and only time with Oliver, nothing progressing further than the blowjob and some third base touching.

Still, I hadn't *intentionally* pursued him. I would never get involved with a man who was in any sort of committed relationship. It just so happened that they didn't feel the same way about me. Happy for me to be their mushroom—kept in the dark and fed bullshit.

"Thanks a lot, Lani," I snapped, a little more than slightly annoyed. "You of all people should know that I would never try anything with someone else's man. Especially not a friend."

She had the decency to look apologetic, her hands reaching for me just as quickly as her mouth sought to explain. "Kitty, of course I know that. I trust you, we're friends. But not everyone is as understanding, and I don't want Eve to turn up on your doorstep one day with an icepick because she turned into a psycho territorial bitch."

While Lani didn't judge me, she judged others plenty. Namely rich women who came from privilege, which Eve happened to be. You'd never know from looking at Lani but she'd been dirt poor most of her life, and she'd sooner trust a drug dealer from the hood than a gallery owner who hailed from the Upper East Side.

"I wish you'd see that Eve isn't like that. And just because she has money, she isn't going to turn into a crazy bitch." I was almost positive the two of them were never going to be able to be in a room together.

"Babe, if you want to be friends with her, that's your own

business. Just maybe next time you're in trouble call Cameron."

I laughed, unable to stop myself. She might be happily in love—or whatever she described her relationship to be—but Cameron wasn't the kind of guy I wanted in an emergency. I mean, if I had an issue with my tax return or the IRS then he'd totally be my first port of call, but anything else . . . I'd take my chances solo.

"I'll be fine, no need to worry about me. But thanks for the offer." I shook my head, hoping my future wouldn't involve instances where I required *anyone's* help. Besides, Dallas and I had our newly minted agreement, which I was positive was going to keep me too busy to get into any real trouble.

She shrugged and turned her attention back to her sandwich, chewing thoughtfully as she listened to how attentive Dallas had been in bringing me pie. I didn't bother to tell her that we had decided to team up and be the ultimate dating deciphering duo. Considering we only had a little time left before both of us needed to be back in our offices, I figured eating lunch was probably more important.

"Hey, you're still going to O'Shea's dinner tomorrow night, right?" I asked, hoping she hadn't changed her mind and decided to spend a fun evening doing a crossword puzzle with Cameron instead.

She groaned, taking a sip from her soda. "Of course I'm going, he's *my* boss. I think these teambuilding dinners at his house are less about morale and more about showing off his fancy penthouse." She rolled her eyes. "If I had a choice, I'd totally get out of it."

O'Shea wasn't my boss, but invited me and the other EAs all the same. Not because he gave a shit about any of us, but because he had a massive chip on his shoulder and wanted to piss off the other executives. Show how much more fun he was, how much he "cared" for his staff and was *one of them*. I went along because he didn't scrimp on the catering and it kept me up to date on office gossip. Nothing loosened lips faster than an open bar, and O'Shea was legendary for his free-flowing liquor. My boss had never asked me to be the inside man—or woman as was the case—but made it very clear that he appreciated my reconnaissance missions. And again, the food was usually really good.

"We can Uber if you want, you can crash at my place," I offered, my lack of a car making the option of being a designated driver impossible.

It just didn't seem practical to waste money on a car when I worked in Manhattan. Besides, I preferred to spend my money on things other than parking garages.

She frowned and shook her head. "Nah, I'll get Cameron to drive, we have brunch plans Saturday morning. But we can pick you up if you like?"

"Snore. Brunch plans." I rolled my eyes, not at all surprised she was forgoing a night at my place to go back home and spend it with her boyfriend. "And it's fine, I'll just get my own ride. It seems stupid for you to come out of your way."

Cameron and Lani shared a modest apartment in Hell's Kitchen, which was a world away from my place in Astoria Park in Queens. So while I appreciated the offer, it made no sense at all.

"The ride is there if you want it." Lani glanced at her watch and cursed under her breath.

A quick check of my phone confirmed lunchtime had ended and we should be getting back to our desks. "Thanks, I'll chat with you later."

We both gathered up our handbags and phones, quickly shoving whatever lunch was left down our throats before heading to the bank of elevators. She was on the eighteenth, while I was up on twenty, so we rode together nodding our goodbyes when we got to her floor.

It was after the elevator doors closed that I heard my phone buzz with an incoming message. I assumed it was my boss, Garrett, needing something in the forty minutes I'd been gone. It wouldn't have been the first time. But when I looked down at my screen, I was pleasantly surprised to see it was Dallas instead.

The smile was bursting off my face until I read his message.

9–1-1 Call ASAP—D

Without even thinking, I dialed his number. While I assumed it wasn't anything too bad, I was happy for the distraction and curious as to what the emergency was. It was Dallas; it literally could have been anything.

"Hey, what's up?" I exited the elevator and walked out onto my floor. I was so engrossed in my call that I didn't notice the hot male chest until I'd walked into it.

"Shit, sorry." I pulled back, eyeing him up and down.

"Sorry for what?" Dallas asked on the phone unable to see my unfortunate—or fortunate, it was a very nice chest—position. It was bad elevator etiquette to talk and walk, and clearly I didn't have the skill to do both, failing to look where I was going.

I shook my head, lowering my phone as I checked out the stunning man in front of me. While I was well aware Dallas and whatever his 9–1-1 had been were still on the phone, I couldn't ignore the sexy man of mystery I'd literally slammed into. Plus, I'd already been rude by walking into him, I didn't want to further perpetuate the rudeness.

He smiled.

The mystery man, obviously, because I couldn't see Dallas.

His sexy lips spreading into a wide grin as he straightened his tie. "No need for apologies."

"Kitty?" My name echoed from the phone being held in my hand. "Are you still there?"

Mystery man glanced down to the cell, grinning even wider. "Sounds like someone is trying to get ahold of you, *Kitty*. See you soon."

And without a plan on when or how that was going to happen,

he disappeared into the elevator with the metal doors closing behind him.

Who the hell was that?

Certainly not anyone who worked on my floor.

Not anyone who worked with the company unless they were new.

Regardless, I was going to find out who he was. After all, he already had my name—Dallas screaming it had helped him get that—so it was only fair I at least knew his.

"Dallas, sorry, I ran into someone." I brought the phone back to my ear as I recovered and walked quickly to my office. "What's the emergency?"

He coughed, clearing his throat. "Okay, it still feels weird talking about women with you. And I could have asked Josh, but he's too busy showing the new guy the ropes, and we agreed this would be our thing."

"Dallas, it's fine. Whatever it is, you can tell me." I closed the door behind me, unsure if the smile on my face was from the mystery man earlier or from how adorable Dallas sounded when he was confused.

He blew out a breath. "Fine, so when a girl says she wants to take you to *church,* is it like when a guy says he's going to take you to heaven? You know . . . in the sack."

My brows furrowed, slightly confused by the question. "Babe, I'm going to need more information. Can you give me some context? She wasn't a nun was she?"

Dallas laughed as I settled into my office chair. "Yeah, I've made that mistake before, but I swear to God—whichever one was her boss—she didn't look like one. Firstly, aren't they supposed to be wearing costumes so we can easily identify them? And secondly, aren't they supposed to be old? I was so confused by how hot she'd been I'd completely overlooked the pamphlets she was handing out. So, while I've had that problem before, I always ask upfront now. Kind of like asking if someone is a cop so they can't get you for entrapment later."

I couldn't help it, the giggle bubbling up my throat as I listened to his theory. "Yeah, probably a wise choice. So you asked her?"

"Sure did. Right at the start when she handed me her cookies."

"Wait a minute." I stopped, the confusion back. "She gave you cookies? That isn't code for something, right?"

With Dallas, you could never be sure. And while it wouldn't be unheard of for a woman to casually and randomly offer herself to Dallas, I'd never heard him call any body part a cookie.

"Not code, double chocolate chip. And they were delicious," he confirmed, a smile in his voice.

"Please tell me you knew this woman and she wasn't just someone you randomly met." I held my hand against my forehead praying I didn't have to give him a stranger danger lesson as well.

"Of course I know her, she's the dry cleaner on the corner. I think her name is Holly, but to be honest she's got an amazing rack so it's hard for me to concentrate. Anyway, today she came in with a plate of cookies and like I said, Josh was busy with the new guy so she had to talk to me. And while I was savoring her delicious baked goods—the cookies, not that I wouldn't take something else if it were on offer—she told me she wanted to take me to church."

While I was both glad and relieved he hadn't been the victim of a roofie via *Chips Ahoy!* I was still no closer to solving his riddle. On the surface, it was flirting. A classic—and still fairly widely used—concept of trying to win over a man by appealing to one of his base needs.

There were three.

Oxygen.

Food and drink.

And Sex.

I'd heard tales about women trying to *Betty Crocker* their way into a man's heart. Turning up on his doorstep with some *pound cake* and hope he'd reciprocate. But I had yet to see it for myself. I highly doubted those kinds of women even lived in New York City, the dying breed hidden away in some place like Arkansas or something.

"Was she flirting?"

"If she was, she wasn't trying really hard." He laughed. "Which was *why* I couldn't work it out."

"Hmmmm." I tapped my finger against my lips, giving it some more thought. It wasn't easy to decipher even with the extra information, but I wasn't going to fail at my first assignment. Hell no, I had too much pride for that. "Wait, when she said wanted to take you to church, did she say *her church* or just church in general?"

I had a moment of clarity, the use of a pronoun important if we were going to unravel *Dry Cleaner Holly's* intentions.

There was a pause, hopefully meaning Dallas was replaying the conversation and able to extract addition information. "Ummm, now that you mention it, she did say *her* church."

Mentally I cheered, excited I'd solved the puzzle—or at least I believed I had—as I pushed my shoulders back proudly. "Then I would safely guess that no, she does not mean anything sexual, and she is probably talking about the actual place of worship."

"Thank God, I checked," Dallas cursed out. "I was literally moments away from agreeing. I mean, she had amazing tits and delicious cookies, I'd have probably agreed to go anywhere with her."

"Well, glad I could save you. Probably a different kind of *saving* than she had in mind." I giggled, imagining poor Dallas sitting in a pew listening to a sermon for a good thirty minutes before he'd worked it out.

"Yeah well, I still think it's a low blow trying to recruit me with tits and cookies. Pretty sure Jesus wouldn't approve with the whole bait and switch."

"Probably not." I wrinkled my nose, amused someone could

work *tits* and *Jesus* into the same conversation. "So anything else I can do for you?"

"Nah, I should probably go back out there and tell her that it's a no go."

My eyes widened, my back shifting forward in my chair as I leaned against my desk. "Dallas, you had her *wait* until I called you?"

"Of course I did," he announced, the pride brimming in his voice. "I told you it was a 9-1-1. If she'd already left, we could have had this conversation later. But she sort of wanted an answer so I told her to hang tight until I got the okay."

I shook my head, both honored he thought so highly of my opinion that he had some girl wait while he verified, and horrified he'd ditched the poor girl while he checked in.

"Dallas, go put the poor girl out of her misery," I ordered. "And next time maybe tell her you'll think about it, and then we can discuss it when it isn't so time sensitive."

"And risk her taking my *maybe* as a commitment? Please, just like the nun, that is a mistake I'll only make once. Thanks, but no thanks." He chuckled.

There weren't many men who could get away with stringing a woman along, but Dallas was a rare breed. Which was why his church-going lady friend was probably still waiting for him despite him needing to take a call. Even if her intensions were only of the religious kind, I didn't doubt Dallas would be charming as he always was. And if she was working some weird angle and we'd been mistaken, then she'd probably be smitten he'd taken it so seriously.

"Bye, Dallas. I have work to do." I sighed, still amused by the conversation. "Call me later and let me know how it all worked out."

"Will do," he promised, saying goodbye before he hung up the phone.

There wasn't a doubt I'd be hearing from him later, and if I was honest I was curious how it went.

My life had never been boring. And I often seemed to find

myself in one or more messes of my own in my personal life. But there was something refreshing and almost exciting to not be the subject of the mess. It literally had nothing to do with me, nor could I be inadvertently dragged into the drama. Plus, it was one time where my past could be of some use. Good, instead of evil. It made me feel giddy, sort of like getting a free coffee when you hadn't realized you'd filled up your loyalty card. A wonderful and unexpected surprise for all the previous times you'd more than paid your share.

With the feel-good vibe still humming through my body, I turned my attention back to my computer. It was another area of my life where my previous determination had paid off. Working hard had earned me not only respect but incredible success too, which was something I wanted to continue.

All good things.

Which was why even though I knew I was going to be buried for the rest of the afternoon under a mountain of spreadsheets, I did it with a smile.

It was good to be at the top of my game, or at least that was where I assumed I was. And until something showed me otherwise, I was going to enjoy the weird feeling of contentment I had going on.

Teaming up with Dallas had been such a good idea.

DALLAS

I WASN'T THE KIND OF guy you'd want in charge of babysitting anyone.

Normally, I'd be the first person to tell you how awesome I was, except when it came to taking care of something important and keeping out of trouble. That was a level of responsibility I didn't care for or want. But taking someone out and showing him a good time, well there was no man better for the job. Just as long as I didn't have to worry about him getting home in one piece. I would take him to the Promised Land, show him the way to all of the spoils, but when push came to shove, it had to be every man for himself.

"So, Mason, here is the deal." I mapped out our plan as I pulled into a parking spot not far from one of my favorite bars. "We go in together. If we're lucky, we'll be leaving separately. This place is like a club but without the required dancing. Which means although it's a bar, it has a lot more women."

"I'm not looking to hook up. But if that's your thing, that's cool, I'll call my brother-in-law for a ride." He tipped his chin at me and grinned.

What the fuck?

OOOOOOOOOOOOOOOOOOOOOOOOHHHHHHHH

I laughed, glancing over at him and giving him a nod in appreciation. Honestly, I was a little disappointed in myself that I'd just assumed he'd be into *women*. I mean, times had changed and love was love, right? And I had zero problems with anyone's preferences. Hell, the more men out of the game, the less competition I had. So he could go on with whatever he wanted, and he'd catch no heat or judgment from me.

"Hey, I feel you, dawg." I put out my fist, waiting for the bump. "There are men in there too. Whatever your flavor is fine by me."

It was his turn to laugh. "I'm not gay, Dallas. I'm just not into random hook ups."

Hold the hell on.

He wasn't into women *or* men? Well that made me really confused.

"Are you . . ." I swallowed hard, having heard about men of his *kind* but never thinking I'd ever see one in the wild. It was New York for Christ's sake, and I was sure those were all gone. I dropped my voice to a whisper. "A celibate?"

Mason grinned, looking pretty pleased with himself considering his dick was basically an ornament. Not sure I'd be so cool about it. "Relax, dude. It's not a disease you can catch. But no, I'm not celibate. I just have to be into a girl before I have sex with her. You know, get to know her mind, her spirit—that kind of thing."

"Umm . . . like with *every* girl you're ever with?" I'd been mistaken, I wasn't with a celibate; I was with a unicorn.

Fine, maybe I was exaggerating. I completely understood that some men preferred to have "girlfriends." They would rather know what was on the menu than rock up at a buffet and take their chances. All good. But given a chance—and a guy was not in a relationship—there weren't a lot of red-blooded males out there who wouldn't at least want to take a sample. It was like going through a supermarket and not taking the free cheese on the cracker when the woman in the apron offered it to you. It's free cheese, why the hell *wouldn't* you take it. Not to mention how are you going to know what you like unless you taste it?

"Yeah, with *every* girl," he confirmed, popping open the passenger side door, hopping out of my Corvette.

With my mind still stuck in the groove that was the new guy's confession, I joined him outside. Maybe I should hook him up with *Dry Cleaner Holly*? She was probably more his demographic than I would ever be. I was still going to eat her cookies though, because they were freaking delicious.

"Huh, well good for you. I guess we'll just hang out then. You still drink, right?" I had to ask, unsure if his aversion to pussy extended to all of life's joys.

"Yeah, I still drink." He shot me a grin. "And seriously, you do you tonight. I don't need my hand held if things go well for you."

Well at least he had that going for him and wasn't demanding we sit in a corner and chat like a bunch of old women.

My head bobbed in silent thanks as I pointed to the door. "Great, then let's go in."

He led the way, walking to the front where we were greeted by two security guards. They grunted an acknowledgment, stepping aside as we walked into the bar, the noise welcoming us like an old friend.

I didn't bother looking for a table, preferring to get a seat up at the bar if it was available. It was not only closer to the booze but also gave you a better view of what was on offer. Besides, while I had no issue with anyone else's sexual preference, I wanted to be very clear about mine. And sitting at a table with a dude didn't exactly do that.

At the edge of the bar I spied two vacant stools, the massive dude sitting next to them looking like he ate the last people who'd sat there. Still, beggars couldn't be choosers, and I wasn't going to stand like a loser all night.

"Hey, buddy." I tipped my chin to the behemoth perched on his seat, hoping English was his first language. I didn't speak Sasquatch, so if it wasn't, we were shit out of luck.

His massive head tilted downward, looking at us like he couldn't believe someone had addressed him. "You talking to me?" His voice rattled down his throat like a train coming off the rails.

"Well, unless you've got some invisible friends," I pointed to the empty bar stools beside him, "yeah, I was talking to you."

He grunted, muttering a *"whatever"* into his beer as he turned back to the bar and ignored us. That was fine by me because having a conversation wasn't high on my agenda either.

"Two beers, Roscoe." I tapped my hand on the bar. "Domestic, you can choose."

It wasn't the kind of place that served draft, the fancier surroundings made sure of that. And even though we were in Queens and not Manhattan, people liked to drink their longnecks with the illusion it was something more than it was. Still, I wasn't complaining because its bullshit makeover got some of the hottest women in town to stay local. And screw crossing the bridge when I had everything I needed right in my own borough.

"Looks like the place to be." Mason nodded as icy-colds came our way. "It's a Thursday night and it's wall-to-wall."

"Dude, it doesn't matter what night it is, there is always action at this place. Why do think I brought you here?" If I was going to be showing the new guy around then I might as well entertain myself at the same time.

He nodded silently, but his look didn't convince me that he agreed.

"So, what's the story with you and all the talking?" Part of me was curious and the other part was making conversation. It wouldn't hurt to know him a little better too, might help me to work out his agenda.

His eyebrow rose as he lowered his beer. "With women?"

The head nod in the affirmative enough for him to keep going.

"You aren't worried you're going to catch it?" The bastard smirked, the sarcasm dripping from his voice.

"You want me to tell King Kong sitting next to us that you think he looks sexy in his jeans?" My chin tipped to our neighbor, who was doing his best to ignore us. Besides, it looked like shooting evil stares at the hipsters across the bar was a full-time job. He was probably too busy to worry about either of us.

Mason's eyes flicked to the big guy and laughed. "Let's say that's a firm no on that. But if you want the truth, I get turned on by their minds, just as much as their bodies. Trust me, once you start finding out what they like and don't like, and what really makes them tick? A whole new world, brother."

He didn't even try to hide his smug grin, looking like he had some super-secret key to unlocking the best sex ever.

"You're so full of shit." I chuckled, feeling sorry for the guy. The only kind of man who needed to stop and ask for directions was a dude who didn't know what the hell he was doing. And trust me, I knew plenty. "I have never had a woman who wasn't completely satisfied. I feel it in their bodies, hear it in the way their breathing changes—I don't need them to tell me when I have an inbuilt compass."

Mason's head shook, disagreeing with me as he leaned in closer. "You misunderstood me. The *whole new world* isn't for them. It's for *you*. It takes the high to another level. It's like getting to drink a really good wine. And once you've had that, you won't be satisfied with the bottle of Boone's Farm you used to think was okay."

Firstly, I hated wine. All kinds. And I especially didn't drink grape juice that was flavored like Kool-Aid so dipshits could get drunk for three-dollars and ninety-nine cents. And secondly, that sun in San Diego must have baked the poor idiot's brain, because if he didn't think I was living the dream, then there was no helping him.

"You been smoking weed, sunshine?" I cocked a brow, not sure if he was serious or jerking my chain. "Josh had to have told you about me, right? Everything about me is top shelf—my art, my ability in the studio and *everything* else." I figured he was a smart enough guy not to need it spelled out.

"Hey, like I said before, you do whatever you like. But you asked me, remember?" He conceded, holding his hands up.

Fuck.

I hated it when someone was right.

Not about me needing coaching in the bedroom, because there'd be a cold day in hell before I'd ever need that. But about being the one who asked.

"Yeah, yeah. Let's talk about something else. Tell me if Joe is still as big a jerkoff as he used to be."

Mason took the hint and diverted the conversation back to his previous life out west. I tried to listen, hearing snippets on how he'd met Joe and become an apprentice. Then rattling more bullshit on how art was his only true way of expression blah, blah, blah.

But as I listened, the shit he'd said earlier ate at me.

Like he knew something I didn't, and I'd somehow missed out.

I didn't usually have issues with my confidence. Pretty sure I had loads to spare. But the douchebag looked so freaking sure of himself. And just a look around the bar at all the eyes of appreciation on him proved he could have any woman he wanted.

And yet, there he was, talking to me about growing up without any parents, and missing his sister, and I swear if he says *art is my life* one more time, I'd probably puke.

"Yeah. Great. Sounds good." I nodded, not sure at what point of the conversation we were at. Hopefully it wasn't anything to do with him being an orphan or something like that. I wasn't a complete heartless bastard.

Mason stopped, looking at me like I'd grown another head. "You didn't hear anything I just said, did you?"

"Of course I did," I scoffed, not willing to admit I'd zoned out like one beer and half an hour ago. "Art is your life," I repeated, the words not sounding any better coming out of my mouth than they did out of his.

He laughed, handing me the next beer he'd obviously ordered while I was pondering, and pointed discreetly to a brunette across the bar. "I said, she's been staring at you for twenty minutes straight. And I was asking if you knew her."

My eyes rose to the hottie who was indeed staring. I'd been so caught up in my own thoughts to even notice. "Nope, but looks like someone I'd like to meet." I shot her a grin, the pink hitting her cheeks as she quickly turned away like she was embarrassed.

Hmmm. *A shy one.* Hadn't had one of those in a while.

"She's kind of cute." Mason lowered his beer, wiping his mouth with the back of his hand. "You want to go over and say hi?"

Go over and say fucking hi?

"Bud, seriously. You know we're men, right? We don't say hi." I laughed, admitting that while I still hadn't worked him out totally, I didn't outright hate the guy.

He had some good qualities.

Keeping an eye out for prospective talent was one he'd already proved. So maybe he wasn't so bad after all.

"Nope, I've let her know I'm interested. Ten-to-one, she'll come over herself. Or, if you like what you see, feel free to go there yourself."

He coughed, choking on his drink. "Thanks, but I highly doubt she's interested in me. And I'm not the kind of guy to make a move on a woman when another guy is involved. That leads to nothing but a mess. Besides, we've already discussed my *feelings* on hooking up in bars."

"Suit yourself." I shrugged. "But there would have been no bad blood on my end. She just seemed more your speed, looked like she might want to *chat.*" I laughed.

My mouth savored the beer, grinning as a pair of blondes shimmied our way. "And I have a feeling something better is about to come along anyway."

Mason followed my line of sight, seeing the twin beauties headed in our direction. He might be up in his ivory tower with the get-to-know-their-minds BS, but I had no problem with getting to know their bodies first. "Be a team player and keep the purity ring under wraps," I coughed out, smiling at the dynamic duo. Given a choice I'd keep them both myself, but I wasn't sure if they were a package deal.

Mason nodded, though I wasn't sure how much of a wingman he was going to be. But I swear to God if he ruined it for me, I was shipping his ass back to California.

"Ladies." I lifted my beer in greeting as I tipped my head in appreciation. They weren't drop-dead gorgeous, but they'd do.

"Hey, Dallas." One of the ladies draped her arms around my neck. "Who's your new friend?"

Firstly, I had no idea who either of them were despite at least one of them knowing my name. And secondly, the smile she was giving me reeked of prior familiarity.

Shit.

"Ahhhh, that would be Mason." I swiveled toward him seeing he had his own blond accessory, trying to throw her hands over him like a scarf. "He's new in town."

I'd hoped one of them—and I didn't care which—would handle the introduction, their names kick-starting a memory or two. I didn't want to commit myself to a repeat performance until I was positive the previous encounter had been pleasant.

"Faith."

"Lucy."

Mine then his responded, their names fired out without any fancy preamble.

And even with the new info, I was still no wiser in who they were or when we'd met.

Well, to be honest, names had never been my forte, so it wasn't exactly a shock on the lack of recall. The one thing I could trust were my hands; the fingers unoccupied by the beer made their way across Faith's waist hoping to get a *feel* in more ways than one.

Ahhhhh so *that* was who she was.

What I'd lacked in memory I'd made up for in tactile recognition, able to know exactly when we'd met and what we'd done as I braille read her body.

Left thigh tattoo.

Butterfly.

Except it hadn't been *her* body I had worked on. It had been some other woman, the *Lucy* she was currently with not the same BFF I'd remembered. Left-thigh-butterfly had cried most of the time, Faith holding her hand. Didn't flirt, didn't acknowledge me—letting me do my work without a single sexy look. It was two weeks later when we ran into each other at a nightclub in Brooklyn that she gave me her full attention.

Didn't even wait to get me home, dragging me into the ladies bathroom where I pounded her from behind.

And then like the perfect one-night stand, she vanished into thin air after we left the bathroom.

I could do a repeat.

Especially since the bar we were in had recently refurb'd the bathrooms.

"So, Mason, where are you from?" Lucy asked, batting her eyelashes at him despite him giving her no encouragement. "You here on business or pleasure?"

While I could tell she was aiming for sexy, she fell short on flirtation. But to Mason's credit, he answered her like she'd asked a genuine question, trying to keep her hands above his belt while he looked at me for help.

"I just started working with Josh and Dallas."

"How fun." Faith moved her body into my lap, smirked at her friend and then turned to Mason. "You're going to love working at Ink Addiction, Josh is fantastic and Dallas is soooo talented."

Usually I loved hearing about my talent—in or out of the sack—but her tone had been off, like she wasn't sincere.

It was too enthusiastic.

The words sounded hollow.

And as much as I hated to admit it, I'd heard enough of those to know the difference.

Interesting.

"Well, thanks for the recommendation," I responded coolly, still unsure if she was trying too hard or she was nervous.

Whatever her angle was, she had no reason to lie. Her friend had gotten a Monarch so freaking realistic it looked like it was going to lift right off her skin, and Faith got two orgasms before I claimed my own. Then she'd done a disappearing act, for which I hadn't even hinted to be mad about.

If she was trying to be defensive for any shade I might throw her way, she didn't have to bother.

"Mason is from San Diego," I offered, deciding more conversation was needed. "And I was pointing out how awesome it is here."

Lucy had given up trying to touch him, deciding pushing out her tits would be more affective. Pity she had no idea that Mason had more interest in hearing her life story than sliding his hand down her top.

"Can we buy you ladies a drink?" Mason asked, being a gentleman and ignoring the breasts that were in his face. That was pretty strong resolve right there.

"Um, no we're fine," Faith answered quickly for both of them. "We had one earlier." She leaned in closer, rubbing her body against mine.

There weren't many women who turned down a drink, but I didn't ask questions. I was too distracted by the sexy dance she seemed to be performing, her body teasing mine without me even asking.

She was making it clear she wanted me to touch her, which wasn't a hardship. My hands were already there, and even though part of my brain was telling me it was a bad idea, I decided to give the girl what she wanted.

To say it felt wrong was an understatement, but not because I was suddenly growing a conscience. There was just something about the way her body tensed despite her flashing me a neon sign that she wanted my hands or anything else from me.

If Mason's preaching had sunk into my brain and ruined what used to be amazing, I was going to have to knock the dude out. I had a relatively pretty girl in my lap and I was doing more thinking than I liked.

A purr spilled from her lips, appreciating the attention I was giving her as Mason unwrapped himself from Lucy and excused himself to go to the bathroom.

Not sure if he genuinely needed to take a piss or his dedication was starting to wane. After all, Lucy was giving him a look that said she'd probably drop to her knees and blow him right there if he'd asked. At the very least he was going to need to re-rack what was in his pants.

Lucy parked herself on the newly vacated stool while Faith leaned in. Her hands moved up my thighs as she brought her lips closer. I wasn't sure if she was trying to tease me or wanted me to take charge, but unless I was reading her entirely wrong, she wanted my mouth on hers.

"Hey, Dallas, we need to go." Mason had either taken the quickest bathroom break in history or had a severe case of performance anxiety.

Oh, and he was cockblocking me after he told me he was going to be a team player.

Not cool.

"What's the rush?" I bit back, my agitation pretty clear as I speared him with a glance.

Faith had pulled back, the interruption cooling her seduction. "You can't stay a little bit longer?" she asked, gripping the front of my T-shirt in what was disappointment or annoyance. And I completely got it too because I wasn't exactly pleased either. Especially when I was trying to be charitable and let the new guy hang with me.

Mason held his phone up and waved it in his hand. "Josh called, said there was an emergency at the shop. We need to go."

While I was bewildered beyond measure that Josh had called Mason instead of me, I would argue about the phone tree later. Josh needed me and that was all I needed to hear, no woman or anything else was getting in my way.

"Sorry ladies, we're out." I almost shoved Faith off of my lap and reached for my keys. "Let's go." I headed for the door not bothering to see if Mason was behind me.

We reached the front door at the same time, the big guy waiting as I pushed through and exited into the street. "What did he say? We heading to the shop?" I talked and walked, my singular focus on getting wherever I needed to be. Josh rarely asked for my help, so the one time he did, I wasn't going to let him down.

"Yeah, the shop." Mason shoved his phone into his jeans as I unlocked my car.

He didn't give me any further instructions, getting into the passenger seat while I took mine behind the wheel. The engine of my Vette roared to life as I hightailed onto the road.

Without thinking I pulled out my phone and started dialing, Mason reaching out and yanking my cell from my hand. "What are you doing?" I spat out, my eyes shot to his as I concentrated on steering.

"Just pull over." He pointed to an abandoned hardware store, its empty parking lot a ghost town.

I shook my head, wondering how I was going to choke him out *and* keep my hands on the wheel, a little tired of his good boy attitude. "Dude, I can drive and talk at the same time. I will put it on speaker, and quit being a dick and hand me back my phone." Pulling over wasn't an option, especially since I had no idea what the emergency was and we were only ten minutes away from the shop.

"Dallas, for real. Stop the car, I don't want you to wreck when I tell you."

My head whipped around almost driving off the road, the situation critical as I thought of every worst-case scenario that involved my best friend. "Stop fucking with me, Mason. What the hell happened to Josh?"

"I lied." He blew out a breath. "But it was the only thing I could think of. Josh didn't call and there is no emergency."

Pulling the steering wheel hard to the side, we skidded to a stop on the curb. Some asshole behind me flipped me off, beeping his horn and calling me a dick as he went past, but I didn't care. I needed to know what the hell was going on and how I was going to explain to Josh our new tattooist had gone missing.

"Listen, Mason." He was lucky I was still using his name and not one of the alternatives floating around in my head. "I don't give two shits about you and your wishes of abstaining. You live your life and keep your balls for decoration, it's all good with me. But don't you dare try and push your agenda on me. Who the hell are you, anyway? Some kind of traveling monk?"

The dude had the good sense to look worried, holding up his hands in surrender. "Dallas, it has nothing to do with that. I don't have an agenda, and I personally don't care if you screw both of them at the same time."

"Then why the hell did you yank the ejection handle?" I fired back, annoyed, with a side order of sexually frustrated.

"Because, while I might not have cared, the dude watching it go down probably would have."

"What the fuck?" I reared back, the words not making any sense. "What the hell are you talking about?"

He thumbed over his shoulder in the direction of the bar. "That woman who was trying to make a move had a dude about my size watching the entire time. Not sure if he was her boyfriend, her husband, her brother, or some other asshole she was trying to make jealous. But he was with his friends, and like five minutes away from walking up to you and taking a shot."

"No, no, no." I shook my head, Mason clearly mistaken and/ or delusional. "Dude, I already had sex with her like three months ago or something."

"Yeah, and how did that go for you?" His raised brow cocked like he was expecting details.

"Hey, I'm not a choirboy like you, man, but I don't go into the play-by-play," I fired back, floored by his nerve. He was the new guy for Christ's sake; I didn't even know him and he'd already pissed me off more times than I could count.

"I don't want to know what you did, dude. All I'm saying is I have witnessed enough bar fights and pissed off boyfriends to see a revenge fuck when it's about to go down."

Now that I thought about it, she had been a little weird.

Didn't want a drink.

Didn't want conversation.

And seemed hell bent on getting me to make the first move.

Ordinarily I'd say it sounded perfect, but we'd already been *there* and done *that* so all she needed to do was ask and she probably would have received.

"Yeah, whatever," I huffed out, slightly annoyed he might have been right. While it wouldn't be the first time I'd been involved with a girl who was already taken, I didn't like the drama that came with it.

Yeah, thanks but no thanks.

"So what, you want to go home?" I didn't need to check the

time to know it was still ridiculously early.

Mason, looked out through the window at the passing traffic. "You want to show me just a regular bar?"

I rolled my eyes, throwing the car into gear and easing back onto the road. "Fine, we'll go to a *regular* bar and sit like a couple of old men in the corner. Just don't try and convert me or anything. I've had my fill of fucking drama tonight."

"Dallas, I'm not even religious. I'm not trying to stop you from anything other than getting a fist in the face." He laughed, relaxing into the seat.

My fingers gripped the steering wheel tight as I muttered under my breath. "I could have taken him."

"Sure you could, it was his five friends I was more worried about."

"That's what you're for. You worried about messing up that pretty face of yours?" I volleyed back not sure whether or not he'd have my back.

He shook his head, a grin spreading across his lips. "Not worried about my face or anything else. I'll even buy the next round."

"Well, I can't argue with that." A free beer was a free beer, and if there was one thing I needed it was a drink. "Okay, celibate. Let's go spend some of your money."

KITTY

THURSDAY NIGHTS BLEW.

Eve was busy with gallery stuff, Lani was on a health kick and trying to talk me into going to Bikram yoga, and the woman who lived in the apartment next door was practicing her Inuit throat singing. She wasn't Inuit or a singer but believed—like Lani with her hothouse yoga—it would give her better life balance.

I didn't need my chakras cleansed or my spirit amplified, and I hadn't hit that level of boredom yet but it was close. Instead I sat on my couch, balancing the plate that contained my dinner on my knees and tried to work out exactly what was the difference between frittata and omelet. I had apparently made a vegetable frittata, using the food delivery service my sister had suggested.

Katy—yeah, our parents were so original—was a year younger than me but was my complete opposite. She was married, pregnant and knitted blankets that she donated to premature babies. She cooked, she cleaned, and had only ever been with one man—her husband. But while it might seem like she had it all together, she hadn't been able to hold down a steady job in forever. She'd changed majors in college four times, barely gaining her bachelor in general studies by the end of it. She could barely choose a job, let alone a career, flipping between working at bars and restaurants, retail stores and then going to do courses like cosmetology which she had no intention of ever using.

Together we would have been the perfect woman. Me, kicking ass in the professional world, while she had the domesticated side under control. And because her dinners looked like they belong on Pinterest, I decided to take her advice and try one of those meal subscription box services. It was idiot proof, they deliver the box with everything you needed to make a healthy, nutritious and well-balanced meal, and you followed the directions. I'll admit that about three steps in I went rogue and tossed everything into the pan, hoping for the best. Which was why I was looking at the mess on my plate trying to work out if it still fit the card description.

It didn't taste great but it was better than another night of takeaway, and the glass of wine helped it go down. Besides, I was so involved watching a whole season of *Project Runway*, I hadn't even noticed I'd finished the unnamable dish until I reached down with my fork and there was nothing left.

My motivation to do the dishes was also at a low, choosing to continue with the next season and dumping my plate on the coffee table while I chilled on the couch.

Boredom.

Which could only lead to bad things.

With my mind and hands idle, my thoughts wandered back to the man I'd seen in the elevator. He was gorgeous, and someone I'd probably like to get to know better.

Fine.

It was his *body* I wanted to get to know better. Wondering if he knew what to do with what he kept hidden underneath that well-fitted suit. I didn't have to see him naked to know he was ripped, the broad shoulders and chest and narrow waist billboarding his toned physique.

He had to be a client.

Leaving Heidi Klum and her fabric militia humming in the background, I pulled up my laptop and logged into the Braxton Hill portal.

As assistant to the CEO at Braxton Hill, I had access to almost everyone's schedules. Made things easier to track down executives, or get a temp up to speed when someone took unscheduled time off.

And oh so convenient when I wanted to look who had what appointments so I could try and work out who the mystery man was. Some might call it misappropriation of company resources, while I preferred to look it at as using all the tools at my disposal. Besides, it's not like I was using the information for anything shady. I was just going to get his name and then stalk him on the internet like a regular person.

As I'd exited the elevator at approximately one thirty, I had to assume the meeting had ended around the same time. Then all I had to do was look through the time blocks and hopefully narrow down my search.

There were three possibilities.

Lyle McCure.

Saxon Banks.

JD Easton.

Three names were better than twenty, each one of them entered into the search engine and hoping one or more of them would have an accompanying photo.

It didn't take long, the winning entry JD—Justin Dean—Easton.

Justin was in his early thirties, a lawyer who worked near Wall Street. Other than his public persona, there wasn't a lot to see which meant I had to be content with just his name.

Oh well, at least my night hadn't been a total wash and with that little nugget of information tucked into my proverbial back pocket, I decided to go to bed.

I stripped off in my bathroom, going through my nightly ritual of cleansing, naked. In my mind it made sense to be bare, taking off my makeup and moisturizing not only my face but also my body. My mom had drummed into both Katy and I that our skin wouldn't stay great forever. And as a woman who looked like she was still in her 40's even though she'd passed that time over a decade ago, I listened to everything she said. Well, almost everything she said. Okay, fine, skin care was probably it.

My parents were great, still together and living in Torrance. I didn't see them as much as they would have liked but they didn't judge me. In fact, they openly supported me and my life choices, which was probably why I was able to get through life with a decent self-esteem despite my many missteps. It could be worse, I could be severely unhappy, hating my job, and have the skin of a Komodo dragon.

While I was thanking my parents and my regimented skin care routine, I heard knocking at my door. Not banging like the dude who lived one floor up from me did when he came home drunk and got the wrong apartment. Like a regular knock, as in someone was at my door and wanted me to open it.

At midnight.

While I was naked.

Yeah, I wasn't *that* stupid.

Disregarding my lotions and potions, I hustled to my bedroom and grabbed a robe. I still wasn't sure what the plan was, but the person on the other side of the door didn't seem perturbed that I had yet to answer.

The knocking continued, my name only heard as a low whisper as I stalked to the door.

"Kitty."

"Dallas?" I called back, confused as to whether it was him or someone who sounded remarkably like him. We had already spoken a few times today, our last conversation either by phone or text, hours ago.

"Yeah, it's me. Can you open up?"

Ordinarily a late-night visit from a man meant only one thing. A booty call.

It wasn't uncommon for a guy who I'd been with once to turn up drunk or horny on my doorstep. Some would text first while others preferred the element of surprise. Sometimes I was up for it, sometimes not so much. And it was only my feelings on the matter that determined whether or not I opened the door.

But it was Dallas and we weren't doing that.

Pretty sure our agreement to help each other being better at hook ups meant we *weren't* sleeping with each other.

"Kitty, you going to let me in or not?" He laughed, reminding me that while I was internally debating I had yet to answer him and/or open the door. And that was just rude.

Deciding I'd left him standing outside long enough, I unlocked it and pulled it open. "Are you okay? What are you doing here?"

His eyes glanced down my body, taking me in like he usually did, but the usually cocky grin that accompanied his "look" wasn't there. "I need to talk to you."

Still no closer to knowing what was wrong, I invited him in and locked the door behind us. It was clear something was bothering him, and it unnerved me a little.

"Tell me." I grabbed his hand and led him to my sofa. "What's happened? Is it Josh? Eve?" The thought of something bad happening to one of our friends was terrifying but the only explanation I had for his somber mood.

It was Dallas—he never got depressed or serious.

"Do you think I don't talk to women?" he asked with zero context.

I narrowed my eyes, trying to get a read on whether or not he was drunk. He hadn't been slurring his speech and he walked just fine when he entered my apartment. No glassy eyes or rosy cheeks, or signs of excess sweating. Then again, he'd only just walked in, so it was probably irresponsible to assume he was sober too.

"Dallas, is this a trick question? You are talking to one right now."

"No, not you." He waved his hand. "Like *other* women."

Yeah, if he wasn't drunk then he was definitely under the influence of something because that sentence made no sense.

I felt his forehead, testing to see if there was any fever. "Honey, did you take something? You talk to women all the time. Like *a lot* of women. You spoke to one this afternoon, remember? She baked you cookies."

"Apparently that doesn't count if you are trying to get them in bed," he huffed out in frustration. "I was drinking with Mason tonight, and there was this girl who was looking to use me to start something with her dude. Now, I don't give a shit what is happening in someone else's relationship, as long as it doesn't impact me. But Mason had said some shit earlier about me not getting the best deal because I don't get to know them or talk to them—shit, I can't remember everything. And I swear, between Bible Holly, the chick at the bar, and then him, my head is completely messed up."

It was obvious he was agitated, and while I didn't know exactly who Mason was and why he was relevant, I needed to know a little bit more about what he said to Dallas if I was going to make any sense of it.

"Babe, you are going to slow down and go over it again for me, okay? Who is Mason?" I turned to face him, his brows pulled tight into a frown.

Given the prompt, Dallas launched into the details, telling me about the newest member of their team. They'd been looking for someone for a while so I wasn't surprised Josh had finally hired. I listened intently as Dallas told me all about the new tattooist, and his theory on women. I didn't interject, letting him get all the way through to the incident at the bar with the woman he'd previously slept with.

"So Mason and I ended up going to Bricks and Mortar near the shop, sitting in a booth like a pair of teenagers on a date." Dallas scratched his neck. "And I can't stop thinking about what he freaking said."

"About the woman trying to make her boyfriend jealous?" I asked, more than just a little agitated someone would use him like that.

Sex for sex's sake was fine when everyone knew the score, but using him as bait wasn't cool.

He shook his head. "Nah, that was dumb. I knew something felt weird, but didn't have my head in the game. I meant about him saying I could have better sex if I got to know them better."

"Ummmm . . . I guess?" I shrugged, not really sure. I mean, how was I supposed to answer? I had no idea what it felt like for him, and if it would improve with the added insight.

His frown deepened. "You mean, you don't know?" The surprise was genuine, like he was expecting me to have an answer.

"How can I know? I can tell you that no two women are alike and what one woman wants, another doesn't. We don't all want deep and meaningful conversations. Sometimes we like it dirty and rough, and don't want to feel like it makes us less than for wanting that. Sometimes we want to wear tiaras and sip tea pretending to be princesses. Women are complex creatures."

"Great, well now I'm even more confused. I was hoping to come here, have you tell me it was all horseshit and have one less thing to worry about." He sighed, leaning back on the sofa seemingly defeated.

I, myself, toggled wildly trying to decide what I wanted. I'd given up on the fantasy, believing a man who would be able to take me as I was and have a longstanding relationship, didn't exist. I'm not sure if it was my fault or theirs that I attracted and was attracted to guys who didn't fit that mold. Possibly because the fantasy didn't exist. It was a dream sold to us by toy manufacturers and movies, leading us to believe that there was someone for everyone and you just had to find them. But that wasn't true, which is why I'd given up looking.

My body relaxed against the couch beside him, our shoulders touching as I shifted my weight. "It sounds a lot like a relationship if you ask me."

"Yeah, and neither of us wants that." He laughed, wrapping his arm around my body and pulling me closer.

It was strange to have him touching me and for it not to be in a way that was sexual. I mean, we'd hugged and stuff like that when we'd seen each other in the past. But his arms around me felt *different*. Non sexual, non-demanding—like he didn't want or expect anything from the touch.

"Hey, we should do it." My spine jacked up from the couch as the idea floated through my head. "We should try it."

"Try what?" Dallas asked, completely oblivious to my brilliant plan.

I waved between us, trying to illustrate the familiar comfort we'd slipped into. "We should try to get to know each other better. Talk to each other. And then, I don't know, in a few weeks or a month, have sex again and see if it is better."

His lips twisted into a gorgeous Dallas grin. "Babe, if you want to have sex with me, you know all you have to do is ask."

"Not now, Dallas." I shoved him playfully. "It's an experiment. To *test* if Mason's theory is right. We already have our baseline; we had sex when we didn't know each other that well. Then we have sex again and compare data."

He screwed up his face in horror. "Now you're just making sex sound like work. Who even does that? Mason has already messed with my head, now you want to take away whatever joy was left."

"It's not going to be like work." I rolled my eyes. "Besides, it's not really different to what we are doing now. We are talking and helping each other. We just need to take it a little bit further."

His eyes dropped down to my breasts, following the column of my throat and back up to my face as a wicked grin spread across his lips. "You want me to handcuff you?"

"Not sexually, dumbass." I elbowed him, fighting my own smile. "I mean we go out and get to know each other a little better."

"Wait a second, did you not just suggest we have sex? How did that get taken off the table so quickly?"

"We *are* going to have sex, later," I promised. "When we know each other better, like Mason would know one of the girls he sleeps with."

It sounded strange, saying those words like I was talking to a stranger, which wasn't accurate at all. I knew Dallas probably more than most of the men I'd slept with, which probably wasn't well enough. Maybe Mason had a point, sure as hell worth finding out.

Dallas looked skeptical, nowhere near as convinced as I was that it was a good plan. "So do we write it on the calendar or something? How long does this getting to know you phase last?"

"Jesus, Dallas. I'm just as in the dark about this as you. I've dated a guy for three months before I found out he was stealing my used underwear and selling it on the internet."

While I did wonder why my collection of panties had dwindled, I just assumed I'd misplaced a few. Or the industrial washer at the laundromat ate them—happened all the time. And it wouldn't have been the first time I'd forgotten panties or a bra somewhere else, usually in a backseat of a car or a boyfriend's apartment. But the dumbass who I had been delusional to believe was my boyfriend happened to leave his web browser open. My previously missing— and worn—hot pink *Agent Provocateur* lacey bikini underwear stared me in the face from the computer screen. They had been up to two hundred dollars and bidding was still open for another three days.

"Let's do a month," Dallas decided. "It will take into account the fact we already know each other. Like when they take into account the time you've already served before they give out a sentence."

I narrowed my eyes, pretending to be annoyed. "Now who's making the sex sound unsexy. I don't think sleeping with me has ever been compared to jail time."

"Are we back to talking about the handcuffs?" He laughed, not buying my pissed off face for a second.

"Dallas, focus," I huffed, my manufactured annoyance starting to become real.

"Sorry, I'm focused," he apologized, actually looking sorry.

My body turned into his arms, looking up at him with excitement. "Okay, so we do this. Any questions?"

He hesitated, biting his lip like before he asked, "What about other people?"

"If you're suggesting a threesome, that's a bad idea." I shook my head, not willing to even consider it. "We won't know them like we know each other and therefore skew the data."

"I meant, are we doing this like you would a real relationship? What are the rules for this?"

He was so adorable, tilting his head to the side with eyes full of sincerity. "Dallas, we aren't dating and I'm not your girlfriend so you don't need to worry about being faithful. If you see something you like, then go for it." It wasn't like we were or ever would be a real thing. So he was free to do what or whomever he wanted. "I'd probably avoid getting involved in a serious relationship until after we're done though. I don't think it's fair to that person if we're spending so much time together and then cheat on them when we sleep together."

I'd been on both sides of infidelity, both cheated on *and* being the other woman. I couldn't decide which felt worse, to be deceived or be part of that deceit. Not like I'd been given a choice, and if I had, I would never choose to do that to another person.

"Chances of me having a girlfriend in the next year—let alone month—are almost nonexistent. And yeah, I would rather not have some douche you're dating wanting to track me down because I gave you a better orgasm than he did," he said with a grin.

"Good. So we see other people if we want to but make sure it's nothing serious until after. Now, it's late. Did you want to stay over?" I yawned, rising to my feet as I stretched.

Dallas joined me, ambling off the couch as he bit his lip. "But I thought we—"

"Not for sex, geez," I chuckled. "You can talk to me while I fall asleep. I hear people do it all the time. I read an article once that says when you get tired and are about to fall asleep is when you're at your most honest."

"Can we cuddle?" His mouth hitched at the side leaving no mistake as to what he was thinking. "No sex, I promise."

"The only reason you want to cuddle is because you want to touch my boobs." I warned. "And we both know it will lead to something else."

If not for the cheeky grin, I'd have assumed he was disappointed. "Yeah, you're right. And if we are going to go to all this trouble, we should probably try and do it properly."

"Exactly." I yanked on his hand and led him out of the room. "Is this going to be your first time sleeping with someone and actually sleeping?"

"Yep, I'm a virgin, baby." He batted his eyes sweetly. "You'll be my first."

"I like that. Now give me a minute to put on some pajamas and I'll meet you in my bed. Start thinking of things we should talk about."

I was still naked underneath my bathrobe and there was no way I was getting into bed like that. Not because I was shy, because being nude didn't bother me all that much. But because it would be too tempting for both of us and that wouldn't be fair.

He nodded, moving into my room and started to undress. I grabbed a long T-shirt I wore as a nightie and a pair of panties and retreated back to the bathroom to put them on.

It didn't take me long, getting into my sleepwear and heading back to my room in a little more than a few minutes. In that time he'd stripped down to his boxer shorts, using all the decorative pillows that I usually piled onto my bed in an effort to make it look pretty, to build a wall down the center of the mattress.

"You went from cuddling to the Great Wall of China," I laughed, amused by the comical sight I'd walked in on.

"Isn't this what PG is?" he asked, pushing an arm behind his neck to look at me. "And looking at what you're sleeping in, it's probably just as well."

I looked down at the faded oversized T-shirt that was about five sizes too big. "If this is what turns you on, then you have serious issues."

The smile on his face stayed locked in place as I shut off the light and shuffled into bed. The pillow wall moved, decorative squares haphazardly falling between us as we got comfortable.

Neither of us spoke, both staring at the ceiling as we breathed in silence. It didn't even feel weird, my body relaxing into the mattress as I felt his toe wander past the pillow border onto my side of the bed.

I didn't move, smiling as we touched more innocently than either of us had being in bed with someone else, the minutes ticking past with neither of us saying a word.

Finally Dallas spoke, pushing a silk rectangle out of the way so he could face me. "Hey, I know we're supposed to talk, but I kind of like just laying here and saying nothing. Can we talk tomorrow instead?"

"Yeah," I whispered back, my cheeks hurting from grinning. "I like just laying here too. Goodnight, Dallas."

"Night, Kitty," he yawned, slowly closing his eyes.

Mine closed too, my breathing slowing as my body drifted into sleep.

It was going to be an interesting night.

DALLAS

THE PAIN IN MY BALLS was almost unbearable.

I groaned, reaching down between my legs and feeling my dick so hard it hurt. Those twenty or so pillows I'd put between us were tossed across the mattress like confetti, zero obstruction from my view of a beautiful and sleeping Kitty.

I wasn't sure if I was glad or disappointed she hadn't moved over to my side of the bed. Her beautiful body was curled up facing me, her hands underneath her like she didn't trust them in her sleep. I didn't blame her, I'd done the same thing. I'd also repeated *"no sex"* at least a million times in my head before I'd fallen asleep. The hope they'd sink in and keep me on my best behavior subliminally.

And what do you know? It worked. My hands—and the rest of me—didn't make a move all night. It was incredible. I had been inches away from a sexy woman, with an incredible body, and didn't even try to cop a feel.

She stirred, the sexy noises coming from her lips making me harder as she moved in her sleep. I wasn't sure what time it was, but I knew it was probably time I bailed before the temptation became too great.

"Kitty," I whispered, scooting over to her and gently touching her arm. "I'm going to head out, sweetheart."

She reached out, her hand hitting my bare chest and rolled toward me into a hug. "Okay, thanks for spending the night." Her face pressed against my naked skin as her fingers rested on my abs.

All she had to do was move those fingers a few inches south and—

No.

I said I was going to take this seriously and I was going to.

"Babe, I can't leave if you're laying on me." I laughed, but it was nowhere near funny.

She yawned, making no effort to move. "But I'm so comfortable, and I don't have to be up just yet."

Not only had she not lifted her hand or head from my torso but she'd brought the rest of her body to join the party. Her legs brushed against mine as she snuggled into my side.

Shit.

Blood drained from every other place in my body and headed straight for the steel rod between my legs. I would have to jerk off for like an hour just to be able to function, the very real possibility that I wasn't going to be able to walk weighing on my mind.

Cursing under my breath—and hoping like hell I was earning some extra karma points or something—I leant down and kissed the top of her head. She purred, not taking the hint as I cursed again and gently slid her off my chest and onto the mattress.

"Ugh, you were so warm." She groaned in frustration, her eyes staying tightly shut as I moved off the bed.

That groan of hers ran right through me, not doing my morning wood any favors as I struggled to stuff it into my jeans. "Then I'll come back tonight and we'll do this again." The offer genuine as I continued to dress in the dark.

I hoped and prayed none of her clothes were on the floor as I picked up a T-shirt and shoved it over my head. It would really suck if I got outside and realized it wasn't my shit I was leaving in.

She sighed, blowing out a frustrated breath as her eyes slowly slid open. "I have this work thing tonight. A stupid party in the city. Not sure what time I'll get back, depends on how quickly I can get a ride home."

And like my good behavior was already being rewarded, the perfect opportunity presented itself. I knelt beside the bed, getting close so my eyes that had adjusted to the dimness of the room could see her.

"Well why don't I come get you? Just tell me where and when."

When I'd offered to come back to her house and be her personal heat pack, I had meant it. Other than possibly hindering my ability to have children later in life, the night had been pretty awesome. I'd slept like a log, completely at ease despite not being in my own bed. I wasn't sure if it was beginners luck or if there was something more to it. Definitely worth a repeat if for no other reason than to see if it could be replicated.

She shook her head. "You don't have to do that, traffic on a Friday night is terrible. Why go all the way into the city if you don't have to?"

The point was valid but not one that would change my mind. I'd been a New Yorker my whole life, a bunch of red taillights weren't going to piss me off, especially if I didn't have anywhere to be.

I'd have offered to pick her up even before our agreement, because that was the kind of guy I was. But seeing her with her eyes all glassy and her hair all messed up from sleep, there wasn't a chance I wouldn't offer to spend another night. "Isn't that what you're supposed to do when you are trying to get to know someone? And think of all the talking time we'll have in the car, means we can go to sleep when we eventually get in bed."

Her eyes widened, a smile as bright as sunshine spread across her face. "Dallas, that would be awesome if you could do that.

Really awesome."

"Then it's done. Send me the details and I'll see you tonight." I lowered my head and kissed her forehead again. "I'll be working late at the shop tonight anyway. Just let me know when you're ready to come home."

She nodded and thanked me again as her eyes started to droop. "Do you want me to walk you out?"

"I'm pretty sure I can find the door." I laughed. "See you tonight."

And like she'd been given permission, she closed her eyes and snuggled back under her blankets.

I grabbed my shoes and socks and walked out to her living room and pulled them on. It wouldn't be the first time I'd left a woman's apartment in the early hours of the morning, but it was the first time I'd done it and *not* had sex. You'd think I'd be pissed about that—somehow feel lacking—but I didn't. Which was as surprising to me as it would be to anyone.

Making sure I locked up behind me, I jogged to my car parked down the street. The sun was just starting to rise and I knew if I hustled I could get home and catch an hour or two more sleep before I needed to be at the shop. But as I tossed myself into my car, it wasn't Zs that were on my mind. It was the hard-on that was pushing itself impatiently against the fly of my jeans.

"Easy, big guy," I laughed, starting my ignition. "I'll get to you in a minute."

⁓⁓⁓

"HEY, SO WHAT DO YOU usually ask a woman before you fuck her?" I walked into Mason's room, his eyes shooting up from the sketch he was working on.

His brow scrunched in confusion, looking around the room for more of a clue. "*Excuse* me?"

"When you're chatting." I strolled to his desk, taking a seat on the chair opposite him. "Is there a list of questions? Like what are the topics you like to cover?"

It had been a busy day, with both Josh and I getting slammed with work. All days were jam-packed, but Fridays were notoriously bad. People liked the idea of getting ink done in time for the weekend, give them a chance to pay attention to the aftercare before heading back to work. Of course there were also the douchebags, the ones who wanted something to show their friends over happy hour. Either way, Fridays were a madhouse, both Josh and I loading up on appointments with neither of us even thinking about leaving before ten p.m.

Mason wasn't required to stick around, not having any real clients until Tuesday, he could have easily bailed around five. But either in an effort to impress the boss or because he didn't have anything better to do, he stayed and helped reset the rooms between clients, and worked on some sketches of his own.

A grin of understanding covered his mouth, the question finally making sense. "Dallas, there isn't a list. You just want to find out more about them, ask them about personal stuff."

"What's personal?" Josh walked in, the last of his clients leaving minutes before.

If it had been any other day, I would have given Josh the lowdown about our previous night the minute I'd walked in. But after jerking off in the shower, crashing into bed, and then needing to jerk off again, I'd woken up a little later than I'd planned. Which meant I was twenty minutes behind when I'd arrived at work, and Josh was elbows deep already.

There was no time to shoot the breeze, my client already sitting in my chair as I waved hello to everyone and got to work. I didn't even stop for a proper lunch, chowing down on a lukewarm burrito in the five minutes I had between clients.

"Okay, so Mason here doesn't sleep with women before he

gets to know them," I announced, tipping my head in the celibate's direction. "Like *ever*."

Josh laughed, the big guy's body shaking as he pulled over a rolling stool and took a seat. "You know, Dallas, a lot of guys do that. I'd say it's almost the norm."

"I said, *ever*," I emphasized to prove my point. "Even you, Mr. Sensitivity, have had a one-night stand or two, especially in the early days."

Josh wasn't like me, and definitely the more *feeling* of the two of us. Sometimes I thought he cared too much about people, sacrificing his own happiness for someone else.

That didn't make you a good person, that made you a fucking sucker.

And while I didn't agree with his *be-good-do-good* bullshit, I let it go because that was Josh. Me, on the other hand, thought it was a better idea to take care of yourself first. Not that I was a totally selfish prick, but I didn't see the need in making myself needlessly suffer.

But even Josh—the perfect guy with the heart of gold—had partaken in the spoils that was casual sex.

"I'm just trying to work out what the rundown is, like what he actually gets to know," I finished, the answer no clearer than when I'd first asked.

Josh shook his head, shooting a look of sympathy over at Mason. I didn't blame him, I felt a little sorry for the poor dude too. "You can head home, man. See you back tomorrow."

"Wait a minute, he still hasn't told me." I jumped to my feet wondering why Josh was trying to sabotage my efforts. "He can't just leave in the middle of a conversation. It is *literally* his thing, to fucking talk."

Both of them laughed, finding the irony as funny as I did.

"The more you know, the better it is." Mason tossed out the riddle like it was something profound, standing up and closing his sketchbook. "I'll see you both in the morning." He grabbed his backpack and his keys and strode out of the room.

"You want to explain?" Josh raised an eyebrow, making it clear that it was more of a demand than a question.

I shrugged, checking my phone for a message from Kitty that hadn't arrived yet and figured I wasn't in a hurry. "Sure, but let's go into my room instead."

As he followed me into my space, I gave him the rundown. Telling him all about Mason's theory and how it got me curious, willing to test it out with Kitty. Of course I didn't go so far as telling him I was going to have sex with her, because I knew he'd probably say it was a bad idea.

And it wasn't.

It was a fucking brilliant idea, and one that I wouldn't be talked out of. Not only did I see it as an awesome opportunity for me— expanding new horizons or whatever—it was the highlight of this whole freaking exercise. Sex with Kitty, a woman who I knew was dynamite in bed *and* had a body of a goddess. The thought of feeling her underneath me in a month or so made me so excited my balls ached. Seriously, if I had to take a vow of silence for a guaranteed night of sin with her, I'd probably do that too. So no, I wouldn't be talked out of it, which is why I saw no reason to mention it.

"Sounds like an interesting concept." Josh nodded, not shooting it down like I'd expected. There weren't a lot of my ideas he usually agreed with, which had me a little concerned.

"Interesting how?" I asked, waiting to see if it was one of the times he was being sarcastic and I hadn't gotten the hint.

He rubbed his chin, his eyes lacking the smugness they usually did when he thought I was being a dick. "The idea of you and Kitty trying to get to know each other, as friends instead of fuck buddies. That's really responsible of you."

I coughed out a laugh, thinking it was hilarious Josh was even suggesting I was trying to be *responsible*. That couldn't be any further from the truth. I wasn't trying to be *responsible*, I was trying to work out if I could have even better sex than I already did. But if he wanted to live in that fantasy world, then who was I to shatter his dream.

"Dude, you know it only happened once. And we agreed," *well more she agreed*, "that we weren't fuck buddies," I pointed out. "But yeah, I think this is a good idea."

"I agree, and I appreciate you taking Mason out last night. Sounds like you guys had a good time." He gave me a half smile. "I know I don't hang out with you as much as we used to but—"

"There's no need to explain. I've told you multiple times, if I had a woman like Eve at home, I wouldn't be wasting my time with you." I laughed, only half joking. "I get it. We're tight, even if you are getting married."

He clapped my shoulder, the years of understanding passed between us with no effort. "And on that note, I'm going to go home to *my woman*."

"Yeah, you should probably go before she wises up and dumps your sorry ass." I rose to my feet, unable to help myself from chuckling. "I'll lock up, I'm picking up Kitty from her work thing in a bit."

"Thanks, D. You really have stepped up these last couple of days. Makes me glad I never fired you all those times I wanted to." He joined me standing, his grin widening.

It was a threat he'd made at least thirty times, and both of us knew it was bullshit. But just like how I liked to tease him about Eve finding someone better, he liked to imply there would be a shop without me. Neither of those scenarios would ever happen.

He didn't prolong the goodbye, shooting me a "see ya," over his shoulder as he left my room.

With no idea how long I was going to be waiting, I flipped open my sketchbook and worked on some of my personal stuff. Even though it was on paper, I still got a thrill out of watching lines form into fully drawn pictures. Easiest way to lose yourself and your thoughts, and it had been my first love.

My only love actually.

Well at least I didn't have to worry about a page fucking me over.

It was probably an hour later when I finally got Kitty's message, her all caps *"COME SAVE ME!!!"* accompanied by an address in the Upper East Side.

I wasn't even bothered that it was my least favorite part of the city, smiling as I left my sketchbook where it was and grabbed my keys. Not sure exactly what situation she needed saving from, but whatever it was, I was her guy.

With Mason's fortune cookie response on what Kitty and I should talk about, I figured I was on my own. Lucky for me I had a decent amount of time to work it out, the distance between Queens and the Upper East Side longer than it needed to be because of traffic. I was so lost in thought that I almost didn't notice I had arrived at the address she'd given me. The apartment building I'd stopped in front of, the pretentious kind that had a doorman.

"Hey." She ran out, not even giving me a chance to find a parking spot. The passenger door was open a second later, her sexy body sliding into the seat as she looked back at the building she'd come out of. "Let's get out of here before O'Shea notices I'm gone and makes me come back for more team building."

I didn't know who O'Shea was, but I automatically didn't like him. Firstly, if Kitty felt the need to get away from him so badly, he was obvious bad news. And secondly, it had been a work thing, so the dipshit probably worked with her, meaning she'd have to see him regularly.

"Who's O'Shea?" I asked, trying to sound casual as I pulled away from the curb and got back onto the road.

She groaned, leaning into her seat and closing her eyes. "One of the executives from work. He's my friend's boss and an asshole.

He has these dinners to prove how rich and powerful he is."

My eyes followed the lines of her body and liked what they saw. Her spectacular figure was wrapped in a black dress that was probably conservative on the hanger, but didn't stand a chance at being anything other than sexy on her.

An asshole who made her feel like she needed to run from the building to escape his company sure as shit didn't deserve to spend time with her. Something I would be more than happy to remind him of, if the reminder was needed. "He didn't do anything, did he?" My body tensed, my knuckles tightening around the steering wheel.

"Oh God, no." She turned to face me, her hand reaching out and squeezing my thigh. "He's just pretentious, gets off on making people feel like they are inferior. But he has never even looked at me in a way that was sexual."

Ha! Yeah, unless the fucker was blind, that statement was one hundred percent false. But pointing that out at the minute would serve no purpose. I didn't want her worrying about the cocksucker thinking about her and second guessing herself at work.

"So if it's such a bad time, why bother going?" I asked, curious to see why she'd waste her time on something she clearly hated. Unless she was like Josh or Mason who had a hard-on for self-sacrifice, it didn't make sense. "Surely they can't make you go."

She sighed, rolling her head to the side, her lips edging into a small smile. "Because it gives me an edge at work. People get drunk and then they talk. I learn more about the business through these stupid dinners than I ever do through a memo. Information is power, Dallas. And if I can use it to my advantage to get ahead, then I'm going to do it."

Wow, of all the things I was expecting to hear, that wasn't one of them.

I'd assumed she'd give me some line about how it was expected and she'd be worried she'd lose her job if she refused. Or that maybe some asshole she had a crush on went and she was hoping to catch his attention. Hell, I'd even settle for the old *it's free food and booze, why turn it down.*

But to know it was strategic, to be used at some other time to help her further her career, made me grin a little wider. Not only were we more alike than I'd thought, but she was more than just a sweet sexy blond with an amazing pair of tits.

Loving the new side of her, I nodded at her to continue. "Tell me everything."

With a wicked grin, she proceeded to tell me all about O'Shea and his *famous* dinners. She talked all about her work, what she did and how she'd worked her way up through the company to be an assistant to one of the biggest honchos there was. From what I could tell, the dude couldn't even take a piss unless he had Kitty's help, the woman beside me flooring me with how smart and driven she was.

Not proud to admit it, but I always assumed she was like some bullshit secretary or something. That she went into work at nine, got people coffee, filed some papers and made copies of important documents. Then when the phone rang, she answered it, and maybe took a message if her boss was out of the office. Little did I know that not only wasn't she a secretary, but that she practically ran the day-to-day operations for her boss.

I barely managed to set my own appointments, bitching at Josh that we needed a person to help us, and Kitty was able to do thirty times that, and not break a sweat.

Impressed was too weak a word, the mix of pride and awe oozed out of me as she spilled her secrets, not laughing at my stupid questions as we drove the entire way home.

She looked at her apartment building, her eyes then finding their way back to me. "You're coming in, right? Spending the night?"

The question was all but redundant as I unlatched my seatbelt and pulled the keys from my ignition. "Are you kidding? Of course,

I'm coming in. I want to hear more about how you managed to get Eve's moronic ex demoted and not have anyone suspect it was you."

She laughed, throwing her head back in pure joy before leaning in closer. "Oliver is just lucky I was feeling generous that day or he would have ended up filing for unemployment. Besides, it gives me a wicked sense of pleasure to know that he has to turn up for work and be miserable. To think he was once the up-and-coming superstar and now is working as the *manager for internal acquisitions*. Oh, and don't let the fancy title fool you, he's basically in charge of the maintenance, janitorial and office supplies. Not even good office supplies because the assistants have their own accounts." She grinned, seeming to be thoroughly enjoying herself. "He takes care of things like pencils and notepads in meeting rooms, the inconsequential stuff that barely anyone uses considering everyone works on laptops."

Not wanting her to stop talking, I stepped out of the car hoping she wouldn't feel the need to stop as I raced to her side. She was already out, closing the door behind her as I locked it and followed into the building.

We climbed the steps, our voices and laughter echoing off the walls of the narrow stairwell, probably pissing off her neighbors. Not that I gave a shit, not bothering to lower my voice until we were both inside her apartment.

"Shit," I cursed, looking around her living room and feeling like a complete ass. "I had a list of questions I was supposed to ask you on the ride home. I got so distracted, I forgot to ask."

I had constructed what I had deemed perfect topics of conversation. Questions asking her about where she'd gone to school, where she'd grown up, family stuff—basically everything I never bothered asking anyone. Not only did I not ask, but I rarely even gave a shit, the thought of knowing about someone's past boring me to tears.

And while I didn't get excited about what was for sure going to be a mind-numbing conversation, I was willing to sit through the snore fest. How else were we going to accomplish the talk-and-get-to-know-each-other shit?

Kitty's eyes shot me an apology, her hands snapping to her mouth in horror. "I'm sorry, Dallas. I have totally been dominating the conversation and didn't even give you a chance. It is completely my fault, we agreed the drive would be our talk time."

"Babe, I could have stopped you at any time. And if anything, I'm just as much to blame. I was the one who asked about your work." I pulled her into a hug, hating that I'd made her feel bad. "You want to do it now?" I asked, not really feeling it but willing to make the sacrifice.

She scrunched her nose, pulling her face into a grimace. "Not really. I know I promised and everything, but I kind of want to get out of this dress and just relax."

Anything that involved getting her out of her dress sounded like an excellent plan, which was why I had to remind myself it wasn't going to be for my benefit. But even without the reward, I was just as happy to give my list of questions a pass.

"Then go get comfy." I grinned, letting my arms drop. "You want to watch something on television or go lay in bed?"

"What about watch television *in* bed?" She waggled her eyebrows with suggestion. "Best of both worlds."

"Josh should be worried. You are on the fast track to replace him as my new best friend." I laughed, letting her pull me into her room.

She tossed me a smile over her shoulder, handing me the remote as she kicked off her shoes. "Since I was the one doing most of the talking in the car, I'm giving you the power to decide what we watch. Strip down to your boxers and hop in between my sheets. I'm just slipping into the bathroom to get ready for bed."

And I'd cut out my own tongue before I would argue with that, pulling off my T-shirt before she'd even left the room.

Screw the questions, the conversation and getting to know each other better. We had a whole month to do that stuff; there was absolutely no rush. Which meant we had all kinds of time, and I was going to spend it doing more important things. And lying in bed with Kitty and watching mindless television had climbed to the top of that list.

KITTY

NORMALLY WHEN I HAD A guy over, I forewent my usual nighttime ritual until he was asleep and I could sneak out to the bathroom without him noticing. I didn't like to skip it entirely unless I spent the night somewhere else and it was unavailable.

But as Dallas and I weren't together in *that* way, I saw no reason to not do what I usually would do. Which was why I closed the door to my bathroom and slid out of my clothes until I was entirely naked.

With my skin bare, I stared at my reflection, removing my makeup before cleansing, toning and moisturizing as I always did. When I was done with my face, my attention shifted to my body, squeezing lotion into my palm before rubbing it along my neck and then continuing down onto the rest of my body.

My mood was euphoric, unable to wipe the smile from my face even though I was alone. The drive home with Dallas was amazing. I had laughed and chatted so much my cheeks had hurt, the buzz still running through me as I continued with an otherwise mundane routine.

The coolness of the lotion felt amazing against my skin, my

hand sweeping in large circles until it absorbed. My nipples puckered as I touched my breasts, my fingers cupping them as I moisturized, my body feeling hot despite the coolness of my hand.

I squeezed more cream into my hand, slipping down my torso and lower belly, and without even thinking about it, my hands moved back to my breasts.

"Ahhhhh." The low moan left my lips without any thought, more lotion added to my hand as I slathered my body so my skin was slick.

It wasn't the first time I'd turned myself on, touching myself sometimes inevitably leading to *touching myself* but usually I'd been alone.

Unfortunately I was not only *not* alone, but I had a man waiting in the connecting bedroom. He would only be too happy to help me "scratch that itch" if that was what I wanted, the thought of Dallas's hands and mouth on me getting me more worked up rather than calming me down.

My eyes darted to the closed door, biting my lip at my dilemma. There was no way Dallas and I could have sex. If we caved, it would completely ruin our chances to test the theory, and we had already agreed to wait a month.

But . . .

I couldn't deny that I was ridiculously turned on and the thought of going to bed like that made me worried for both of us. Not even a pillow wall would save us, my hands mauling him and riding him until he made me come the minute I slipped in between the sheets. It would be too tempting, reasons why flying out the window the minute either of us touched. I wasn't sure he'd stop me either, which was a problem since one of us had to be the stronger more rational one.

Tonight, that person wasn't me.

"Ahhhhh," I moaned again, my fingers slipping in between my legs and coating themselves in my wetness. It felt good, my body shivering as I swiveled my hips against my hand.

I'd just have to do it.

Make myself come in the bathroom, and *then* go to bed. It was my only option, and one I was very quickly making peace with as I stuck a finger inside of myself and felt my body clench.

"Yes." I closed my eyes, both agreeing with my decision and feeling the heat travel up my spine. Oh, it felt so good, my breath coming out in short and fast bursts as I moved my fingers faster.

"God, that is goooood," I whispered to the empty room, my thumb sweeping across my clit as I teased myself. I was so close to coming; the knowledge that Dallas was in the next room, completely unaware of what I was doing, made it even hotter.

I wondered what it would feel like if he watched, his eyes on me while I pleasured myself. My mind quickly decided he'd touch himself too, reaching down to his impressive cock and giving it a tug.

My back hit the wall, using it for leverage and stability as I continued with my fantasy. With my eyes firmly shut, I saw every inch of his perfect tattooed skin. The flashes of color up and down his arms, the intricate designs across his chest, all of it popping against crisp black outlines.

The metal bars that pierced each nipple caught the light, reflecting a kaleidoscope of color. My tongue flicked across my lips imagining licking each of his nipples, pulling gently against each bar with my teeth.

But that wasn't the only place he was pierced, a large ring with a ball at the end that went right through the head of his cock had made me come so hard I almost blacked out when we'd had sex.

I remembered exactly what it looked like, conjuring up the memory and rearranging for my own purpose. It was like my own private porno, the images running through my head in vivid detail.

The glint of the silver would flash as his hand pumped up and down his shaft, making him harder as he watched what I was doing.

His tongue licked his lips desperate for my body, just as mine were dying for his—our mutual pleasure and torture bringing me to the brink of insanity as I sunk deeper into my own mind.

"Yes, yes, yes." My body and mind got lost in the mix of fantasy and sensations, seeing every inch of him as clear as if he was standing beside me.

My legs buckled from under me, sending my body crashing to the floor as I came hard against my hand. Waves of pleasure spread across my skin as my core continued to pulse.

I might have been in that room alone, but the man on the other side of the wall was just as responsible for my gratification, the thought of him jerking himself off to completion almost making me come again.

"Kitty?" Dallas knocked, his voice sounding concerned as it traveled through the door. "I heard something fall, are you okay?"

"Yes," I managed to squeak out, unable to move as I braced myself with one hand on the floor. The other still hadn't moved from between my legs, the reminder of what I'd done still echoing through my body.

There was a pause as I tried to calm my breathing, not sure how much he could hear through the wood. "Babe, are you sure you're okay? You need me to come in?"

My lower body throbbed, not satisfied by the orgasm I'd given myself when it was suddenly presented with the man of the fantasy himself.

"What the hell is wrong with me?" I cursed under my breath, hoping like hell I could pull it together. I had literally just fingered myself in the bathroom while a man I was attempting to *get to know* was waiting for me in my bed. And because that wasn't bad enough, I'd been thinking about him the whole time.

"Kitty?" He knocked again, reminding me I had yet to answer.

My eyes went to the door, the lock not engaged because I hadn't anticipated taking that long and I begged for him to open it.

No.

Tell him you are okay, and will be out in a minute.

The confusion of what I wanted clouded my mind as my mouth opened and nothing came out. I tried again with no more success, the rush of air the only thing that passed my lips as I kneeled on the bathroom floor in silence.

My heart pounded as the knob turned, my body buzzing with hyperawareness as I watched the door slowly open. I was paralyzed, unable to stand or even cover myself and not entirely sure I wanted it even if I had the ability.

Open it.

See me.

The idea that when he did it would justify the decision to throw myself at him and lose myself in what I knew he could give me.

And just as I was about to be revealed, expecting the door to open and show me exposed on the floor, it stopped.

"Babe? Do you need me?" His voice was louder and more concerned without the wooden barrier.

Like a bucket of ice water had been thrown at me, my momentary insanity evaporated. What the hell was wrong with me? It was like I was some kind of sex-starved fiend unable to be friends with a man and *not* have sex with him.

Quickly I grabbed a towel from the rack and covered my body, mentally spewing expletives as I metaphorically gave myself a good shake.

"I fell," I croaked out, only telling half a lie as I wrapped the towel around myself tighter.

The door swung open without hesitation, Dallas filling the space. His body was naked except for his boxers, every inch of skin exactly how I'd imagined it a few minutes before taunting me. I swallowed hard as he dropped to the floor, the metal bars piercing his nipples mocking me as they shimmered in the light. "Shit, are you okay? Did you break anything?" He was on his knees beside me, his concern making me feel guilty.

If he'd only known what I'd been doing when my legs gave way I was sure his reaction would have been different. But I kept my mouth shut, my knee actually hurt as the endorphins from the orgasm evaporated.

"Can you move? Did you hit your head? Shit, do you have a concussion?" His questions fired at me as his arms went around my body. "Can I lift you? You didn't hit your back right? I don't want to make you a paraplegic because I moved you if you severed your spine or something."

I laughed, unable to stop myself even though his concern was both heartfelt and endearing. "No concussion and my back isn't broken I promise. I'm just an idiot," no truer words ever spoken, "and fell."

His arms engulfed me, my back pressing against his strong capable chest. At least I could no longer see those menacing nipples while he was behind me, that was about the only positive I could find as I felt his muscles flexing

"Jesus Christ," he huffed. "No wonder you fell, you are completely covered in goo. It's like a seal jacked off on you."

I laughed even harder, at both the silliness of his words and the irony behind them. "It's body lotion, I was trying to moisturize."

"Babe, I think we could grease the cylinders of my Corvette with what's covering your body. Maybe use a little less next time, pretty sure that isn't recommended use." His strong arms pulled me to my feet, keeping me steady as he turned me to face him. "Anything hurt?"

"No." I shook my head. "I'm fine."

Or at least I would be.

He kept his arms around me, seeming to be unsure of whether or not I was going to fall again. I didn't want to point out that the excessive lotion wasn't responsible as I allowed him to keep me steady. Plus, I liked his hands on me, liked the way they felt. Hugging was allowed, we hugged all the time, so what we were doing was well within the rules of getting to know each other better.

"You need help getting dressed?" he asked, his eyes dipping to my cleavage. Ironically the question not accompanied by the cheeky smirk.

I couldn't remember the last time Dallas looked at my breasts and didn't at least allude to the fact he wanted to touch them. In fact, I didn't think it had *ever* happened. It surprised me, catching me off guard as I hitched up the towel a little higher annoyed with myself that I was disappointed.

And for the millionth time in the last hour I asked, *what the hell was wrong with me?*

"No, I think I can manage. Give me a few more minutes and I'll be right out." I forced an empty smile still wondering why I was feeling weird. I should be grateful he wasn't making it uncomfortable or using the situation of being almost naked to his advantage.

It was what I'd wanted.

Or at least what I had thought I wanted.

He slowly released his hands, drawing them back with hesitation. "Okay, yell out if you need me." He took a step back, testing my ability to stand on my own feet before edging toward to door. "I'm literally just out there." He thumbed over his shoulder reassuring me he wasn't far.

I nodded, doing some reassuring of my own that my battle with gravity was over and I'd have no further issues with remaining upright. And I assumed he'd believed me until he left the bathroom but didn't pull the door all the way shut. The edge had been left ajar so all that would be required would be a push and it would swing open.

Ignoring the door, my feelings and the confusion that had taken up residency in my mind, I turned my attention to my body. Not in the same way I had before—I wasn't a complete masochist—instead using the towel to wipe off the excess lotion and make myself presentable. I quickly pulled on my sleep shirt again and a clean pair of panties, not bothering to check out my reflection in the mirror as I switched off the light and left the room.

Dallas was already in bed, the side he'd occupied the night before filled with his delicious body while my side was awaiting me. And this time around there was no pillow wall, the decorative squares and rectangles piled sort of neatly onto a chair I kept in the corner. I could tell he'd tried.

His eyes followed me as I slid under the covers, ignoring the television entirely. "I'm fine, Dallas, honestly. I'm just a klutz," I lied, tempting fate by scooting closer to him.

If he was worried about being next to me he didn't show it, stretching out his arm and giving me more room. I decided that I'd take whatever inches I could—even if they weren't the ones I'd been thinking of—settling against his body in a warm snuggle.

"What did you choose?" My attention turned to the screen, a cartoon playing in the background. "You put on the Disney channel?"

Granted the chances of us getting down and dirty were greatly reduced while there was a kid's show in the background—I wasn't a complete degenerate. But I thought we could watch something a little closer to our demographic. Maybe a comedy? Or an action movie? Something that involved a lot of blood and guts perhaps? Nothing sexy about seeing someone's brains smeared on a highway.

"It's *The Lion King*." He tipped his had to the screen. "One of the last hand drawn Disney animations. While technology is awesome, giving us realistic almost lifelike pictures, they completely lack the warmth of the hand drawn stuff."

Huh?

I turned my head, the confusion obviously showing on my face as I watched Simba prancing around singing about being unable to wait until he was king. The colors, the action, the flashes of activity spilled into each frame filling it completely.

"See, people had to sit there and draw every single cell by hand. There were no machines to do it for them. So while it meant that the result was less than perfect, it just feels different. Like a really good childhood memory or a warm hug. The skill these guys had is ridiculous, I mean, just fucking look? Every single time there is a slight change—a blink, a hair blowing in the breeze, a toe heading in the other direction—someone had to draw it."

"I haven't really looked at cartoons that way," I admitted, giving the movie more of my attention. My eyes widened as I watched the characters running, jumping, laughing, singing with so many changes it would have taken thousands of drawings.

"Pretty fucking crazy, right?" He leaned his head against me. "Everyone thinks it would be a walk in the park—just a kids movie—but that is an insane level of skill. Sadly it's becoming a lost art, all the animation now is being done on computers."

I continued to watch, fascinated with my new insight. "Have you ever done it?"

"Animation? God, yeah. When I was six or seven all I wanted to do was leave school and work for Disney. It was literally my dream, to sit in a room and get paid to draw all day. But I soon found out that it didn't work that way, and the idea of working on a computer makes my skin itch. Plus, you have to be really smart to do it. They make you go to college, and I couldn't do that, so that wasn't even an option."

The confession was startling, never expecting to hear that the heavily tattooed and pierced guy that I was currently snuggling with harbored dreams of working for Disney. It seemed as unlikely as me saying I'd wanted to be a mechanic. And I *hated* getting my hands dirty.

"Why couldn't you go to college? Was it a money thing?" I asked, realizing only after it had left my mouth that I had no business asking it. Hell, the last thing I wanted him to feel was that I was judging him. I didn't care whether he went to college or not, he was far from stupid. "Hey, sorry. That was really rude, you don't have to answer that."

"Nah, it's okay." He chuckled, giving me a soft kiss on the top of my head as he pulled me closer. "I didn't do great in school. Reading is *really* hard for me. I have to read something two or three times before it starts to make sense and in the end it's just exhausting, so my brain shuts off. I hated it, made me angry that everything just seemed like a struggle. Soon, I just stopped trying and my grades reflected that. I mean, I wasn't a drop out or anything, I graduated. But there wasn't a chance I would sign up to do it for four more years. Besides, in that time Josh and I were already inking each other in marker, and I suddenly found a new way to express myself. One that didn't involve me torturing myself for years."

I lifted my head, concerned about what he'd told me. "Dallas, have you ever been tested for dyslexia? Clearly you're not stupid, and your trouble reading was probably something they could—and should—have helped you through."

"Babe, it's fine. I am literally living the dream. Well, the *new* dream." He chuckled. "I get to go hang out every single day and be with my best friend. And as for the actual work, it's sort of like being an old school animator. Every single piece I do is different. I get to change styles, and challenge myself—and what I do is on someone's body for life. Think about it, some person liked what I drew so much they are willing to have it on their skin until they die. Screw reading, I'm a fucking God." His eyes shone with pride and mischief.

"That is *so* cool," I agreed, the need to overinflate his talent and skill level not needed despite the size of his ego. "I would let you tattoo me any day."

"Really? I thought you preferred Josh?" He seemed surprised, scrunching his brow in confusion.

Josh was an amazing artist, which was the reason I'd sought

him out to do the very large and detailed Birth of Venus that covered most of my back. I didn't even know Dallas then, not meeting him until after I'd already made an appointment with Josh.

"I didn't prefer Josh, I just knew of him," I explained, the choice made out of nothing other than a recommendation. "He'd done a forearm piece for a friend of mine and I didn't want someone I knew nothing about working on my back. But I would totally trust you to tattoo me. Actually, I think we should schedule a time and do it. I've been meaning to add more ink anyway, but you guys are always so busy that I never got around to making a booking. You think I can get preferential treatment since we're *getting to know* each other?"

"Are you fucking kidding?" His eyes lit up, squeezing me tighter. "I would *kill* to work on you. I'd fucking love it. And just so you know, as good as the Botticelli is on your back, what I draw for you will be a million times better."

While I didn't doubt that he would give me a masterpiece, it was a pretty bold statement. Josh's Botticelli was stunning; I couldn't imagine anything better. I'd be happy with just as amazing, excited to see what Dallas would come up with. "Well let me know when you're free and I'll make the time. And the preferential treatment I'm asking for is just for the booking. I fully intend on paying you for it, I wasn't trying to get a freebie."

"Please, I'm not taking your money." He rolled his eyes. "Firstly because I *fully intend*," he threw my words back at me, shooting me a grin, "on enjoying every single second of it. And secondly, because Josh has this no sleeping with clients rule. And again, I *fully intend* on sleeping with you. So, yeah. You aren't paying me."

Back in the bathroom I'd assumed his lack of attention to my nakedness was out of loss of interest. Or because he'd decided that since we'd agreed to wait a month, he didn't see any point in trying. Why waste the energy only to get turned down? I'm sure he had other outlets, and we had already decided that because it wasn't a relationship he had no reason to be faithful. So it came as a surprise that he'd mention it, my body heating at the suggestion.

"Fine," I conceded, resolving to find another way to pay him back. A gift worth a similar amount of money that he'd have no option but to accept. "I don't want to do anything that would jeopardize our agreement. And for the record, I *fully intend* on sleeping with you too." I admitted readily knowing fully the kind of fire I was playing with.

Disney movie or not, I couldn't ignore the hot, muscular body of the man I was very much attracted to laying beside me.

"So here's a question." Dallas breathed out, his finger trailing down my arm. "Does making out count as getting to know each other?"

I swallowed, focusing on his lips. "Yeah, I think so. Our mouths would get to know each other better for sure."

There had been no rules about *not* kissing. As far as I remembered, it was only sex that wasn't allowed. People even kissed on first dates and even by that standard, we were at least on our second. Possibly even third.

"Well thank God for that." His lips came crashing down on me, kissing me before either of us changed our mind.

I didn't hesitate, giving my mouth to him with full commitment as he slid in his tongue and deepened the connection.

It was hot, and seductive, with the right amount of tease, toggling between deeply passionate and light and sexy. His lips and tongue testing how far they could go before backing off and giving me sweet. It was making me dizzy, my body hot and excited even though he kept his hands respectably away from anything that was sexual.

We'd kissed before—hot and heavy, leading us right to sex—but what we were doing was nothing like that first time. He was patient, not willing to rush it as he took his time exploring my mouth. The desperation was there but tempered, simmering slowly underneath as he ebbed and flowed, making me hotter even though he was barely touching me.

My body arched into his, my breast involuntarily rubbing against him as they sought more than what he was giving us. And suddenly I couldn't remember why we weren't ripping each other's clothes off and screwing each other's brains out. Who needed a month? We knew each other just fine, and whatever stupid data I was hoping to find wouldn't even come close to how good he could make me feel right now.

He turned, his body opening to me as I hooked a leg onto his hip and brought myself even closer. He was hard, his cock grinding against my core as his hands stayed locked around me, not reaching for my breasts like I was sure he wanted to.

"I didn't fall in the bathroom," I admitted, losing my mind between the kisses and the feeling of his hard-on teasing my clit. "I was touching myself and my legs buckled when I came." I breathed out the words in between the heated kissed.

"Fuck that's so hot." He groaned in appreciation. "I would totally have loved to watch."

I twisted my hips, my sleep T-shirt riding up so the only barrier between us was my panties and his boxers. The friction of his hard-on and his piercing both maddening and delicious. "That's what I imagined. You watching me while I did it and you jerking off with me."

"Kitty." He purred out my name so low and raw it almost made me come. "You're driving me fucking crazy right now."

I wasn't an expert, but I was fairly sure that what we were doing no longer qualified as just kissing. Before I could think—and talk myself out of it—my hand slithered between us and breeched the waistband of his boxers. The head of his cock jerked as the tips of my fingers made contact, all five of them wrapping around his girth as I gave it a firm and decided tug.

If I'd been worried about crossing the line before, the question was no longer relevant.

"Tell me to stop," I panted into his mouth, unable to stop my hand from sliding up and down his shaft as my body used his firmness and my hand to find its own pleasure.

"Are you fucking crazy?" he panted back, his tone completely devoid of its usual cockiness. "Your hand is on my dick and it feels amazing, why the hell would I do that?"

"Because we're supposed to wait." I kissed him, unable to stop. "Talking." His lips owned mine. "Other stuff." The rest of the sentence lost with the possibility of never being spoken. And who gave a shit any way, I was positive it wasn't even as close to being as important as what we were doing at the moment.

A primal rumble traveled up his throat as his hands moved to my ass.

"Screw the agreement."

DALLAS

I'D CHOSEN FOR TWO REASONS.

One, the animation was freaking spectacular, and I genuinely enjoyed watching the work.

And two, other than some pretty obvious sexual tension between Simba and Nala, there wasn't any danger of me getting any more turned on.

I say *more* because I'd been rocking a semi since finding Kitty on the floor in the bathroom wearing not much more than a towel. Never had I been so glad for an accident—and equally glad she hadn't hurt herself—making me able to focus on something other than those fantastic boobs poking out from the top.

If I'd swung open the door and found her standing there and well, I'm not sure I would have been able to stop myself. Even though all the good bits were tucked away, the suggestion enough to test my resolve.

But the thing about my resolve was that it wasn't very strong in the first place, deciding that kissing her should be my next move. Not because I was hoping it would turn into sex—I'd already made my peace that wasn't going to happen—but because Jesus Christ,

I really wanted to.

And trust me, I *really* freaking tried to be good.

My hands stayed out of bounds, keeping decent while my mouth did no such thing. But then her fingers decided to wander and all bets were off.

Jesus, it felt good. Her hand tight and rough, locked around me as it jerked me off. Then she asked me to stop her like she thought I was capable of being rational.

Not. A. Chance. In. Hell.

Even a rational person wouldn't have been able to, because last time I checked super strength wasn't a real thing. That wasn't even taking into account what she'd told me just *before* the hand job, the reason she'd been on the floor in the first place.

If there'd been any blood left in my head when we'd started kissing, it had flowed right to my cock at the mention of her touching herself. I was lucky I didn't pass the hell out, the idea of her doing that while I waited in bed watching Mufasa was so hot I was positive it broke some kind of federal pornography law.

It wasn't fucking decent, that was for damn sure. But as her hand slid up and down my dick, I was more than willing to serve any jail time.

"Kitty." I said her name over and over again as my hands moved from her ass and yanked up the T-shirt she seemed hell bent on sleeping in. If it was supposed to be unsexy, then it hadn't worked, the shapeless cotton as effective as Victoria Secret's lingerie.

Her back arched, giving me enough room to slide it up her body and uncover all the good bits. Her tits stood up at attention like two cherry sundaes just begging to be licked. And what can I say, I really, *really* liked sundaes.

My mouth dropped to her nipples, swirling my tongue around each of them as her hand continued inside my boxers. Her tugs hadn't stopped but the rhythm was no longer smooth, her hand slowing as she gripped me like a vise. Just as well too, because any faster and I was going to come in her hand whether I wanted to or not.

The other shit I'd planned to ask her when she came to bed went right out the window. There was nothing else on my mind other than kissing and touching her.

Not what school she went to.

Not whether she enjoyed Pina Coladas.

Not if she liked getting caught in the rain.

My hands, mouth, and anything else she'd let touch her on every square inch of her hot and sexy body.

That was it.

"Can I suck you?" she asked, biting her lip suggestively as her bright green eyes lowered to the dick she still had in her hand.

I was going to stroke out.

The image of her lips wrapped around my cock so freaking vivid I was positive at some point I'd actually lost consciousness and had started to hallucinate.

My head nodded, not bothering to wait for my mouth to catch up and give her the *yes* we both knew was coming.

Whatever the plan had been, the new one was infinitely better, my hands giving her breasts one last squeeze until she maneuvered out of my reach. It was bittersweet; my mouth having nothing left to do while hers would soon be full.

"I need to lick you." Unlike her polite request, mine hadn't been a question. My need to put my mouth on her so high I was unwilling to accept any other outcome.

Her answer was given to me physically—a method I highly appreciated—tossing the covers back as she swung her body on top of me. I'd barely pushed her panties to the side when I felt her take me in her mouth. My groan muted against her pussy as I tasted her.

Neither of us had bothered to rid each other of our underwear. The time spent removing either or both wasted when we could be doing other things. Namely what we were doing.

So with my boxers yanked down enough to expose my cock, and her panties held out of the way by my hand, we'd problem solved like the badasses we were.

Every single suck, lick and jerk against my shaft was amplified as I thumbed her clit and fucked her with my tongue. But even the mouth skills of a goddess weren't enough to undo me until I'd felt her get off, my body flat out refusing.

"Dallas." She pulled my cock out of her mouth long enough to scream my name. "Oh God."

She didn't need to say anything else, her body shaking as it clenched around my fingers and gave me its precious honey. My tongue lapped at her, teasing out every last shiver until there was nothing left.

I'd barely had time to enjoy it, the pride of getting her off so quickly tossed aside as she repositioned her mouth back on me. And with the satisfaction of a job well done, my balls saw no good reason to wait any longer.

"Kitty, I'm going to—"

I'd tried to warn her, give her the option of pulling me out, but it seemed my resilience was spent, giving me its middle finger for waiting so long. There was no time to say anything, spilling my load down her throat as I came in hot hard bursts.

If she wasn't pleased, she hadn't bothered to show it. Continuing to take greedy pulls of my cock until I was convinced the stroke I hadn't suffered before was minutes from happening. Not that I cared, the softness of her body on top of mine something worth dying over.

My tongue flattened against her, wanting another taste as she did the same. I was positive we should stop but couldn't find a compelling reason why.

She made the choice I hadn't been ready—or willing—to make, easing her body around so she was no longer inverted. Nestled against my chest, similar to how she'd been lying before we'd gotten severely sidetracked, she kissed my pecs with her smiling lips. "So that happened."

"Don't tell me you regret it, Kitty. I won't believe you." I smiled back, unwilling to accept what we'd done had been anything short of perfection. "And *that* was so far from a mistake it isn't funny."

Her nod told me I wasn't wrong, her body still warm as she wrapped her arm around me. "You're right, that wasn't a mistake. And technically, we didn't have sex, right?"

Clearly she subscribed to Bill Clinton's rules and regulations regarding what constituted sexual relations. And she wasn't going to get any argument from me. Didn't have any time for it considering I was still enjoying the after glow of her spectacular oral skills.

"Yeah, no rules were broken, we're all good," I agreed, turning my attention back to the television screen. Pretty sure every time I watched *The Lion King* from here on out, I was going to get a hard-on. But that was a problem for another day, so no point beating myself up for being a deviant.

She yawned, her body relaxing against mine. "Do you have to work tomorrow?"

"Yeah, but not until eleven. You have plans for tomorrow?"

"I was going to see Eve's new exhibit. I feel bad I haven't made time yet but work has been kind of crazy."

Eve's gallery—and by hers, I mean she owned it—had been rotating shows on a fairly regular basis. She concentrated on local artists, but had a great eye for picking up raw talent. Oh, and she was also a pretty freaking phenomenal artist in her own right, her latest showing opened a week and a half ago.

"You want some company? Josh is closing the shop tomorrow at three, I could swing by and we could go together?" I offered, the words so easy in my mouth I hadn't even considered she might have plans for a Saturday night.

I was expecting the brush off, telling me that she preferred to go earlier so she could go do whatever later in the day. After all, we hadn't made plans and a girl like that didn't sit around on a Saturday and paint her toenails.

She tilted her head, her eyes fixing on me. "Really? Haven't you seen it already though?"

It wasn't what I'd been expecting to hear, her concern about whether or not I'd seen it taking the place of the mention of plans I assumed she had.

"Yeah, of course I have. Doesn't mean I'm not happy to go again." I kept it casual, making it seem like it was no big deal either way. "Besides, I still need to thank Eve for agreeing to marry the bastard. And that kind of thank you needs to be delivered in person."

All of it was true, even if it wasn't entirely accurate. I'd be happy to see Eve, and enjoyed walking around her gallery and contemplating the stuff she had on the walls. Not all of it was my personal brand of whiskey but I appreciated it all the same. And I had no doubt that my appearance would earn me all kinds of good karma with Josh, which was another awesome incentive. But all of those reasons weren't even close to why I'd offered, the *why*, pressed up against my chest.

"Well, okay, then. I guess it's a date. Hey, maybe after we can go get something to eat and we can go through your questions." She smiled, looking like I was doing her the favor when it had been the other way around.

"See, I knew you were smart." I kissed her forehead, excited for my weekend plans.

We didn't talk after that, didn't need to. Instead we lay in the bed together watching animation, relaxing into the mattress until we fell asleep. I hadn't even noticed when it happened, my eyes sliding open sometime in the early morning and finding the television still on.

Kitty was right where I remembered her, lying across my chest with her hand on my abs. I shuffled gently, doing my best to reach the remote control without waking her. She whimpered a little but didn't wake as I shut off the tube and plunged the room into darkness. I half considered getting out of bed and heading home but I thought better of the idea and stayed right where I was instead. I saw no point in leaving, and I had nowhere I needed to be. So instead of doing what I'd done the night before, I closed my eyes and went back to sleep.

I wasn't going anywhere.

cllep

THE SOUND OF A COFFEE grinder woke me, as did the smell of cooking bacon. I didn't even bother checking the time, willing to be late for work if bacon and coffee weren't just figments of my imagination.

Kitty was already out of bed—something I probably could have guessed without checking her side of the mattress—so I kicked off the covers and strolled into the kitchen. She was wearing the same T-shirt I'd peeled off her, her blond hair a mess as she moved around the space cooking what was obviously breakfast.

"Why are you up when you don't have to be?" I leaned against the kitchen counter appreciating the view.

She spun, waving the spatula in her hand like a magic wand. "I'm so used to getting up during the week, I struggle sleeping in too late on the weekend. Besides, I was going to bribe you with breakfast so you'd agree to drive me to the grocery store."

"Of course, the bribe isn't even needed." I winked, happy to play taxi for as long as she wanted. "Although it will be a cold day in hell before I turn down breakfast, so don't think you can take it off the table now that you've offered it to me."

Her smile was everything, beaming from ear to ear as she flicked her hair out of her face. "Don't get too excited, cooking isn't one of my many talents. It's only bacon, coffee and toast. I didn't have any eggs left, and obviously I need to shop."

"Babe, does this look like the face of a man who'd complain about food?" My finger circled my head for illustration. "Bacon and coffee sounds amazing. Let me just grab my phone and tell Josh I'm going to be a little late." He wouldn't be happy about it, but I would deal with it later.

Her brow rose, looking at me strangely. "Do you have something else to do? If you have plans I can catch an Uber or call a cab to the store."

I should have kept my mouth shut, and honestly still wasn't sure why I'd brought it up in the first place. All I had to do was pretend I was going to take a piss, send Josh a message, and go about our business like it was no big deal.

Regardless, I wasn't going to allow work or Josh's possible shitty mood to stop me from doing what I'd committed to and *wanted* to do.

"No, no plans other than this amazing breakfast you are promising and taking you shopping. But I have to be at work at eleven and just need to let him know."

Her eyes widened, the confusion of my earlier statement replaced by shock. "Dallas, it's *seven*. I'm not sure how long you usually take to eat breakfast but I can assure you I can get my shopping done in less than an hour. That includes getting there, coming back and putting it into my cupboards."

What.

The.

Fuck?

I couldn't remember the last time I voluntarily woke up at seven in the morning. Certainly none where I was happy about it.

"*Seven?* Are you sure your clock isn't broken?" I rubbed the back of my neck, a faulty timepiece the only explanation as to why I was upright, alert, and wearing a smile.

"Here." She pushed her phone into my hand, the time at the top of the screen confirming that it was seven-oh-two. "See, not broken."

While seeing the numbers confirmed it, I couldn't remember a time I saw seven in the morning and was glad about it. Unless you counted the times I hadn't been to bed yet, but that was a whole other story.

"Yeah, I guess we're good then," I answered, wondering if you could roofie someone in reverse. You know, where you put something in their drink and they end up alert and awake, the situation still not making much sense. Not that I was complaining, not when my view included a beautiful woman who was serving me up coffee and bacon.

We ate breakfast, and then Kitty went into her room to shower and dress. I had casually suggested I could help her with either or both those tasks but she decided to give it a pass. I figured it was more about time constraints because she was more responsible than I was but didn't push my luck. Besides, I wasn't sure how firm she was going to be on this no sex for a month thing. Last night hadn't really been the plan.

She emerged from her bedroom looking more amazing than should have been possible. Dressed down in a pair of jeans and a top that had the back exposed so her ink was visible. And as an added bonus it also showed she wasn't wearing a bra, her boobs unhindered against the material was probably going to test the last of my resolve.

"You want to go put on some pants?" She pointed to my boxer shorts, my attention being too focused on her to worry about my lack of preparation.

I nodded slowly, not even trying to hide I was openly gawking at her as I smiled. "Yeah, not sure I want to now that I've seen you."

She laughed, rolling her eyes as she pointed to the door. "Dallas, while I don't regret what we did last night, I'm serious about us trying to keep our hands off each other. Actually I was thinking about it all morning. While we didn't break any rules, we should try and stick to other things until the month is over. I don't trust myself to do what we did again, and not want you inside of me."

Instant hard-on.

Her words were a shot of Viagra right into my cock, getting me hard without even touching it.

"Yeah, not sure how the hell you expect me to walk out of here when you're saying stuff like that?" My head dipped to the bulge in my boxers. "But if it helps you any, I'll try and be good."

I wasn't making any promises, the loophole of *try* the only one I was willing to commit to.

Her eyes dropped, widening as they took in the view. "Maybe you could use some time in the shower?" she suggested. "There's still some lotion in my bathroom."

It was my turn to laugh, the idea she was suggesting I jerk off while she waited, hilarious. And while the thought had crossed my mind, I already knew my hand wasn't going to give me what I wanted. "Yeah, maybe later. I'll be right back."

Back in her room I pulled on my clothes and shoes without the cold shower I desperately needed. I would try and get one of those before I went to work, needing to go home and change before I headed to the shop anyway.

I grabbed my keys and phone and found her back in the living room. She already had her purse and was waiting for me as she sat on the arm of her couch.

Without even thinking about it, I put my arm around her and we left her apartment. It felt like the most natural thing in the world, walking to my car as we spoke about nothing important. She laughed when I told her I was going to find out where she bought that top from and buy a million others just like it. I was serious about it too; it was my new favorite thing.

When we got to the store, I got out of my car automatically.

Even though she hadn't asked me to come in, I enjoyed being by her side as she shopped. I'd even stopped being distracted by her boobs, checking out what kind of groceries she was tossing in her cart, and asking why would anyone buy quinoa.

"It's supposed to be good for you." She didn't sound convinced, pulling it out of the cart and inspecting the packaging. "Katy has been trying to get me to eat it forever."

"Who's Katy? Please don't tell me you have some bullshit life coach because I will for real lose all respect for you," I warned. Praying to God she wasn't signed up to a daily newsletter that gave her crockpot affirmations and let someone other than herself decide on how she was going to live her life.

She pushed me playfully, tossing the quinoa back on the shelf and continuing down the aisle. "Katy is my sister, moron. And she is better at food stuff than me."

"Babe, you can't be *bad* at food stuff. You see food you eat it—it's literally the easiest thing to do." I grabbed some double stuffed Oreos and added them to her haul. "That's for when I visit because if you're listening to *Katy*, I don't trust there are going to be any decent snacks at your place."

I'd half expected my Oreos to meet the same fate as the quinoa and find its way back on the shelf. But she left them right where they were, my contraband cookies polluting her otherwise healthy options.

And since I'd been given permission, I decided to add a few other things she'd obviously forgotten off her list. She didn't bat an eye at the cereal or potato chips, ignoring each new colorful addition until I tossed in the large box of condoms.

"Really?" She anchored her hand on her hip, tapping her foot impatiently.

I shrugged, unable to hide my grin. "Safety first, babe. It's a staple like coffee and bacon, and frankly I'm surprised I had to remind you."

"How do you know I don't have a month's supply already?" Her eyebrow rose. "Only an amateur buys them one box at a time."

Wow.

What. The. Hell. Did. She. Just. Say?

"I know I joked about this before, but I am seriously considering replacing you as my new best friend." I grabbed her hand and pulled her into a hug. "I swear to God, I had this exact argument with Josh."

My words seemed to please her, a satisfied grin spreading across her lips as she shimmied in delight. "Not everyone can be as brilliant as us."

"Nope, we're a rare breed, you and I." I nodded, the secret understanding passing between us.

She was so much like me.

Obviously she was a woman—and everything that went with that—but underneath that hot body, we were the same.

She giggled. "Yep, a secret society. I'm even thinking up our special handshake. But all of that will have to wait until later." Her finger pointed to the cart. "That double fudge ice cream you decided was lacking in my life is going to melt if we don't get me checked out and these groceries home."

I agreed, not only because she was right—melted ice cream wasn't happening on my watch—but the thirty minutes or so we'd planned on spending in the grocery store had already stretched to an hour. Who'd have thought walking down the aisles making fun of what kind of toilet paper she bought would be so much fun.

"Here let me." I helped load up her groceries onto the conveyor belt, watching the crazy mix of healthy things and junk food travel down the line and zapped by the sales associate.

And without even thinking about it, I pulled out my credit card and handed it over as the last item was scanned and tossed in a bag.

"No, Dallas, they're *my* groceries," Kitty insisted, digging into her bag and yanking out her own card. "Use this one." She waved at the woman behind the counter who had already taken mine.

"Ignore her," I laughed, nodding to the lady to go ahead and charge the card. "Besides," I turned to Kitty who still thought she had a chance at paying. "Half that stuff is mine, and I didn't want to do the math for what I owed you."

"I would have been able to cover your ice cream and cookies, Dallas." She rolled her eyes. "Next time, I'll make you wait in the car."

I didn't bother arguing with her, grabbing our bags and carrying them out to my ride. Regardless of what she said, there was no way I was waiting outside while she shopped. If she was going to get really upset about it, she could pay for her boring crap and I'd take care of all the good stuff. That was about as big a compromise as I was willing to make.

"We should go." She looked down at the time on her phone, the morning slipping away. "I don't want you to be late. Just drop me off and I'll get the bags up into the apartment by myself."

I waved her off, putting the bags into my trunk not at all concerned. "It's fine. Don't worry about me," I said, having no plans about doing any of that. "I have plenty of time."

So I'd skip the shower, it wouldn't be the first time I swiped a washcloth under my arms and tossed on some deodorant. All I needed was a few minutes and I could be out the door. And making sure she didn't struggle up stairs hauling bags upstairs was more important than my beauty routine.

"Okay." She smiled, hoping into the passenger seat. "But only if you are sure."

I answered without any hesitation.

"Positive."

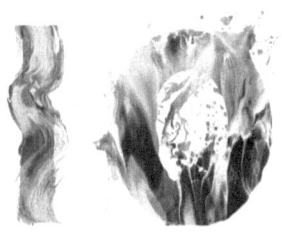

KITTY

AFTER DALLAS LEFT, I CLEANED up my apartment and then spent the afternoon rearranging my closet. I had been meaning to do it forever but I always found an excuse not to. But my morning had put me in a really great mood so I decided since I had no other plans I'd take advantage of feeling so upbeat.

It wasn't half as bad as I'd made it out to be, moving quickly through my clothes and designating what I wanted to keep and what was going to be donated to charity. Not even sure why I had put it off for so long, the neater and more organized closet making me feel super satisfied as I closed the door.

Not only did I accomplish a boring meaningless task and not hate every single second of it but it also helped pass the time. And before I knew it, it was time to start getting ready to go to Eve's gallery with Dallas.

We'd agreed to meet up at the gallery around six. He'd argued of course, telling me that since we lived so close it made more sense for us to go together. But he had already done so much for me, and I didn't want him feeling like he'd been relegated to my personal driver.

Plus, that would be like a date and we were definitely not dating. Well, not like *real* dating. It was for experimental purposes only and the last thing I'd do would be take advantage of Dallas.

He conceded—barely—but only after I reasoned it might alter our ever-important data. I could tell he still wasn't on board with meeting me there, but he didn't continue to argue.

I'll admit that my life would probably be a little easier if I had a car. Even though it would probably spend most of the time sitting idle while I took the subway to work. But part of me liked the freedom, and I had no problem with getting where I needed to be. Which was why I reassured Dallas that I was fine catching an Uber and meeting him there.

I'd showered again, the time spent in my closet making me sweaty. So I freshened up and flat ironed my hair straight. Even though it wasn't a date, I didn't want to turn up to Eve's gallery looking like anything less than my best. Important people turned up all the time—fancy people with their designer clothes and important jobs, and you never knew when you would need to make a good impression. Which was why I was making an extra effort on my appearance, and putting on a nice dress.

Well, at least that was the reason I told myself I was doing it, noticing the nice dress was my backless silver cocktail dress that meant I couldn't wear a bra. It also showed off my amazing tattoo, which was the other thing Dallas loved. *Boobs and ink*, I was two for two on the list of his favorite things. Ironic that the top I'd worn earlier in the day had a similar theme and Dallas had liked it. Pure coincidence of course.

My gut tightened as I pulled up to Art Addiction, Eve's gallery, and I hoped I didn't seem like too much of an idiot. I knew that Eve, Josh or Dallas would never judge me like that, but knowing how much it was a part of all of their lives, it was the first time I was nervous about it.

I thanked my Uber driver, stepping out on the sidewalk as I

tried to reason with myself I was being stupid. Nobody cared what I thought about the art—probably wouldn't even ask—and I was there supporting a friend which was what was important. With the pep talk still looping in my head I walked through the doors and into the main space.

While I loved to support Eve, I didn't go to the gallery as often as I should. The artwork didn't always make sense, the stuff on the wall sometimes looking more like a kindergartner's art project than something that should cost thousands of dollars. I was more traditional in my tastes, liking the calmness and perfection of the Renaissance masters. Sure a lot of my friends preferred stuff that was more avant-garde, but the busyness on the canvases just seemed like noise to me.

Art Addiction wasn't a traditional gallery. It was an old hotel that had been purchased by Eve and completely refurbed. It maintained some of its old rustic charm, while the floors and ceilings had been polished and updated.

"Kitty!" Eve saw me first, throwing her arms around my neck and welcoming me with a hug. "Josh mentioned you might stop by."

Eve was the definition of polished perfection. If a hair was out of place, it was by design not accident. Which is how she was able to still look like she belonged in a magazine despite wearing a messy bun.

I hugged her back, the nerves I was feeling a little earlier starting to quell. "Hey, I'm sorry it took me so long to come check out your new stuff. We've been getting slammed at work."

"It's probably just as well." She laughed, pulling back to look at me. "If you'd turned up on opening night, no one would probably have paid any attention to what was on the walls. That dress is stunning."

I waved her off, pretending like the outfit was no big deal. "Please, this old thing? I just found it this afternoon while I was cleaning my closet and decided to throw it on." Not entirely a lie considering I had been cleaning my closet.

"Well then, you should clean your closet more often." She gently yanked on my arm. "Josh and Dallas are already walking around, and I'm positive you'll have more fun with them than me. I have a buyer coming at seven and need to schmooze so let's go find them."

I followed her through the space, the place still mostly empty. It was still early in art hours, artsy people being more night owls like Dallas than morning people like me.

Dallas had his back to us, standing next to Josh, while they were deep in conversation looking at a drawing on the wall. He was in his usual uniform of head-to-toe black, the color coming from whatever skin was showing, and tonight that wasn't much.

Wearing a black button down un-tucked, over black jeans he had somehow managed to keep his edge while still fitting in. It was amazing to me that no matter where he was, he genuinely didn't care what people thought of him. I loved that about him, glad he didn't feel some stupid need to conform or change what he looked like.

Like he'd heard my thoughts, he turned and smiled. His hair was extra glossy, like he'd slicked it back with some kind of product, while the shorter side looked freshly clipped and neater than I'd seen it earlier.

The rest of him hadn't been so clean-cut, his unshaved jaw making him look even sexier. His hazel eyes fixed on me in what I hoped was appreciation, and regardless of who was standing around, his attention was mine alone.

"Looking good, Dallas." I sidled up to him, bumping his shoulder casually. "Who are you trying to impress?"

"You're impressed?" He laughed, ignoring my shoulder bump and pulling me in for a hug.

He smelled good too, not of cologne but of soap and shampoo—manly and fresh. I liked it, the scent pure and unpretentious.

Allowing myself a quick hug—anymore and I was liable to start groping him even with an audience—I pulled back and smiled at Josh. "Hey Josh, great to see you again. And thanks again for saving me the other night."

I'd assumed he'd told Eve, my unfortunate evening probably earning them both a laugh. Not that I cared, I found it funny too now that I was no longer tethered to my headboard.

"Don't mention it." He tipped his chin in greeting, his arms finding their way around his girlfriend's waist.

"Hey, I'd like to point out that I was instrumental to the rescue. *And* I brought pie." Dallas mirrored his friend's behavior, one of his hands resting on my hip.

I tried not to think about how much I liked it, or that I had no intention of asking him to move it. After all, we touched each other all the time so his hands on me weren't anything new or suspect. What *was* new was the knot in my gut getting even tighter and my pulse picking up pace, but I decided to ignore it, convinced I was overthinking.

It was while I was trying to not overthink—something I wasn't doing very well—that my eyes glanced down to Eve's hand and saw the massive and very stunning engagement ring.

"WOW," I said louder than was probably expected in a place like we were in. My hand grabbed hers and brought it in closer for inspection, the diamond reflecting every single light source like a disco ball.

"It's beautiful." My words directed more to the ring than to anyone else considering I'd yet to take my eyes off it. "I can't remember if Dallas told me you guys got engaged or not, but that ring is freaking amazing."

Eve wriggled her fingers, the sparkle in her eyes matching the impressive diamond on her hand. "Thanks, it only happened a few days ago. And I told Josh this ring was way too much but he's being stubborn and won't even think of downgrading."

"Like I would give my future wife anything but the best," he scoffed, biting back the grin. "I only plan on doing this one time, and that ring isn't even close to how much you mean to me."

"You're lucky I haven't eaten yet, or else I'd be ready to puke." Dallas groaned, clutching his stomach.

I elbowed him, standing up straighter as I turned to Josh. "I think it's adorable and the ring is perfect. It's exactly the kind of ring Eve would wear too. He did an amazing job."

"Can we not talk about how great Josh is?" Dallas rolled his eyes. "I already told you how close I was to puking."

"He is all yours, Kitty." Josh winked, backing away slowly and taking Eve with him. "We're going to go say hi to some more people and leave you guys to it. And D, if you're still having the urge to get sick, use a bathroom for God's sake. Don't mess up Eve's floors."

He took his laughing fiancée with him as they wandered back through the room.

"You can't honestly tell me that Josh and Eve aren't the most adorable thing you've ever seen." I glared at him, challenging him to disagree. "Because that ring and how loved up they are is freaking beautiful."

He rolled his eyes, leaning in closer as he whispered, "Of course I think it's great, I love them together. But if I tell Josh shit like that he will start getting a head swell, and I can't have that. Who is going to keep him levelheaded now he has a hot woman who has agreed to be his wife? If anything, I'm going to have to work doubly hard so he doesn't believe his own press."

"You can't be serious," I laughed. "Out of the two of you, *you're* the one with the bigger ego."

"That's not the only thing that's bigger." The flirty grin across his mouth got wider.

I shook my head not at all surprised he'd taken it there. "I'll take your word for it. Now walk around with me while I try not to look stupid when I look at these paintings."

My admission shocked him, his cheeky smile dropping as he stopped. "Why would you look stupid?"

"Because I don't get it." I shrugged not bothering to pretend. "I just don't see what you guys see."

He looked confused, not understanding what I meant.

"Usually I just stand in front of them, looking like I know what it's supposed to be," I explained. "While I get there is probably some brilliance there, I don't really understand it."

"Kitty." He purred my name sending a shiver down my spine. "You're one of the smartest people I know, you couldn't look stupid if you tried. And lucky for you, you're going to get your own personal tour." His hand tightened around my hip as he brought me in closer. "And I'm going to be your tour guide."

Only Dallas could make the words *tour guide* sound illicit, making me laugh as I nodded. I wasn't sure exactly what he had in mind, but I was pretty sure I was open to almost any of his suggestions.

What I expected was we'd walk around, and Dallas would whisper dirty innuendo in my ear about what was on the canvases. Tell me where he saw penises or which one looked like a vagina. But instead he spoke about composition, about how things were placed and why. He compared them to tattoos, talking about positioning the art so it fit properly or lined up with curves of the body. It wasn't just about the picture; it was about *where* the picture was placed.

Then he moved onto color and tone, and how they could be used to represent emotion and movement. He pulled up the sleeve on his shirt and showed me an intricate cross on his forearm. The entire piece was in grayscale, the light and dark graduated tone. It looked so real, so lifelike even though the only color used was black. Then he pulled up the other sleeve, the forearm on display a stunning portrait. The girl was in color, saturated and bright, the harsh black outline making everything else pop.

"You have to be able to tell the story without saying a word."

He pointed back to the wall. "Whether it's with a brush stroke or a tattoo machine, you need to let it whisper in your ear."

We stood in front of a canvas, the erratic mess of red lines seeming to say nothing. It was like I was deaf, or blind, not able to hear or see anything anyone else could. "I just don't see it," I groaned in frustration, trying to focus even harder, which didn't help.

"Ok stop." He stood behind me, holding my waist encouraging me to continue to look. "Just tell me what you do see."

"Red." I blew out a breath, stating the obvious.

"And . . ." He waited for me to continue.

I looked again, hoping for a strike of brilliance that didn't come. "I don't know—lines, a mess—randomly messy red lines," I huffed in frustration knowing it wasn't the right answer.

He didn't flinch continuing to hold me still as he leaned in behind me. "And how does it make you feel?"

"Honestly, angry. I feel frustrated and angry, trying to see what isn't there. It's agitating, and makes me want to look away because it just makes me more irate."

He chuckled softly in my ear, amused by my obvious lack of understanding.

"Hey, you asked, don't mock me because I got it wrong." I turned around, jabbing him roughly in the chest.

"Read the plaque, Kitty." He pointed to the small rectangle beside the canvas.

I shook my head, no longer interested in the painting. "Dallas, let's just move on."

"Just do it," he insisted, pushing me gently in the back so that I stepped forward.

I rolled my eyes, moving closer to read it for no other reason that to appease him. I glanced at the rectangle and read the title.

Inner turmoil

"I wasn't *mocking* you." His arm wrapped around my waist.

"I was laughing because you were seeing it exactly right and didn't even know it."

It shouldn't have made me as proud as it did, but it thrilled me nonetheless. Maybe I wasn't as artistically dense as I'd first thought. Or maybe it was about having it explained to me in a way I could understand.

My gold-star effort earned me an amazing smile, Dallas and I continued to walk along the walls and talk about what we saw. I still wasn't any closer to liking the more abstract stuff—preferring the old school masters—but at least I no longer felt inept.

In the time we'd been walking around, the space had filled. We hadn't even noticed the people around us, too engrossed in our own world to worry about anyone else.

"You want to go get something to eat?" He tugged on my arm, pulling me closer to an exit. "I know a crazy good steak place around here. Pretty sure they don't serve quinoa, but I'm positive we'll find something on the menu you like."

I glared at him, blowing out a breath. "I put it back on the shelf. And for your information, I'm not a fussy eater and I love steak."

"Then it sounds like the perfect place. Let's go."

He didn't wait for my answer, leading me out the door before I'd had a chance to say goodbye to either Eve or Josh. "Aren't we going to say bye?" I asked, already on the sidewalk before I'd managed to get the words out.

"Nah, Eve is always really busy and Josh likes to do the supportive thing. I don't want to ruin their vibe." He looked over my shoulder to the door we'd just come out of. "We'll order them dinner and have it delivered later. It can be like our little thank you card," he laughed. "But better since they'll both be starving and won't have to cook."

I liked his idea, and it wasn't only thoughtful but incredibly sweet. Not at all what I was expecting. "That's a fantastic idea. But I get to buy."

He was ready with his protest, my hand covering his mouth before he had a chance to tell me no. "You paid for most of my groceries, letting me pay for dinner seems fair."

My hand was peeled away from his mouth, letting him vocalize what I'd tried to stop. "But it was my idea, you don't think I'm going to let you take credit for *my* idea do you? You can buy me dinner next time, but this one is on me. I get to be the hero tonight, baby."

I was almost positive it was bullshit, but it kind of sounded like him too. He *did* like to get credit, especially if an idea was his. So part of me thought it was more about making him look good than not letting me pay. "One way or another, I *will* be paying you back," I insisted, making it clear I wasn't a push over.

"Good, I'll look forward to it. Make sure you take me somewhere decent though, I'm not interested in some fru-fru place where I can't pronounce the menu." He smirked, agreeing to let me take him to dinner.

To say I was surprised he hadn't asked for a blowjob as payment was an understatement. I'd assumed the minute I'd mentioned *paying him back* he would have chosen currency of a sexual nature. I didn't even blame him; I probably would have too given the choice. But hearing him agree to dinner made me irrationally excited and I wasn't sure why. Maybe I really wanted the experiment to work, or possibly I just really liked spending time with him and hoped he enjoyed my company too.

I held out my hand deciding to make him shake, trying not to look ridiculously happy. "Deal."

"Really?" His eyes dropped to my hand and laughed. "Okay, babe, whatever it takes." He shook my hand. "Now let's go."

He led me to the back of the hotel, where there was a small parking lot. It had obviously been used in the past for staff or special guests, the light not great as we made our way to his car.

"So this steak place," I asked, waiting for him to unlock the passenger side door. "They have dessert?"

A grin spread across his lips. "Would I take you somewhere that didn't? You know I'm a big fan of *sweet.*"

If what he'd tossed into my cart that morning was anything to go by, it was a wonder he wasn't a hundred pounds overweight and rocking borderline diabetes. But I had a hunch that wasn't what he meant. "Good. I'm looking forward to it already."

He waited until I was settled into my seat before walking around and sliding into the driver's side. The ignition rumbled to life, his speakers blasting *Jane's Addiction* before he turned it down.

"You don't have to turn it down, I love this band." I fastened my seatbelt, reaching my hand across and edging up the volume.

"Really? I'd have picked you for more a mainstream Top 40 kind of girl." He looked genuinely surprised, nodding in appreciation as I sang along with the lyrics.

"I like all kinds of music but 90's alternative is my favorite stuff. Nirvana, Jane's, Stone Temple Pilots, Soundgarden—it's all I listen to when I workout."

"Get out of here!" His voice lifted, punching over the vocals of the song as he glanced at me. "90's alternative is my thing. I swear, my playlist is loaded with it; it's what I put on when I need to get in the zone. And I'm not even going to pretend that I didn't cry like a baby when we lost Weiland and Cornell."

The death of the two lead singers was something I'd cried about too. Not only because we'd lost two amazing artists, but because their music and lyrics had spoken to me in a way that current music didn't seem to.

Katy thought I was insane, preferring "happier" music as she put it. Translation—anyone who'd won X-Factor or American Idol. She'd also threatened to have me committed when I'd shown her my tattoo, telling me that I would regret it and why the hell did it have to be so big.

"That's so cool, Dallas. I bet your playlist is awesome." I rolled my head toward him, reaching out and squeezing his thigh.

He nodded, sitting up a little straighter in his seat. "When we do that tattoo of yours, I'll let you wear my *Beats* and you can find out."

I couldn't help but smile, the idea of a new tattoo done by Dallas while listening to his curated playlist sounded amazing.

The rest of the trip was relaxed, neither of us talking as we listened to music. It was different than it had been in the past, not just with Dallas, but with people in general.

Almost everyone knew me as the party girl, the one who was always out and doing something crazy. And for the most part, that was true. But every once in a while I craved a time where I wouldn't have to fill the silence. Where just being there would be enough. Not for them, but for me.

I'd never expected that moment to come while I was driving toward a steak house with a guy I'd assumed was only ever going to be a one-night stand listening to "Been Caught Stealing" blaring through the speakers.

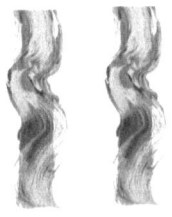

DALLAS

THE NIGHT HAD BEEN AWESOME.

And I wasn't just saying that because she looked drop-dead gorgeous, although, it had taken some serious mental strength not to stare at her all night.

The dress she had on took everything I'd loved about the top she'd worn earlier, and put it on steroids. It was tight, showed off every freaking curve of her body, and of course had an open back.

No bra.

But for the first time in a long time, it wasn't just her amazing tits that got my attention. Sure, I looked, because I hadn't become blind in the last twenty-four hours. But it was her sexy back tattoo that got me thirty levels of hard. Didn't even care I hadn't been the artist to put it there, so freaking turned on that she had it on display, not giving a shit who saw it and what they thought.

That kind of confidence made me so hard I wasn't positive I was going to get through the night without needing to excuse myself to go jerk off.

But I managed to keep my shit together, kept my dirty thoughts to myself and had possibly the best dinner I'd ever had.

Kitty and I talked about music while we ate steak and then

shared a slice of eight-layer chocolate cake. It was hilarious, the two of us attacking the cake like it'd owed us money—it was a fork match to the last bite.

I didn't even tell her how fucking sexy she looked with chocolate on her lips, too busy laughing at her when she said she was going to marry the cake and have little cupcake babies.

It wasn't until later that it occurred to me that I still had that folded up list of conversational questions tucked in my back pocket. Not my actual pocket, because I was fairly sure it was in another pair of jeans I'd tossed into the laundry hamper. I'd have to remember to pull out the paper before I washed them.

But as I drove her back to her place, there was no other way I would have preferred it. I didn't even care that I probably wasn't going to sleep with her, the status of how handsy we were allowed to get with our *agreement* still up in the air.

She didn't ask me to come in but I followed her to her door. I'd spent the last two nights there and I kind of hoped there might be a third. At the very least I was going to kiss her goodnight. I mean, we'd already been doing that and I didn't see the point in stopping.

The minute the door had shut, I pulled her toward me. I wasn't sure what it was—the amazing night we'd had or the quietness of her apartment—but I felt like if I waited another second I was going to lose my mind.

She whimpered against my mouth, taken by surprise but only needing a second to catch up. The softness of her lips and her body, an invitation I wasn't capable of turning down.

My hands grabbed her ass, pulled her up onto me, her legs wrapping around my hips exactly like I'd wanted. I wasn't sure where it was going—too busy doing to think—but I could keep kissing her exactly like that for hours if she'd let me.

Our mouths tangled, tongues and lips fighting for position as I felt myself get hard. It had been a challenge all night, to keep my dick from straining against the front of my jeans. Between the sexy dress, how amazing she looked and how fucking adorable she'd been when we'd been looking at the art, I'd put in an effort that seriously deserved an award.

As for dinner, well that couldn't be helped. Watching her eat chocolate cake while she moaned in delight was only going to get one result from me.

Rock. Hard.

But I was able to hide it under the table so it didn't count.

Didn't have that kind of cover anymore and not that I wanted it, my hard-on grinding against her as we continued to kiss.

Her back arched, giving me more contact as one of my hands slid from her ass to her thigh and lifted the hem of her dress. It was short but not short enough, needing the thing bunched up around her waist so there were less barriers.

The situation was almost critical by the time I'd backed her against the wall.

Man, I wanted her. Wanted to kiss her and watch her writhe against me while I made her come. I didn't even care if it was with my dick or my hand, I just wanted to hear those breathy little noises and know I'd been the reason.

"Wait." She stopped, lifting her head away as her hand pressed against my chest. "This isn't what we're supposed to be doing."

"I don't care." My lips moved to her neck, no longer giving a shit about anything other than continuing exactly what *we were doing*.

She pushed again, this time getting my attention. "No, we can't."

There wasn't any hesitation in her voice. No maybe, like she wanted to but didn't want to say. She was saying no, and was very clear about it.

I stopped immediately, pulling back to look at her. "Kitty, I'm sorry. I thought . . ."

There was no point finishing the sentence because I hadn't

been thinking. Or at least I hadn't been thinking with the part of my brain that mattered.

"Shit. I'm sorry." I lowered her to the floor, her feet making contact but she kept her hands on me.

"No, I wanted it too, trust me." She shook her head, a smile edging up her lips. "I just . . . so this is really stupid."

She blew out a frustrated breath, her eyes on me the whole time. "This is what usually happens. I meet a guy, we have an awesome time, and then it ends up with sex." She gestured between us and to what we were about to do.

"And then it ends badly for me, and I didn't want that to happen for us. You're a really good friend, Dallas. And I like spending time with you. This crazy idea we had about trying to help each other is the most fun I have had in a long time. But you have to know if we sleep together now, that's going to be over."

I got what she was trying to say, but didn't think it applied to us. We were different; there was no pretense with us, no bullshit. We'd already had sex before and still managed to be friends, so why she thought it was going to crash and burn didn't make sense.

"Not necessarily. No one has a crystal ball." I was honest, because that was what we did. And the truth of the matter was that neither of us knew what would happen in the future.

She eyed me suspiciously, probably guessing I didn't buy that us having sex was a bad idea. And maybe it was because I was so caught up in wanting to be with her that I couldn't see reason or maybe the reason—whatever that was—didn't exist.

"How many ex-girlfriends do you still talk to and are on good terms with?" she asked, no accusation in her tone.

I laughed, pretending like I couldn't remember. "Jesus, Kitty, I don't know. It's not like I keep tabs on that kind of thing. A few."

"A few?" she asked, not buying my bullshit.

"Fine, not many. But that's because I usually end up with fruitcakes. I can't be held responsible for our lack of friendship if they're crazy." My past history with psycho exes was the reason Kitty and I had been spending so much time together in the first place. But it wasn't because I had planned it that way, it was just the luck of the draw and I'd just been unlucky.

"Well I'm friends with none." She leveled me with a stare. "*None*, Dallas. If they don't end up being total losers, the only reason they keep my number is on the off chance they need a booty call."

"Then they're fucking idiots," I fired back, pissed off on her behalf that some douchebag would treat her like that. Sure she was hot, but she was more than a slamming body and a pretty face.

She rested her head against the wall, sighing and blowing out a breath in frustration. "I'm sorry, I guess tonight when I was out with you. It just felt like we had something . . . real. It didn't feel like a date, or that you were trying to get into my pants. You are so easy to be around, you make me laugh so much. It's like I can shut the world off and just be there in the moment. And I don't want for it to end by me doing something stupid."

"Babe, I am glad you felt that way." With no intention of kissing her again, I moved closer and brushed her hair out of her face. "I had an awesome night too, and you're right, it didn't feel like a date."

I couldn't put my finger on why; I just knew that it *felt* different. Like she understood me, and I understood her. Neither of us attempted to impress each other. Neither of us had to try.

"Wow, did we just friend zone each other?" I laughed, the idea that I'd voluntarily give up sex with someone like Kitty so freaking out of character I was positive I must have been dreaming. "I don't think I've ever done that."

She laughed too, her beautiful smile lighting up her face. "Yeah, I think we did. And as much as I'd love to sleep with you Dallas, I'd really miss you as my friend."

"Yeah? I would be pretty bummed too if you suddenly started hating me," I admitted, loving the last few days. "Especially with

Josh getting married, I doubt he's going to have much time for my shenanigans. I'm going to need someone who has my back."

And as much as Josh was my brother, I knew without a doubt that his soon-to-be wife would come first.

As it should be.

But I wasn't going to pretend that a part of me wasn't going to miss having him as my wingman. Just knowing that all I had to do was call, and he'd be there no matter what mess I'd gotten myself into.

"Soooooooo." I deliberately left the sentence hanging, not sure where that put us and our agreement. "We going to stop hanging out?"

Her eyes flashed to mine. "God, no. Of course not. I love hanging out with you. I just think we need to do it without it turning into sex. At least not until our one month agreement." She stopped, thinking a minute before qualifying, "Or anything *close* to sex."

"Yep, got it. Totally friendship." I held up my hands as I backed away. "Nothing even close to sex." I said the words I wasn't convinced of.

She laughed, amused by my very literal hands-off approach, and stepped away from the wall. "As much as I'd love for you to stay, you should probably go." Her eyes moved to the door.

I didn't want to leave either but I figured it was a good idea. "Yeah, I can do that. Hey," I paused, biting my lip. I couldn't believe I was even thinking it, let alone even saying it. But regardless of the outcome, I wasn't going to start being a pussy. "Are you sure you're still going to want to go through with this one-month thing? Not that I'm trying to talk you out of it, but I don't want you to think I'll be pissed or anything."

There was no denying I wanted her.

Today.

Next week.

Next month.

That wouldn't change, and I knew it to be undeniably true.

Because no matter what happened, how many nights we spoke about music, or ate dinners where we fought over dessert—my dick would always think it was a good idea.

But make no mistake; it wasn't worth losing her over.

"Dallas." She took a step closer and rubbed her hand across my cheek. "Of course I will. Hopefully by then I'll have worked out a way to do it and not have it mess everything up."

Yeah, I wasn't convinced but I wasn't arguing either. "Okay, baby." I kissed her forehead. "I'm going to go home. Let me know if you want to hang out tomorrow."

She shook her head. "No, it's okay, tomorrow is your day off. You should go out with your friends or . . . or whatever it is you usually do on your day off."

It didn't need to be said what my days off usually consisted of. Catching up with friends, drinking at a bar or two and then ended up in bed with some chick I'd usually picked up at the bar. It wasn't every weekend, but it was close to it. Which was going to make it interesting because for the first time in forever, the idea wasn't appealing.

"Yeah, well I don't have any plans so if you change your mind, let me know. Talk soon."

I fought the urge to reach down and check my balls as I walked to her front door. Not sure when it happened but I was fairly sure I'd lost them somewhere. Lucky for me there weren't many witnesses—Kitty not the kind of girl to say anything—so I could get myself home and work out what the hell was wrong with me.

"See ya, Dallas." She waved, watching me grab the knob and open the door.

"Yep. See ya." *Could I sound any more ridiculous?* "Bye."

Before I could embarrass myself any further, I left. I jogged down to my car, hit the ignition and drove myself home. I wasn't sure when the last time I'd been there that early on a Saturday night was. Not only was I going home early, but I was doing it alone, and the kicker—I didn't care it was early, I was home or that I wasn't with some random girl.

I walked into my empty apartment, tossed the keys on my kitchen counter and went straight to my room to strip off. I was in for the night, so I might as well be comfortable, my clothes dumped in a corner as I picked up my sketchbook and some pencils and made my way back to the living room.

No point going to bed when I knew there wasn't going to be a lot of sleeping going on when I felt so wired. And if I was going to be alone, then being productive sounded like a good thing to do.

And with Kitty still on my mind, I started sketching. I'd promised her a tattoo and it wasn't something I was going to pick off a picture on a wall. Nope, she would get a Dallas original, something only for her.

And it had to be perfect.

❦

MY HEAD LIFTED OFF MY pillow and I felt weird.

Might have been because I hadn't actually been sleeping on a pillow, the stack of magazines my head had been resting on sticking to my face as I opened my eyes.

Man, I felt rough. Like I'd been drinking all night but hadn't had more than a couple of beers. I didn't even remember falling asleep, my pencils and sketchbook still scattered around me right where I'd left them.

I'd been trying to design a tattoo.

Not just any design either, it was for Kitty and nothing I drew seemed to be good enough.

I yawned, stretching my arms out hoping it would make the crick in my neck feel better. It didn't, which was just the occupational hazard of sleeping on the couch. I'd been there before; it was just the first time I'd been there *and* been sober.

I pulled off the T-shirt I'd been sleeping in, grabbing my phone to check the time. My stomach was grumbling which meant it was probably lunchtime. It was when I usually woke up when given the choice, especially when I knew I had the day off.

What.

The.

Fuck.

My eyes tried to focus on the numbers on the screen, a quick blink and reopen confirming I wasn't seeing things.

It was seven a.m., and this time I didn't have the smell of breakfast to blame.

There was no reason for me to be awake, I had no plans and no woman in my bed I was trying to escape from. I was literally awake with nowhere to go and nowhere to be. And what was worse is that I didn't think I could go back to sleep if I'd tried.

The way I'd left Kitty last night didn't sit right with me. I got that we'd been dancing a line, getting pretty close to spending more time with our clothes off than on. But I hadn't seen that as an issue. She did though, and that made all the difference. And if she wanted to keep our status completely clothes on, then I'd fucking do it. Wouldn't say I was ecstatic about it, but I'd do it.

What I wouldn't do, is be a prick because she'd turned me down. And avoiding her wasn't an option either.

I couldn't remember whose idea it was that we not spend time together during the days I had off, but whoever thought it up was dumb. There was no fucking reason why, especially when we had some pretty amazing days up until that point.

It was my time off and I'd spend it how I wanted to, which was why I didn't hesitate, threw myself into the shower and got dressed.

I may not have had a place to go when I woke up, but I suddenly had a new game plan.

Redressed and looking half decent, I left the mess of sketches and pencils on my living room floor and left my apartment. Keys were in my ignition before I'd even bothered to think, starting my car and driving back to Kitty's.

It was a blessing and curse that we lived so close, the time getting there minimal but also not long enough to think up what I was going to say.

Was I really just going to land on her doorstep and knock with no invitation?

Yes, yes I was.

So with that little seed of doubt put to bed, I climbed up the stairs to her apartment. The knock on her door came right after.

It took a bit, needing to knock a couple of times before I heard some movement, her voice sounding husky as it came through the wood.

"Dallas? What are you doing here?"

I waved to the peephole she was probably looking through, waiting for her to open the door. "I woke up early."

It might have been a lame excuse, but she didn't question it, pulling open the door to reveal her sleep shirt I was so fond of.

"Did you want some breakfast then?" She yawned as she watched me walk inside, not questioning why I was awake or why I was on her doorstep. "I can make us a frittata."

"What the hell is that?" I wasn't sure if it was the words she was saying or that her ass looked amazing in the long T-shirt that had me so confused. But either way, I had no idea what she was talking about.

She turned, shooting me a grin. "Sort of like an omelet."

"So why not say an omelet." I shrugged; happy to eat anything she was willing to give me.

"Because you know what an omelet looks like and I don't want your expectations too high."

"Well then, let me assure you." I stepped closer, dying to touch her but I didn't. "I have no expectations."

With a promise that I didn't care what she put on a plate or what she called it, I followed her into her kitchen. She got out a bowl and some eggs, cracking them before adding some other stuff.

"I'll make toast and coffee." I decided to put myself to good use and joined her in the tiny space between the kitchen island and her stove.

As much as I would have liked to use the opportunity to brush up against her accidently I didn't, not willing to risk her throwing me out on my ass because I couldn't be trusted.

My hands might have held her waist a couple of times when we were passing each other, but I kept it as PG as I could. And between the two of us we had something that resembled breakfast. I wasn't going to say it looked good, because if I hadn't seen it being cooked in front of me I would assume someone had already eaten it. But it tasted decent, and more importantly, the company was awesome.

Since I was already dressed, I offered to do the dishes while she took a shower and got ready. She probably assumed I was going to use her being naked and wet as an opportunity, giving me a warning look. But I crossed-my-heart-and-hoped-to-die promised her that I would stay in the kitchen, reminding her we had an agreement.

I was a lot of things, but a lying pervert wasn't one of them.

She walked back into the kitchen looking too freaking fine for words, the dress she was wearing shaped like a long T-shirt that came to her mid-thigh. But unlike the old faded oversized one she slept in, the one she had on fit her very well. The material clinging to her body hinted at the treasures underneath, and calling her beautiful would have been a gross understatement.

She lifted her arms, letting them drop at her sides dramatically. "Now what?"

"I haven't really thought that far ahead, do you always need a plan?" I cocked a grin as I watched her shrug.

"No, not always. But it helps if we're going to do anything

other than sit in my apartment."

I pulled out my keys, dangling them between my fingers. "Well then let's get out of here and find out."

KITTY

WE SPENT THE DAY LIKE it literally had no purpose.

First, we drove to the park near my apartment, laying around on the grass and baking in the sunshine. Then we ate giant slices of pizza while we looked across the river at Manhattan. We didn't go anywhere in particular, ditching the car at Socrates Sculpture Park as we walked around. I wasn't even sure we were looking at the art to be honest, laughing so hard and talking so much we didn't even realize the day had totally evaporated.

Of course that meant Dallas was hungry again, the guy constantly needed to eat or risk getting moody. Which is how we ended up at his place, on his couch as we ordered in.

"Wouldn't it have made more sense going to my place?" I opened what seemed to be a ridiculous amount of Chinese food. "I don't have a car to drive myself home."

He didn't even bother dishing it onto a plate, attacking the Mongolian beef right from the box. "So stay. I stayed at your place before, you can stay at mine."

As much as it sounded logical, having already kicked off my shoes and made myself comfortable, it probably wasn't wise.

"So, I'm going to stay and *nothing* is going to happen?" I casually fixed myself a plate of fried rice and sweet and sour chicken.

He rolled his eyes. "Has anything happened so far? Come on, there's a horror marathon on, and I get jumpy when I'm by myself."

I laughed, finding it hard to believe that Dallas was the kind of guy that scared so easily. "They look so fake, and even if they are real, it's just a movie. When the credits roll, that's it."

"Dude!" He dropped his fork, looking almost offended. "*The Blair Witch Project.* Josh and I went to the midnight screening thinking it was some kind of fucking documentary and I couldn't sleep for a week. You think it's all bullshit, but let me tell you. I got lost in the woods for three hours when I was ten and that shit stays with you. Every time I closed my eyes I saw that chick with the flashlight against her face screaming. I had to sleep with the light on."

I didn't mean to laugh, but he was so serious it was adorable. That someone who looked like him—muscles, tattoos, multiple piercings—would be afraid of the dark.

"I'll stay and hold your hand," I promised. "But I have to work tomorrow morning, so I'll need to get up early so I can get back to my place and change. I promise I'll be quiet and not wake you though."

He shook his head. "You're not sneaking out of my apartment like a criminal, Kitty. I'll get up and drive you home."

"But that's silly, why would you get up—"

He raised his hand, stopping me midsentence. "Since when have I ever done anything unless I wanted to? It's not like I have anything better to do on a Monday. Besides, think of it as payback for staying with me for the horror fest."

Arguing wouldn't have done me any good, especially since his logic didn't necessarily sound unreasonable. I didn't live far, and if he did drive me home, I'd make him breakfast. I could only improve, right?

So, with the rest of our evening mapped out, he turned on the television and started the first scary movie while we ate dinner. I wondered if the horror fest had taken a graduated approach, the first one being so bad it was laughable. Which we did, repeatedly, laughed as we yelled at the dumbasses running into an empty room only to meet their death.

Dallas gave me one of his T-shirts to wear as pajamas and after falling asleep on the couch during the third movie he carried me to his bed.

His face lingered close and for a second I thought he was going to kiss me but he retreated with my lips remaining untouched by his.

I wouldn't have stopped him.

But I wasn't going to start it either.

And then, without a pillow wall or even a discussion, we were able to fall asleep side-by-side without it ending in sex. We *may* have gravitated toward each other through the night—our bodies intertwined when we woke up—but it was a touch of comfort rather than one of seduction.

As promised, Dallas got up, showered, dressed and drove me home. Then I fed him, which he didn't expect, earning me all kinds of smiles and a string of compliments.

"Just put the dishes in the sink and I'll get them when I get home." I checked the time, knowing I needed to get in the shower and get to work.

He waved me off, disregarding my directive and turning on the faucet. "Just go get ready, and then I'll drive you to work."

"Dallas, I work in the city."

"Babe, I might not always take notice of the details, but I know where you work."

As much as I appreciated the sentiment, driving me to work wasn't happening. "It's faster if I take the subway, the traffic will be crazy at this time."

"I'll drive fast."

"No." I waved my finger at him making it clear I wasn't budging. "If you want to be helpful, you can do the dishes but that's all."

He pouted like a little boy who'd been told he couldn't have any ice cream, folding his beautiful strong arms across his chest as he showed me exactly how displeased he was. "Fine, but I'm going to take you to the station."

I let him have the battle, because I knew I won the war.

And when I said goodbye to him before I got on my train, I couldn't help but smile. "I'm getting one of those food boxes delivered today, want to come over tonight and help me screw it up?"

"Only if I don't have to read the directions, my strengths are definitely with my hands." He waved his fingers in case I'd forgotten.

Quick tip: I didn't need the reminder.

"Who reads the directions?" I scoffed. "Those are for the weak, not warriors like us." I flexed my barely-there muscles, not sure I was convincing anyone.

"Done. Maybe I'll get to those questions I've been meaning to ask."

Shit.

I had completely forgotten about those, his list of conversation starters that were guaranteed to get us better acquainted. "Sure, whatever you want. I'll text when I'm on my way home."

I waved and headed for the train while he waited in his car and watched me go. There was a warmth that filled my body, and I really liked having it there.

Clearly we rocked this friendship thing, because I had just spent possibly the greatest weekend of my life.

And I couldn't wait for it to continue.

ellee

"ARE YOU SURE THAT'S CHICKEN?" Dallas looked at the

baking dish as he pulled it out of the oven. "Is it supposed to be that color?"

It was burnt beyond recognition, neither of us remembering to set the timer and getting distracted by a fierce discussion over which superpower would be most beneficial. I argued for flight, while he tried to convince me that invisibility was boss.

"I'd say it's a little overdone." A waft of *burnt* filled my nose. "Yep, trash it. Looks like we're doing takeaway."

I wasn't sure if it was either of our intention, but we'd settled into a routine all week. Dallas would meet me at my place when he got done from work, and then we try and cook something edible without following the instructions.

We'd had some success, but other times we ended up getting our salvation at the hands of UberEats. Other times, we ate cereal and vegged out in front of the television.

The nights were spent together too—staying at my place or his—crawling into bed and sleeping together.

Just sleeping.

There *might* have been a little cuddling, but it never got anywhere close to inappropriate. He hadn't tried to touch my boobs in so long I was beginning to think he forgot I had them, the two of us acting more like best friends than anything else.

He dumped our failed effort into the trash, trying to clear the kitchen of the smoke that had accompanied our dinner. While I ordered pizza, doing my part for the team.

"Josh and Eve set a wedding date yet?" I asked, tossing the phone back on the coffee table.

"I think it's more Eve than Josh who is driving that train," he laughed. "Not that he seems to give a shit, the guy is so freaking happy he doesn't even care."

The pizza arrived and we continued to talk, the television providing background noise but our attention was on each other.

"How is the new guy settling in? Mason?"

Dallas hadn't mentioned any more "conversations" the two of them had shared, but from what I could tell he seemed like a nice guy. "We should drag him out one night with us," I offered. "That might be fun."

"And give up a night of almost setting fire to your apartment?" Dallas looked horrified. "What kind of fantasy world are you living in Kitty? We have a mission here and I am not the one who punks out early."

"Well the mission can wait, you must be bored out of your mind spending every night with me."

I'd regretted it the minute it left my mouth, hoping to God he wasn't. While the time we'd spent together was awesome, he was probably tolerating it for my benefit.

He stopped chewing his slice, dropping it back into the box before wiping the grease off his hands. "Why would you say that?" He was serious; the words not accompanied by a flirty smile or joke like I was used to.

"I don't know," I admitted, wanting it desperately to not be true.

"Are you bored?"

"No," I answered, unable to get the word out fast enough.

"Neither am I."

I wasn't sure if I leaned in first or he did, but before I could work out what was happening, we were kissing.

It wasn't a sweet, friendly kiss either, our mouths tangling with each other like they were animals just let out of a cage.

The rest of us followed too, hands that had previously behaved were running rampant, touching each other like it was the first time.

"Fuck," Dallas groaned against my neck as he palmed my breast. "Tell me you want this, Kitty. Because I'm fucking on fire here."

Those were not the words of a friend, his eyes licked with desire that made a shiver run down my spine. And hell yes I wanted him, his touch making me feel so turned on I was probably going to come before I got naked.

"I want this, I want you." I gripped the front of his T-shirt and yanked it over his head. "God, I want you."

It was all he needed to hear, his hands getting busy on my clothes and building a pile of them on the floor. He didn't waste time, getting himself naked as soon as he was done with me.

I ran my hand along his muscles, watching them flex under my fingers. His gut tightened, the metal in his nipples catching the light as he moved down my body.

"This isn't going to stop at oral sex, I am going to fuck you." He leaned me back against the couch, spreading my legs apart so he could see me bare. "I'm going to be inside of you, Kitty. Not just my mouth or my hand, all of me."

If he was looking for me to uphold my half of that bargain, it was an easy promise to make. I nodded, watching as he lowered his head between my thighs, desperate for him to touch me.

"Dallas, please," I begged, not able to take it any longer. I hadn't realized how sexually frustrated I'd become, the week and a half of not touching each other slowly driving me crazy.

His tongue dragged across my core, making me cry out at the contact. I didn't care what we had agreed or that we were supposed to be just friends, unable to think straight when he was doing something that felt so good.

My hands gripped my breasts, feeling my nipples pebble underneath my palms as he lapped at me again. His tongue moved to my clit, teasing it mercilessly.

Oh. My. God.

He was so good with his mouth.

I rocked my hips against him, wanting more.

More of him.

More of *everything*.

He didn't stop, pushing a finger inside of me while his tongue circled my clit. He might have threatened to use more than his mouth and his hands but at that moment it was all I needed.

"Dallas." I screamed out his name in a rush, the explosion taking me by surprise as my body shook all over. "Dallas, Dallas, Dallas." I couldn't stop, mumbling his name as every single part of me felt electric.

He leaned back, looking at me with a satisfied grin, letting his fingers travel down my legs. "I'm taking you to bed, Kitty. And this time, not to snuggle."

Not sure I was able to talk, I nodded, my eyes wide as his hand gripped my waist. He was on his feet and had me on mine in record time, tossing me over his shoulder like I didn't weigh a thing.

"If you're worried about me running away, trust me, it's not an option," I panted, my world upside down as he carried me to my room.

He slapped my ass, his palm landing a soft thwack on my skin as a chuckle traveled up his throat. "I'm not worried about you running, I'm conserving your energy because you're going to need it later."

My back hit the mattress in a rush, the pillowy surface compressing as soon as he joined me, his body covering mine. He groaned, grinding his hard-on against me as his lips found my mouth again, kissing me senseless as I felt myself get wetter.

"Jesus, Kitty." His tongue swirled down my neck and circled my breast. "I need a condom, right now."

"Let me." I shuffled up as much as I was able, reaching out my hand toward my nightstand and trying to open the drawer blind.

He chuckled, watching my effort before taking over, grabbing one of the packets and opening it with his teeth. I felt the pressure against me ease as he lifted off my body, his hand stroking himself as he slid on the condom.

The ring in the head of his cock disappeared under the latex, the rest of the shaft following quickly behind. I couldn't help but reach out for it, licking my lips and desperately wanting to touch it too.

"No, baby." He pushed my hand away gently, lining himself up against my opening. "My dick hasn't gotten any attention other than my hand since the last time you sucked it. You touch it now and this isn't going to last long, and believe me, I want it to last very long."

He pushed in slow, inching in a little at a time as his focus stayed locked on my eyes. I gasped, arching my back, wanting more of him as he slid inside.

"Kitty," he warned, his hands holding my hips still as he bottomed out. "Just give me one second before you move," he panted, his lips at my throat and sucking hard.

He didn't need more than a second, starting to thrust against me before I did, filling me whole with each rock.

"God!" I whimpered, tilting my hips to match each of his thrusts, the sensation building inside of me again. "It feels—"

"Amazing," he finished for me, dipping his head and kissing my breasts as he continued to fuck me. "You feel so amazing."

I couldn't argue, my body tingling all over.

There was no way our first time had felt that good, the memory of how amazing it had been still vivid but not even close to how it felt at that moment.

He hooked one of my legs against his hip so he had room to thumb my clit. He drove in deeper, making my body shake.

"Dallas, I'm going to come." I was so close to the edge I wasn't sure I'd be able to finish the sentence, every muscle in my body tensing before dissolving into a wave of pleasure.

He dragged his cock in and out of me while I continued to come, my pussy pulsing around him as he groaned. "That's it, baby. God, I love feeling you like that. Right there, Kitty. I am right there with you."

He exploded into me, coming in a rush and shouting my

name, his hips not stopping as he teased every last drop from both of us. "God, Kitty. I don't think I've ever wanted anyone as much as I want you right now."

My hands reached around his neck pulling him toward me and kissing him. We might have had sex but I didn't want the contact to finish, needing more of him while we stayed connected.

"I wanted you too," I mumbled against his mouth. "So much."

He pulled his lips from mine "Shhh, baby. Are you going to let me do that again, or was that a one-time deal?"

"Right now?" I asked, my eyes widening.

"Might need a minute," he chuckled. "But I'm not done worshipping your body, Kitty. And I would really like the opportunity to continue."

"Yes. More." The words spoken between kisses.

"Good, because neither of us have to be anywhere tomorrow." His wicked grin got wider. "And the only thing that is getting up early is my dick."

I liked that plan.

I liked that plan a lot.

DALLAS

WAKING UP WITH KITTY IN the morning was awesome.

Waking up with Kitty in the morning when I'd spent most of the night inside of her was even better.

And no, it hadn't been my plan. I'd expected to spend the night being the big spoon, trying to angle my hard-on so it didn't hit her in the ass. But when she looked at me on the couch and thought there was a possibility I was getting bored, I couldn't stop myself from kissing her.

God, I'd missed her mouth, happy to have left it at just kissing if she'd pulled away. But lucky for me she didn't leave it there, pulling me closer and giving me more of her beautiful fucking mouth.

Once she started touching me—her hand on my ass pulling me toward her—I knew it wasn't only kissing that was on her mind.

And wow was it good, every single inch of her tight body as perfect as I remembered it. I thought I was going to blow my load before I'd even got to the good bits, the sound of her moan when she came on my mouth making me unhinged.

She mumbled beside me, shuffling closer toward me while she slept and even though we'd had sex more times than I could count, my dick got instantly hard.

I wasn't sure I'd ever wanted a woman as much as I'd wanted her, wanting to touch her constantly even if it was just my hands on her while we slept. It wasn't natural and sure as hell wasn't normal, and I reminded myself to check the internet what the symptoms for sex addiction were. Not sure whether I wanted a cure though, the feeling of freaking contentment making me feel like a superhero. Obviously a superhero with invisibility, because who gave a shit about flying.

"What time is it?" The words spoken into my chest, her lips pressed against my skin. I liked her mouth there, and if I had any say about it, it would be spending a lot more time there too.

My hand brushed her hair, starting at the top of her head and working its way down the soft blond waves. "Early, we don't have to get up yet, remember?"

It was Sunday, which meant that other than each other, we didn't have to do anything. I still hadn't worked out what I was doing awake, but if I had to take a guess, I'd say the straining rod between my legs was probably responsible.

"I hate not being able to sleep in," she groaned. "Just once I want to wake up at lunchtime."

My hand moved down her back, flattening against her spine and feeling her warm skin. "Well, lucky for you, I am pretty fucking awesome at it. The easiest way is not to talk, keep your eyes closed and tell your body there is no reason to be awake. A few mornings of trying, I bet we can get you staying asleep at least until nine."

"Yeah, well considering I'm not having this conversation with myself, I'd say you aren't as awesome as you claim." She laughed, running her fingers against my chest.

Shit.

She was right.

My body froze trying to remember the last time I slept in. A week ago? Maybe two? It couldn't have been that long, maybe I'd gotten the days confused.

What else had changed?

I searched my mind, trying to categorize everything and see if there was anything else out of place.

She lifted her head, her green eyes latching on to mine. "What's wrong?"

"Nothing, why would there be something wrong?" I tried to huff out a laugh.

"Because we were talking and laughing then I made a joke and I felt you stop and now you're looking at me weird."

She'd always been smart, and to be fair, there was a possibility she might have a better read on it than I did. Sometimes it was easier for someone outside of the issue to see the problem; hell it was the reason why I'd gone to her in the first place. Have her give me an insight that I couldn't see myself.

"I haven't slept in recently."

Her brow scrunched, like she couldn't understand the problem. "O-kay."

"I mean, I haven't done it since waking up with you." I figured if I offered a timeline, it would be useful. To know that it hadn't been that way before.

"Is this your way of saying you don't want me to spend the night?" She chuckled but I could tell she was forcing it. "Because I gave you a choice lots of times and you said you wanted to stay."

"Of course I wanted to stay." *Why the hell wouldn't I?* "I don't know what the hell is wrong with me."

It wasn't just the sleeping in thing; there was a lot that was different.

I was different.

I couldn't remember the last time I wanted to go hang at a bar with my friends, or even look at another woman.

"So what *are* you saying?" Kitty shot me a look of concern.

If only I knew.

"Nothing." I shrugged, feeling stupid for even bringing it up. "I was just thinking out loud."

She nodded, scooting out of bed.

"Hey, I thought we agreed we had nowhere to be?" I protested, not liking that her body was no longer laying on mine. "Seriously, Kitty, I'm just being an idiot. Who even cares what time I get up?"

Last thing I wanted to do was make an issue where there wasn't one, especially if it upset Kitty.

"I know." She leaned across and kissed me. "But I'm making you breakfast and then we need to talk about what happened last night."

"Can't we just eat and have sex again?" I grinned, hoping she'd come around to my way of thinking.

She looked over at me and smiled. "Nice try, but I'm hungry and just because we had sex, doesn't mean we're going to stop talking. That was what we were supposed to be doing in the first place anyway."

Well, at least she wasn't annoyed, grabbing the oversized T-shirt she hadn't bothered to put on last night and strolling out of the room.

I laid back in bed, knowing I should probably get up and help her but the weird feeling in my gut was still gnawing at me.

What else had changed about my life in the time we'd been together?

The whole idea was for her to help me with other women, yet since we'd started, I hadn't been with anyone else.

Knowing I wasn't going to find the answer staring at the ceiling, I got my ass out of bed and walked back to the living room where my clothes were and threw on my boxer shorts.

Kitty was making my favorite breakfast, the bacon and coffee competing for what was making my mouth water the most.

"Have you slept with anyone?" I asked, leaning against her kitchen counter.

She stopped, spinning around with a spatula in her hand. "Did you get amnesia between the bedroom and the kitchen? You know we had sex, right?"

God she was adorable, and could make me laugh on a dime. "I meant with anyone *else*."

"Babe, we've been together almost every second I'm not at work. When would I have had the time?"

She made a valid point; we had spent a lot of time together. "Yeah, that's true." I chuckled, not sure why the uneasy feeling I'd had in the bedroom had followed me into the kitchen.

"Dallas, is that why you're acting weird? You want to sleep with someone else and you're worried to tell me?" The bacon crackled behind her but she kept her attention on me. "Because if that's what's going on, I need you to be honest."

"Fuck, Kitty. I don't know." She wanted honesty, so I was going to give it to her. "I haven't seen anyone I wanted to if that's what you're asking."

Unable to ignore the bacon, she switched off the stove and moved the pan from the burner. "But there is a part of you that does want to. I'm not mad, Dallas, I knew what I was signing up for when we started this."

"What does that mean?"

It would have been a good time to call or text Kitty and ask her for the interpretation, except Kitty was the one I was having the conversation with.

She clearly wasn't mad, and trust me, I knew the difference. But her words didn't sound good either.

Her head tilted to the side, her hair falling across her shoulder as she smiled. "It means that I think that maybe we should spend less time together."

"Is that what you want?"

"I think it's what we both *need*." She took a breath and looked at me. "Dallas, you are an amazing person. I honestly think you are great, and you don't need to change who or what you are for anyone. And I'm not going to be the person who tries to clip your wings. I don't want that. I think you should go out with your friends, do things you want to do and not worry about me."

"Is this a test where I agree and then you get pissed because I'm not supposed to agree?" I asked, honestly confused.

She shook her head, walked to where I was standing and put her hands on my chest. "I'm not trying to trick you. I'll never lie to you or play mind games. That stuff, that's for all those other idiots in the world but not for us. Do you understand?"

If I agreed, I'd be lying because I really didn't. "So what, we don't see each other anymore? We stop being friends? What exactly are you saying, Kitty? You know I'm not good at this stuff, so you have to help me understand."

She smiled, kissing me lightly on the chest. "No, we never stop being friends. This is exactly what we are. We are friends. And I do not regret last night, or anything I've ever done with you but it can't happen again."

"Sex? We're not having *sex* again?" My hand went to her waist, steadying her in case she decided to move away. "But why? We're *awesome* when it comes to sex. Why would we stop?"

"Because we weren't doing this for sex, remember? And because I don't want to lose what we have right now." She looked away quickly clearing her throat. "So I'm going to feed you and kick you out. I want you to spend your time off doing whatever it is that makes you happy."

"You're saying to go fuck someone else?"

She had her back to me, fussing around with the pan of bacon and the coffee pot. "I would never tell you what to do, Dallas. Never. I'm saying that whatever you do, you will always be my friend."

Fuck breakfast, I needed to see her to check that she meant it. I stalked behind her, spinning her around and looked at her.

She had the most amazing green eyes, and when I had their attention they calmed me. "Kitty, this just feels weird."

Her hand lifted to my cheek. "Then let's make it not feel weird anymore, okay?"

Out of the two of us, she was probably the best one to make the decisions so I nodded and agreed. And despite the weirdness not really leaving my chest, we ate breakfast together and I got dressed. We hugged but didn't kiss and then I promised to give her a call later.

She nodded, telling me to have fun and that she'd see me soon.

And even though I had no idea what the hell was going on between us, I knew she meant that.

ellee

OUR WEEKEND WAS SUNDAY AND Monday, Tuesday starting our workweek in the shop. Not that it made a difference, I loved my job so going there and working was no hardship.

But today was different, I was edgy and agitated and I hadn't slept worth a shit. Last week had been our first with Mason actually working and he'd taken some of the load. It was still busy, but having another artist sure as hell helped. But today I was really looking forward to seeing him, and not for his brilliant art skills.

Oh no, I had an entirely *different* reason than that.

Josh was already there when I walked in the door, sipping his coffee while he looked at the book we wrote our appointments in.

"You do realize it's only nine?" Josh looked at me in shock as I strode to the front desk. "Nine in the *morning.*"

I pulled off my shades and rolled my eyes. "Yeah, yeah. You should be encouraging me, not giving me shit."

"Dude, I'll give you all the encouragement you want, I'm just not sure when the last time was you were here this early. Pretty sure it was when Eve was working as our front desk person, and you had an ulterior motive." He folded his arms across his chest, looking at me for an explanation.

I shot the bastard a grin, unable to help myself. "Yeah, well she was worth getting here early for."

"Too bad you didn't stand a chance." He laughed, not taking the bait. "And since my future wife is no longer your motivation, you want to tell me what brings you in so early?"

I shrugged not wanting to admit the truth, especially when I wasn't sure of it myself. "I spent the weekend chilling at home working on some sketches. I woke up earlier than usual this morning, I just decided to come in."

It was half accurate, but not even close to how I'd spent my weekend.

Josh clapped, accompanying the round of applause with dramatic wipe of a fake tear from his eye. "Just like an adult would do. I'm so proud of you, little buddy."

"Hey, easy with the *little buddy*." I shot him a warning. "And don't get too excited, I'm still not sold on this early morning bullshit."

I wasn't even sure why I'd woken up, my eyes flying open at seven like they'd been pre-programmed to do so. It had been like that on both Sunday and Monday, thinking back to Saturday morning where I was sitting in Kitty's kitchen eating breakfast. I'd been almost hoping if I woke up at that hour, bacon and coffee would miraculously appear like it had that day. But I was sadly disappointed when not only was there no smell of bacon grease or freshly brewed coffee wafting through my apartment, but there was no Kitty in it as well.

Not only had I been inflicted by the need to wake early, I'd barely left my apartment the entire two days. No bars, no clubs— just sitting on my couch watching television like an old man.

And Mason assured me the celibacy thing wasn't catchy, yeah, right.

"Well whatever the reason, I'm glad." Josh reached out and popped me in the arm. "And since you have some time before your first appointment, maybe you can go through the supply closet and see what needs reordering."

"C'mon, man." I tossed up my hands in protest. "Isn't good behavior supposed to be rewarded, not punished? And besides, I've got some artwork I'm working on so was hoping to get some time at the desk."

"For a client?"

"For Kitty."

"Ahhhhh, yes Kitty. So what's happening there? You guys still *friends*?" Something in his tone pissed me off, made even worse by the smirk he was wearing.

"Yes, we're still *friends*, dipshit," I fired back, the barb hitting me a little harder than he'd probably intended it to. "We just really like hanging out. But I am totally doing her next tattoo, and unlike you, I don't need someone else's ideas."

"Dallas, she literally asked me for *Botticelli's Birth of Venus*. You do realize when putting something on a person *for life* that you give them what the hell they ask for, right?"

"Tell yourself whatever you like, J," I scoffed. "But I'm going to give her my own *masterpiece*."

He didn't bother arguing, instead nodding in agreement. "Can't wait to see it."

"Hey guys, did I miss a staff meeting?" Mason walked in, all smiles with a backpack strapped to his shoulder like it was his first day of school.

Josh tipped his chin hello. "Nope, just giving Dallas a hard time. Why don't you go get settled in your room and I'll be in there in a minute to give you the rundown for the week."

"Yep, sounds good." More smiles. "See you guys in a minute." He gave us a wave as he strolled down the hall.

I waited until the door shut. "Hey, give me a second with the new guy."

"D," Josh warned, his face harder than his tone. "I thought

you agreed to be nice to him, you were great last week, please don't screw it up now."

"Whoa, whoa, whoa." I held up my hands defensively, shocked he'd think I'd be giving the kid a hard time. Sure, that had originally been my plan, but I was a changed man. Well, mostly. And what the hell was I going to do? Haze him with a tattoo machine? Besides, all I wanted to do was chat.

Just talk.

And that was something he *loved* to do apparently, so what was the fucking harm?

Yep, no harm at all—or so I kept telling myself.

"I just want to ask him about his weekend, see how he's settling in. Since he's always trying to impress you, I figured he'd be more relaxed if it was just me and him."

The relief in Josh's face was instant, the tension in his shoulders coming down a notch too. "Sorry, dude. I just assumed—"

"The worst." I finished for him. "I told you I would be cool, and I'm going to keep my word. Maybe just trust me, okay?" I added, slightly hurt that he'd think I'd really do something to jeopardize his business. Fun and games were one thing, but I wouldn't screw him over.

"Again, sorry. That's my bad. And I do trust you." He had the decency to look sorry, throwing his hand out and waiting for mine.

I grabbed it, giving it a shake before letting go. "Okay, now let me go talk to the new guy before he assumes we're out here talking about him."

"We kind of are," Josh laughed.

I flipped him off, turning around and heading down the hall.

Mason had set up his room so meticulously I wasn't sure if he planned to tattoo in it or shoot a photo feature for *Ink Magazine*. His desk was angled so he could see the door, while his tattooing chair took prominence in the middle of the room. He'd lined the walls with glossy pictures, but instead of them just being snapshots of his work, they were professional photos mounted in frames.

"You do realize it's Josh's fiancée who owns the gallery, not him?" I pointed to the walls, the pictures obviously going up when I'd been too distracted to notice.

Mason raised his head, following my line of sight to his previous work on display. "Ha, yeah. One of my buddies was studying photography in college so I let him shoot my work. Kind of worked out for both of us, he got portfolio pieces and I—"

"Yeah, yeah, whatever." I interrupted him, not wanting to hear any more of the fucking story. "So what did you do this weekend?" I asked the question, praying to God he wasn't going to give me an itemized account of every hour.

He looked at me curiously, like he didn't trust the question. "Ummm, I hung out with my sister, brother-in-law and my niece."

"The entire weekend?" My eyes widened, wondering why the hell a guy new to the city would spend the whole time he had off playing house. You'd think he'd go out for a little while—meet some new people, go "talk" to women so he could get to know them. All he did was sit in his sister's house?

He eyed the door, rising to his feet cautiously as he swung his gaze back to me. "Did something happen?"

"Did something happen?" I laughed, taking the few steps from the door to his desk and grabbing him by the front of his shirt. "Yes, something fucking happened. What kind of voodoo shit did you do to me?"

He might have been bigger than me but I didn't care, my head not quite right since I'd walked out of Kitty's apartment. While I agreed with her and our plan to be just friends, I hadn't planned to put my dick into retirement. And yet every single time I even thought about going out and finding some action, I couldn't make myself get out the door. It was like I'd been hexed, an invisible force field put around me that stopped me from going out and finding a good time.

"What are you talking about, Dallas?" His eyes dropped to my hand still on his shirt. "I didn't even see you this weekend."

"You didn't do anything?" I barked at a laugh. "Then why the hell since that night at the bar haven't I been able to go and find random women and get laid? It's like you got into my head and messed up shit in there."

His brow scrunched in confusion. "This is about you having sex?"

"Well we all know you're sure as shit not having any. *Yes,* it's about me." I let go of his shirt, frustrated. "Ever since that shit you said, I'm having problems." I huffed out a breath and stalked around the room.

"You can't get an erection?"

Goddamnit. Why did I have to promise Josh I wouldn't kill the guy? Clearly he was begging for it.

"I can get an erection just fine, dipshit," I warned, prepared to pull out my dick just to prove the point. "I've been hard so often I'm astounded I still had enough circulation in my legs to walk."

"Then what do you mean?" His eyes followed me as I continued my restless pace around his room.

My chest heaved out a heavy breath wondering if I was going to have to draw a fucking diagram. "It means, I sat in my apartment the entire weekend like you did. I didn't want to go out and get laid. And trust me, before you and that "talk," I always wanted to go out and get laid. Now what the hell did you do to me? Did you freaking hypnotize me? Am I going to cluck like a freaking chicken?"

Incidentally, it had been one of the things I'd seen on television. Some dude in Vegas was able to get people to do what he wanted them to do just by whispering some words in their ear. They weren't even words that would flag suspicion, just some random mind-altering bullshit that gave him the ability to burrow into their head like a worm.

"Dallas, I swear to you, I didn't do anything. I wouldn't know how to hypnotize someone if I tried. Honest, all I did that night was talk."

"Then why?"

"Do you think that maybe some of what I said possibly made sense and resonated with you?"

"What the fuck are you talking about?"

"I mean, maybe speaking to me, got you thinking that you want something more than just random sex?"

"See, this is exactly the kind of shit I mean." I held my fingers up in a cross, backing away to the door. "Keep out of my head."

I didn't wait for his response, hightailing out of there before he could do any more damage. *We just talked,* my ass!

As I shut the door to my room, I cursed out a "fuck" and continued my agitated pacing in my space. He might be unwilling to admit it, but something wasn't right. There was no fucking way I was going to tell him about Kitty, because A. I didn't know the bastard enough to trust him, and B. I didn't want his paws on anything to do with her. But before that night he and I had gone out, Kitty and I had been on track to help each other avoid the crazies on our random hook ups. I wasn't trying to get to know anyone better and I wasn't making deals to fuck someone a month later who I ended up fucking before then anyway. And I didn't feel like shit when I walked out the door of a woman's apartment after we'd had sex. I swear to God, if his bullshit had screwed things up between Kitty and me, I was going to put his head through a wall. Because, none of this had happened before.

It was *all* his doing, putting ideas into my head and making me second guess myself. And he had the nerve to think he wasn't responsible?

Whatever, champ.

KITTY

I'D ALMOST FORGOTTEN ABOUT JD Easton.

His name being something I'd looked for after our chance meeting at the elevator. So it was just as big of a surprise when I almost plowed into him for a second time.

"Shit." It slipped out of my mouth as my face met a chest. "Sorry." My eyes flicking up and seeing it was him.

"Kitty." He said my name with a smile. "We've got to stop meeting like this, people are going to start talking." His laugh was both charming and infectious.

"Ahhh." *Do not say his name and admit you cyber stalked him.* "It's you, from the other day. Sorry, we didn't have a chance to properly meet."

His arms steadied me as I backed away, giving me a minute before he let go. "I'm Justin, Justin Easton. And I didn't get a chance because you were on the phone. Lucky for me, this time around I have your *full* attention."

His eyes followed the lines of my body up and down, pausing when they got to my breasts. His smile widened, bringing his focus back to my face with the attention he had bragged I was giving him.

I laughed, amused at how brazen he was being. He wasn't even hiding the fact he was flirting. "You lawyers are all the same, and you could have still introduced yourself. I can multi task."

"How do you know I'm a lawyer?" he asked, my big ass mouth advertising my extra-curricular research that I had managed to avoid earlier.

Crap.

"Lucky guess?" I smiled, hoping he was too busy flirting to ask too many questions. "I figured it was that or a stockbroker on Wall Street, the suit gave you away."

"Wow, I *do* work on Wall Street. You're really good at this game." His eyes twinkled with mischief, not suspecting anything despite my little slip.

No more, Kitty. I reprimanded myself. "I'm thinking of setting up a little booth somewhere and charging fifty dollars to read people's fortunes." I chuckled trying to not sound as nervous as I was.

Despite him being attractive and obviously interested, it wasn't either of those things that made me nervous. No, not only had I been off since Dallas left my apartment on Saturday morning but I didn't want to inadvertently reveal that I had gone through the company's central appointment system to find out who he was. Thank God, I wasn't stupid enough to search him in the company database. While me looking at the appointment schedule wouldn't raise any red flags, searching for a client I or my boss had nothing to do with would have definitely earned me some questions.

"And what do you see in my future?" he asked, his lips quipping into a smile as he leaned in. He smelled nice, but not like Dallas. His scent was polished, his cologne obviously expensive, tickling my nose as I breathed it in.

I pressed a finger to my lips, taking a minute to guess. "An appointment?"

It was lame, but I figured it was better than trying to flirt back. Not because he wasn't exceptionally hot, but my work place wasn't a pick-up joint. I'd made the mistake once with Oliver, and I wouldn't risk my job for anyone else.

"Maybe I over estimated your ability." He chuckled. "I was hoping you'd say dinner with me."

If I thought he was brazen before, he'd reached an entirely new level with that line. Not that I hadn't been around assertive men in the past, and sometimes, it was actually kind of hot. But other than my name, the guy knew nothing about me.

"I'm sorry, but I don't date . . ." *What was he? A client? One the firm's lawyers?* "People I meet at work." I finally settled on, not wanting to be outright rude, but not encouraging the situation either.

"Well then lucky for you, you probably won't be seeing me here again. I just completed my business with the firm."

If what I'd said had meant to be a rejection, he sure didn't take it that way. He continued to smile and made no effort to leave.

"I guess I really *won't* be seeing you again." I couldn't decide if I was glad or disappointed. "I hope you enjoy the rest of your day."

He took my have-a-nice-day and ignored it, adjusting his tie. "Why don't you meet me tonight at The Knight's Templar for a drink. Six o'clock?"

"Other than your name and your occupation, I don't even know you. What makes you think I'm going to go to a bar for a drink?" I scoffed, a little impressed by his amazing self-esteem.

He might have been cocky, but he wasn't stupid. He hadn't demanded anything or made any suggestive advances. In fact, both times we'd crashed into each other it was because I was barreling through without looking where I was going. And despite his obvious attempts at flirting, he'd not once tried to be improper, keeping his hands and all other parts of his body to himself.

"I'd give you more of an introduction, but you already said you don't date people you meet at work. Therefore, our official *meeting* won't be happening here." And without waiting for my answer, he strolled past me and went into the elevator, the metal doors making him disappear.

Two weeks ago I would have been high-fiving myself and been excited for the invitation. He was good looking, had a job and chances were a lawyer didn't have a criminal record. All excellent points which would make going out with him a good idea. Plus, I'd totally been attracted to him, our brief encounter the first time running into each other, prompting me to super sleuth until I got his name. That wasn't the behavior of a woman who wasn't interested, so of course him asking me out should be awesome. And, whatever business he'd had with Braxton Hill was over, which meant I didn't have to worry about any conflict of interest, completely taking away any concern I had of breaking any company policy. So why—with all those positive ticks in the yes column—had I even hesitated?

He hadn't asked me to sign over the next twenty years of my life, or meet him in a secluded warehouse in Harlem. It was a drink in a popular bar in Manhattan, where there'd be lots of other people around. He hadn't even asked for my address or phone number. So if I decided to go have that drink and then pretended to go to the bathroom and slipped out the door, he'd have no way of contacting me. Unless he decided to come to my work—a place he admitted he no longer had business at—and tracked me down like a stalker. Which meant he couldn't randomly turn up on my doorstep or call me three thousand times asking why.

It was not only safe, but came with completely no expectations. No strings, no complications and best of all, he seemed sort of nice. Not in a boring way like Lani's boyfriend Cameron, but *nice* in that he was good looking and didn't seem like a dick.

So why the hell was I not excited?

"Probably because of Dallas, you moron," the voice in my head whispered.

No, I wouldn't become that girl.

The kind that had feelings for a guy when we'd decided to be friends.

Accepting I was acting ridiculous, I decided to get back to work and resolved that I *would* be meeting Justin for a drink.

One.

He deserved that. And if nothing else it would give me something interesting to do that night, not having made any plans. And if it all went to shit and he ended up being a douche just like all the other guys I'd dated, I'd kick him to the curb and move on.

Missing the excitement the decision should have given me, I squared my shoulders and walked into my boss's office. Garrett was sitting behind his desk flipping through the property section of a newspaper.

"You know you'll find more current listings online." I smiled, sitting in my usual spot opposite his desk. "They're able to include color photos and more details without having to worry about printing space."

His eyes rose, shaking his head as he pushed his glasses up the bridge of his nose. "I know that, Kitty, but if I'm online I get interrupted by emails and interoffice memos. I like the idea of being able to take a minute and enjoy the paper."

Garrett hadn't become CEO through a fancy degree or family prestige; he'd worked his way up the company the old fashioned way. He'd started at the bottom and clawed his way to the top, learning as he went along. But in recent times, he was starting to show a decline. He was impatient with computer programs and people, and hated sitting in on meetings. And while he was the one still leading the company, I was doing more than I should be as his assistant.

"So I looked over those projections finance gave you, and something in the numbers looks off. I think you should get a second opinion before signing off on the budget." I waited for his response, hoping he was done with checking out beach houses in Montauk.

He sat back in his chair, pushing aside his paper. "Look off how?"

"I don't know exactly, just there is something about the calculations that look weird. Everything is there as far as I can see, but it just . . . I don't know, accounting was never my strong suit, which is why I think you need a second opinion."

While my level of involvement and increased authority was largely kept under wraps, I was positive some of the other executives had noticed. Even O'Shea had tried to grill me at his team building dinner, asking me if I thought Garrett was looking to retire soon. So given the rumors were out there, it wouldn't surprise me that some people were gunning for his departure. After all, Garrett's exit would create a vacancy, giving people like O'Shea the opportunity to rise to the top.

"Yeah, maybe." He gave a non-committal shrug. "See if we can organize an independent accountant to look over it. And as always, don't mention it to anyone."

They were his usual parting words, asking for my silence in return for an inflated salary. It worked for us, and while I knew eventually he would leave and I'd have someone else to report to, I loved having the free reign I currently enjoyed.

I grabbed the financial report from his desk and carried it back to my office. While Cameron—Lani's boyfriend—didn't have the most exciting personality, numbers were definitely his thing.

Being discreet as always, I locked my office door and dialed his number. I didn't like the idea of asking him to keep something from his girlfriend, but it was business so he shouldn't have a problem.

"Hey, Kitty, everything okay?" he answered, wrongly assuming I was calling him because I was in some kind of trouble.

I rolled my eyes not bothering to set him straight because I knew it wouldn't make a difference. Just like I thought he was a bore, he thought I was a hot mess, so there was no point arguing.

"Yep, everything is great. I was just calling to see if I can hire you in a professional capacity."

"What do you mean?" He cleared his throat, sounding slightly uncomfortable.

Really?

What did he think I was going to ask him for? To launder drug money for my secret shady business? Or perhaps he thought it was my life's mission to seduce every man, even though I never had and never would make a move on him.

"I need you to go through some reports for Braxton Hill, see if the numbers add up. You *were* a forensic accountant the last time I checked." I pushed away my annoyance and dealt with him like the professional that I was. "And one other thing, I need for it to be done confidentially."

"Of course, I never discuss clients with anyone," he affirmed. "And that means Lani too."

"Good, I'll have these over to you by this afternoon. If you need any additional information let me know and I can get it to you."

We said our goodbyes and I slipped the reports into an envelope. While I usually could have organized a courier, I didn't want to raise any kind of suspicion. Besides, Garrett had asked me to take care of it and that meant I was going to hand deliver them myself.

It was just after lunch when I'd decided to leave. Checking with Garrett first, I faked a headache and got one of the other PAs to fill in for me when I left to go "home." With the amount of extra hours I worked, no one would bat an eyelid with a few I took for *personal time* on the company's dime.

And with a few concerned looks, and some added get-well-soons, I was out the door and making my way to the Financial District where Cameron worked. It was also coincidentally the place I'd be meeting Justin for drinks later, which despite trying to push it out of my mind, I couldn't stop thinking about.

It wasn't only him and our impending date that had filled my thoughts, the guy I had been avoiding for two days was also in there.

Dallas.

Saturday with him had been the most perfect evening ever. I was almost positive I hadn't enjoyed myself so much with anyone like that in a long time. Even with friends I'd known longer, with Dallas, I just felt like he understood me.

So after our *amazing* week, and our *amazing* dinner, it was only natural that we ended up kissing like sex-starved fiends who'd just escaped from the asylum.

And the sex.

Well, it had been amazing.

But it had to stop.

Not because I didn't want to. LORD, I couldn't think of anything else I would have preferred to do. But we were more than just a quick fuck, our friendship going beyond what it had been. And in a couple short weeks, I'd felt closer to him than I'd ever had. I wanted it to continue, to have that one person I could always count on. I'd never had that, not really. Lani and I were friends, but she wasn't the person I told all my secrets to. And Katy, well, I loved my sister but she would have a fit if she knew all the kinds of things I got up to. Eve was great, but she had a crew of awesome besties. And Josh, well, he was a good man, but he and I would never be close like that. Dallas was the only one, the only *friend* I'd ever had who I literally couldn't imagine hiding anything from. Who I knew I could talk to and would get not one raised eyebrow or scowl from. And the thought of losing it when it was just beginning was terrifying.

I'd seen the indecision in his face the morning after, maybe wondering if I was trying to trick him into a relationship and I knew. I knew that he had doubts, and I wouldn't allow myself to be one of them.

Not us.

We had to be a sure thing.

I didn't care what Mason said, sex and friendships never worked out for me. And as much as I wanted him in my bed, I wanted him in my life more.

Which was why I told him it had to end.

Somewhere deep inside I had deluded myself, thinking that in a month things would be different, and we could have sex and it not turn into a dumpster fire. But I was going to have to push that aside and let that be a problem to deal with later. Because we hadn't waited a month, and the sex had been more than it probably should have been. And while I hadn't changed my mind about us, it wasn't going to be about only what Dallas wanted, it had to be what was right for me too.

So, even though I was not in a relationship with Dallas or anyone else, and it was unreasonable to believe I was going to give up dating, I still felt guilty about meeting another man.

Like I was cheating.

I'd been so lost in my own thoughts that I had walked the entire way to Cameron's building. The intention to catch the subway or a cab pushed aside in favor of getting some time alone with my own thoughts.

Not that it had done me much good, I still had a friend I wanted to be in a relationship with, and a date I didn't really want to go on.

"Hey, Kitty." Cameron welcomed me to his office once I'd been cleared by his secretary. It was the first time I'd been privileged enough to see his beige-on-beige décor, noting how much it matched his personality.

I settled into a chair—also beige—and pulled out the envelope with the reports. "Thanks so much for doing this, Cameron. I know you're busy."

"My pleasure, at least with you I know I'll get paid. Some of the bigger clients drag it out, make us send three invoices before they'll cut a check." He held out his hand and waited for me to hand over the documents. "Any reason to suspect your accounting department isn't doing their job?" He opened the envelope and flicked through the pages.

"No, not really. But I've seen figures come across my desk before, and something about these just seems off." While accounting made me want to breakout in a cold sweat, I could write a thesis on Excel. And the entries of numbers and formulas Garrett had been given were just messy considering they'd been done by professionals. "I brought an electronic copy too, just in case." I pulled out a thumb drive and added it to his pile.

Cameron nodded, his eyes following the lines. "Great. Well I'll give you a call when I'm done going through it. Not exactly sure how long it's going to take."

Of course I didn't think he was going to be able to look at it and be able to find the problem immediately. That would have been too easy and obvious, especially if someone was trying to do something shady. But not having a timeline made me edgy, especially when Garrett needed to sign off on them by the close of business Friday. It was already Tuesday afternoon and the clock was ticking.

"The sooner the better. I'll pay you double if you can have it done by Thursday afternoon." I stood, thinking he'd probably get it done a lot faster if I got out of his hair and left him to it.

His head lifted along with his brow. "I haven't even told you how much I'm charging yet, and you're offering to double it?"

"I handle Garrett Brown's accounts, and trust me when I tell you this is a priority. So whatever it costs, it costs." Because if there was something amiss and Garrett did sign off, he'd be losing more than just money. Possibly his job. Maybe even mine too.

He nodded giving me the first smile I'd seen that wasn't directly attributed to his girlfriend or a spreadsheet. "Then consider it done. I'll call you if I need anything else."

I showed myself out tempted to remind him to keep it to himself but I didn't, not wanting to piss him off when he'd already assured me confidentiality. Besides, Lani hated talking about work—both her own and his—when she was out of the office. Other than asking how his day was, she didn't want to hear it.

Since it was early and I had all kinds of time before returning to the city for my date, I decided to catch the subway home. The rock against the tracks was comforting, getting me to Queens faster than a cab.

But instead of going home and obsessing over what I was going to wear for my date, I found myself somewhere else.

In front of Ink Addiction, the very tattoo shop where Dallas worked.

Like my legs had a mind of their own.

Deciding it would be rude to pass by without saying hello, I pushed open the door, the jingling bells announcing my arrival.

It had been a while since I'd been inside, the splash of colors on the walls reminding me how much I loved it.

"Hey!" Josh stepped out from the hall giving me a smile. "What are you doing here?"

Well wasn't that the question of the minute. *What exactly was I doing there?*

"I finished work early and was on my way home. I figured I'd say hi!" I stammered hoping it sounded halfway convincing.

His eyes looked me over, hopefully my work attire corroborating my story. "Well, *hi.*" He waved casually, not even pretending he bought it.

"Hi," I repeated, mentally kicking myself for being so awkward.

"You want me to pretend a little longer or can I just go get Dallas?" he asked with a smirk. "As much as I like our friendly hi exchanges, I've got someone in my chair."

Nope, hadn't been fooled for a second.

"If he's not busy. I can come back if he's with a client. I don't want to be a pain." The words rushed out making me sound like a moron.

It wasn't like I assumed he'd be sitting around, having all kinds of time to talk to me when I walked in. But I didn't want to get Dallas in trouble with Josh either. I probably should have thought it through before I showed up at his work unannounced.

"He's in between clients, next one is due in about ten. Why don't you wander back there? I'm sure he'll be happy to see you." He folded his arms across his chest looking smug.

"Thanks." I started down the hall before stopping and turning around. "We're just friends, you know."

"So I've been told." He laughed, not sounding convinced.

Choosing to ignore him I walked toward Dallas's room. The door was open, his head was down with his ears covered by a pair of red *Beats* as he drew.

He didn't hear me approach, not bothering to look up until I'd almost reached the edge of his desk.

"Kitty!" His grin was freaking amazing, instantly spreading across his face as he pulled his headphones from his ears. "What are you doing here?"

"I came to say hi." I gave him the same lame excuse I'd given Josh because it had worked out *so well* for me the first time.

Unlike Josh, he didn't bother to say hi, instead jumping to his feet, walking around to my side of the desk and wrapping his arms around me in a hug. "I've missed you."

"I've missed you too," I confessed, feeling weird that it had only been two days apart and it had felt like forever. "I had to leave work early and all this shit was going around in my head. And before I knew it, I just ended up here."

I could never lie to Dallas, and now that I was in front of him, I wouldn't have wanted to. "I know you only have ten minutes, but do you think we could talk?"

He tipped my chin, inspecting my face before he answered. "Did something happen at work? That O'Shit didn't give you a hard time, did he?"

"It's *O'Shea*," I laughed. "And I barely even see him at work, he's Lani's boss not mine."

"Still didn't deny that something happened at work though," he probed, picking up on my side step.

See, I could never lie to Dallas.

"A guy asked me out," I blurted out, hoping that the sooner I said it the better I'd feel.

His face hardened as his eyes flashed to the still-open door. "Did he touch you? Try to kiss you?"

"No, he literally just asked me out. On a date. Tonight."

"Okay, so were you scared to say no?"

"Well, he didn't really pressure me for an answer. Just told me a place and time and left it up to me on whether I turned up. He didn't even ask me for my phone number."

His hand dropped my chin, walking to the door and shutting it before returning back to me. "Is he hideously ugly?"

"No," I responded, stopping short of mentioning how good-looking he was. "He isn't hideous."

There was unsteady quiet in the room, the silence making me edgy. We had never had that before, the lulls in conversation having never felt awkward. But as we stood apart from each other, there was a chill I didn't understand.

The smile from earlier was gone.

His body was rigid.

And if I didn't know better, he was holding back.

"So what's the problem?" he asked when he finally spoke.

"I don't know if I should go?" Only half admitting what was in my head.

He took a step back, taking a breath. "Then don't go."

It was irrational how happy it made me to hear him say that, the words I'd been hoping to hear coming out of his mouth. But something about it was all wrong.

"So you think I should blow him off." It was a statement more than a question, wanting to know what he was thinking.

"Or not. Maybe you should go."

I wasn't sure what I wanted when I'd arrived at the shop but standing in front of Dallas, I knew that I wanted him to tell me not to. To give me some bullshit reason not to go on the stupid date because I wanted *him* to want *me* not to go.

Make sense?

Yeah, logic had clearly left the building.

"So I should go then?" I asked again, giving him a chance to change his mind.

It was insanity. We were friends, we had agreed—more me than him—to be friends. And yet I was the one who was conflicted.

It wasn't fair. I had told him I wouldn't change him or ask him to be something he wasn't. Yet there I was, wanting him to be different.

I didn't get to change my mind like that, he deserved better.

"Kitty, if you don't want to go, don't go. But if he isn't hideous and isn't an asshole, I can't see why you wouldn't want to. Weren't we supposed to be dating other people? What's the point of us trying to work out how to do it better and avoid the crazies if we're just avoiding it all together?" He laughed.

He laughed.

I swallowed, the sound of him being so glad and sure about being with someone else making my throat tight. Had he already met someone and was just waiting for the chance? I was probably being irrational but I hated the feeling all the same. "Yeah, I guess so. Makes sense."

What else could I say? That no, it didn't make sense and that *none* of it made sense. That maybe I wanted him as more than a friend but I was too scared to admit that—to myself *and* to him.

And that if I did find some kind of courage to say the words, that I hoped he would feel the same way.

Oh.

Shit.

I was such a fucking idiot.

I didn't just want Dallas as a friend, I wanted him as a *boyfriend.* The very thing he literally *repelled* against. Spending time with, getting to know him—it was all leading us to . . . a *relationship.* Something I had repeatedly told myself I hadn't wanted until I realized it could be different. That what I'd had with other men in the past wasn't even close to the connection I'd shared with him. We'd blindly crossed that fucking line without even knowing. And all that bullshit I'd told myself about not wanting the sex to mess it up was because I knew if I slept with him again, I wouldn't be able to deny it.

That there were *feelings.*

Real feelings that had nothing to do with sex, but came from a place in my heart.

I was so freaking screwed.

"So you're going?" He broke what had become another awkward silence, my panic making me too worried to open my mouth. Who knew what I was liable to say?

I nodded knowing there was no way out of it. "Yeah, yeah, I'll go."

"Great, sounds good. Did you need anything else, babe?"

I bit my lip stopping myself from asking for things I had no right to ask for.

"No, I'm good. I'll give you a call tonight?"

Even though I had made my decision, I still wanted his voice to be the one I heard before I went to sleep.

He ran his hand through his hair, pushing the longer part over to the other side. "Yeah, sure. Mason and I are planning on getting messed up tonight but try me anyway. I'll call you back if

I miss the call."

He was moving on too.

My head nodded, powered by sheer will as I tried to smile. "We should hang out sometime this week. Compare notes," I added lamely.

"Sounds like a plan. I'll look forward to it." It might have been his voice but it was stilted and unemotional.

I threw my arms around him again, pretending to be flippant but I knew if I didn't get out of that room soon I was going to make a fool of myself.

"Well, thanks for the chat. I don't know what I'd do without you." It was the truest thing I'd said since walking in the room. I knew I had to let him go but I didn't want to. "I'll call you."

"Great," he answered, letting his hands drop. "I should probably see if my client is here."

"Yeah, yeah. Of course. Talk later." I walked backward toward the closed door, something hitting my butt making me spin around.

He laughed, walking toward me and opening the door. "Here, let me get that for you."

"Yep, wouldn't want my ass to receive any more unwanted attention." I laughed, wondering if I could be any more pathetic.

He ignored the joke about my ass and joined me outside, no words said by either of us as we walked down the hall to the front of the shop.

Sure enough, there was a skinny guy who barely looked eighteen sitting in a chair waiting for him. I had been so caught up with Dallas and our conversation I hadn't heard the bells jangling to alert us someone had walked in.

"I'll be a minute, dude." Dallas nodded to the skinny kid, opening the door and walking me outside.

I faced him, not wanting to prolong the goodbye and make it any more awkward than it already had been. "Thanks again. See you soon." I gave him a quick wave and turned away, not paying any attention to the direction I was walking.

His eyes were still on me until I turned the corner. I felt him watch me until I disappeared, but he didn't call me back. It was better he didn't, not sure I wouldn't tell him I'd been wrong and confused and didn't want to be with anyone else.

It wouldn't be fair.

It had been my choice.

And I had chosen to let him go.

KITTY

IF I HADN'T BEEN EXCITED to go on my date before, I'd become even less enthused as the afternoon wore on. I was lethargic, taking my time showering and getting ready with no urgency at all.

But whether I wanted to or not, I was going on that date.

Not because I thought that Justin was going to be the man for me—I was almost positive he wasn't—but because I needed to get back on the horse and forget about the mess I'd created.

It was funny how I hadn't wanted to have sex with Dallas because I thought it would ruin a good thing, turns out, I was wrong. It hadn't been the sex at all.

Instead, I just got too close and developed feelings, the lines of friendship getting muddled in my head so I began to feel like I was falling for him.

Crazy.

I could not fall in love with what had become—without even realizing—my best friend.

So instead I would go out with Justin, who smelled nice and had a pretty face, and pretend like it was business as usual. Because that was what I needed to do until I could forget about what I was *feeling,* and deal with reality.

I went through all the motions.

Nice dress.

Put on makeup.

Did my hair.

Then I Ubered my sorry ass back to Manhattan on a Tuesday evening. To go to a bar, and have my agreed upon one drink. Any more than that and I could possibly get emotional and I didn't need to get weepy at a bar full of strangers.

He was still wearing the same suit—obviously having come straight from work—but was facing the door despite sitting at the bar. It was like he saw me at the same time, his eyes lighting up in surprise as though he hadn't been sure I'd turn up. Well at least he didn't think I was a forgone conclusion like most men—he earned extra points for that.

As I walked toward him, he stood like a gentleman, waiting for me to get closer before he leaned in and said in my ear, "You look amazing, I'm so glad you came."

"Thank you." I smiled, hoping it looked sincere.

He didn't touch me—he was really racking up those points—gesturing to the back of the bar. "There's some seats back there, it's quieter too."

Just have a drink. Make conversation. And then leave.

My itemized list of instructions looped in my head as I followed him to the back of the bar. He was right, it was quieter there, with most of the customers preferring to drink near the front.

There were a few vacant tables, and he chose the one that didn't back up against the wall. It surprised me, the table near the wall affording us more privacy in the off chance we decided to have "a moment." Not that there was any danger of that, but as far as I knew he couldn't read my mind so I assumed he would think there might be a chance. He even held my chair out for me as I sat down, taking his own seat after I'd gotten settled.

"You have really good manners," I heard myself saying, wanting to compliment him on something but fishing for something non sexual.

He chuckled, his eyes giving me their full attention. "Not sure who you've been dating, Kitty, but real men don't act like pigs when they're with a lady."

It was not what I was expecting him to say, but it did make me smile. The tension in my shoulders started to ease as I leaned forward. "Now pigs, that's something I have experience with. I've dated so many of them I'm surprised I haven't ended up with swine flu."

He laughed, seeming to be amused by my cheesy joke. "Then it's a good thing you agreed to come out with me. I'll be glad to show you we're not all like that. So tell me, beautiful, what can I get you to drink tonight?"

I liked being called beautiful just as much as the next girl. It was silly that we'd invested so much stock in our appearance, but yet, we liked to hear it all the same. But as lovely as it was to hear—and he sounded sincere about it—it felt wrong coming from him. And there was no way I was letting a man I didn't know get me a drink.

Not because I believed a man *shouldn't* buy a drink for a woman, because I had no issue if he wanted to spend his cash.

No, my issue was that him buying me a drink meant walking to the bar, getting the drink and then bringing it back. All the while leaving my drink out of my sight and giving him ample time to slip something in it.

And while I made stupid decisions about relationships, the same couldn't be said about trusting random men with my safety in a bar.

"Let me get the drinks." I stood before he had a chance to stop me. "It will give *me* a chance to show *you* how real women reward good manners."

He joined me on his feet, looking a little stunned by my sudden need to stand. "I'd prefer if you let me pay. After all, I asked you out."

I wasn't sure if he was being sweet or trying to secure his opportunity, but either way, I wasn't bending.

"But I ran into you twice, so I should pay as way of apology." I grabbed my purse, making it clear I wasn't backing down. "So what are you having? Beer? Wine?"

"Wine, a merlot," he conceded, shoving his hands into his pockets. "I'm buying the next one, no arguments," he warned, having no idea that there probably wouldn't be a *next one*.

With his drink order secured, I walked back around to the bar. I ordered his merlot and got myself a dry white, carrying them both to the table. He stood again, taking the glasses from my hand and setting them down in front of us.

After waiting for me to take my seat, he picked up his glass and took a sip. "Now we're no longer at your work—which would have ruled me out of your dating pool—let me introduce myself." He held out his hand waiting for me to shake it. "I'm Justin Easton, I'm a lawyer and work on Wall Street, but you already knew that since you're a fortune teller." He winked. "I love the mountains, hate the beach, and probably spend too much money on my wardrobe."

"Well I guess we have one thing in common. I spend too much on my clothes too." I moved my hand from his. "I'm Kitty Donavan, and I'm an executive assistant at Braxton Hill. I love all places, don't hate much, and think the fortune telling thing was a fluke so hope you won't be disappointed when I can't give you the Powerball numbers."

He laughed taking another mouthful of wine and savoring it. "So which one of those assholes is your boss? Let me guess?" He swirled the stem of the glass in his hand. "Martin Braxton."

"No, and Martin is a sweetheart," I corrected, the eighty-year old not only the founder of the company, but had believed in Garrett and made him CEO. "Garrett Brown is my boss, who is also *not* an asshole."

"Fair enough, I guess in my line of work I see another side to people. Most of the time *not* the nicer side." He grinned as he set his glass down. "Should I take it personally if Martin isn't a sweetheart to me?"

"He just takes a while to warm up to people and especially until they earn his trust. It took me a year before he'd even let me in his office," I admitted.

I had been holding my glass of wine and had yet to take a drink, so I lifted it to my lips and swallowed. The wine was cool, so I took another sip, letting myself relax a little. "So now that I've told you who I work for, why don't you tell me who you were there to see?"

I already knew his appointments had been with Matthew Crisp, I had seen that the day I stalked the appointment schedule. But talking about work was safe, it meant there was less chance he could ask me more about me. And as much as I had agreed to go on the date, I wasn't looking to reveal too much of myself.

"Ahhh, couldn't tell you that. Client/attorney privilege." He smiled, taking a deep breath and trying to look sympathetic.

"Which you're not breaking simply by telling me they're your client, especially if you no longer work with them."

"Wow, smarter than you look, I see." He lifted his glass to toast me. "And here I was distracted by your beauty."

It wasn't the first time someone had assumed I was dumb because of what I looked like, and most of the time, it didn't bother me. Who cared if they assumed I was an airhead? I didn't need their approval, but suddenly I had to wonder if that was all people saw when they looked at me.

Pretty.

Nice body.

Someone for a good time.

All of those things were accurate, except I was more than that. And suddenly I didn't want the empty admiration. Treated like a pretty picture in Eve's gallery.

"Look, Justin. If you want to make small talk and finish our drinks, we can do that. But I'm not a bimbo." If I was going to be spending time with a man I didn't really want, then he wasn't going to treat me less than what I was.

He reached out and touched my arm, which other than the handshake we'd shared earlier was the first time he'd touched me. "Kitty, I'm sorry. That was rude of me and I apologize. There I was telling you all men aren't pigs and I proved myself wrong. Please stay and finish the drink, I know you're not a bimbo."

I wanted to believe he was sincere, but I just didn't know. Still, I was there and with no reason to hurry home, I figured I might as well finish my drink. "Thank you." I accepted his apology. "So tell me more about yourself."

His body relaxed, easing back when he saw I wasn't leaving. "What would you like to know?"

"What branch of law are you in?"

"Corporate."

"Hmmm, I guess you can't get me out of my speeding tickets then." I played along, trying to be funny since flirty was out.

His smile widened. "I bet I could, why don't you let me see if I can and earn myself a second date?"

Shit.

"There are no speeding tickets, I don't even have a car," I admitted, not wanting to continue the lie. "I was just joking."

His smile didn't falter, taking another sip of his wine. "Well then, I'll have to work out another way to earn that second date."

We talked some more but neither of us volunteered much information, and while it hadn't been completely unpleasant, I was ready to go home by the time he suggested a second drink.

"So soon?" He stood, looking disappointed. "I thought we agreed I'd buy the second drink, now it seems I've become indebted."

"It's fine, honestly. I have to get up early for work tomorrow and I live on the other side of town. I should go." I collected my handbag, ready to go.

He looked to the door and then back to me. "Then at least let me drive you. You don't have a car, and it will make me feel less like an asshole for what I said earlier."

"It's fine, it's already forgotten."

"Not by me."

There was nothing about him that seemed suspect, and other than being cocky and that little slur earlier he actually seemed sweet. But as much as my brain was telling me the only reason I didn't want him to drive me home was because he might be a serial killer, it was because I didn't want him to attempt to kiss me.

I wouldn't kiss him.

Not when the only kisses I wanted were the ones given to me by Dallas.

I'd rather go without.

"That is really generous of you, but I'm honestly fine. Thank you."

He clearly wasn't used to rejection because he almost looked shocked. But he recovered well by walking me out and waiting while I hailed a cab.

He held the door of the taxi, watching me step inside. "Give me your number, give me a chance at a second date."

"You're just going to remember it?" I looked at his hands around the door, no effort to get his own phone out to enter it.

"Don't underestimate my memory, Kitty. Or my desire to get to know you better."

I didn't know what to say, rambling the numbers off quickly without giving him a chance to get ready. I wasn't sure I wanted him to remember but if he did, he'd probably have earned the second date. He smiled, closing the door behind me without bothering to repeat them back and the cab took off, leaving him on the curb.

I was incredibly tired, my eyes closed as the rock of the car threatened to send me to sleep. I just wanted to get into my own bed and sleep.

DALLAS

"I'M NOT SURE WHY I'M here, Dallas." Numbnuts pouted from his seat beside me. We were sitting at the bar like real men, not in a booth like a bunch of losers.

"Because, asshole, you got me into this mess, you need to get me out of it." I took another pull on my beer, draining it dry. There would be more where that came from, I hadn't been drunk in a while and it seemed like tonight was as good a night as any.

After Kitty had left and told me all about some dick who probably wanted to screw her brains out, I'd barged into Mason's room and told him we had plans for the evening. By the look on his face when he'd agreed, he'd probably been too scared to say no.

Not my concern on how we got there, just that we did.

And knowing I was planning on giving my liver a workout, I'd agreed to let him drive my car. I'd also generously let him spend the night at my apartment, something he didn't seem too excited about—ungrateful ass. But he was smart enough—or scared enough, I didn't care which—to agree.

My objective was simple.

We get me drunk, him looking less like a tattooed version of a bible salesman, and get us both laid.

Or just me laid because I honestly couldn't give a shit what he did with his dick as long as the curse was off mine.

"I promise you, there is no hex. I didn't do anything."

It was what he'd been saying the whole time, and hearing it again didn't have me any more convinced.

"Blah, blah, blah. You know you talk a lot? Use some of those words to order us another drink."

He rolled his eyes but did what I said and got me another beer, while he switched to what looked like a Sprite. I shook my head, knowing it was going to take at least another five more of what was in my hand to get me even close to feeling good.

"So, are you looking for anything in particular?" Mason sipped his soda as he looked out into the crowd. "Blond, brunette, red-head?"

"Jesus," I scrubbed my face with my hand. "It's not a fucking catalogue, you can't just pick one out."

"Isn't that what you told me you used to do?"

Yep, definitely wasn't drunk enough.

"Didn't I tell you to stop talking?"

He shut his mouth shaking his head as he went back to his drink. Thankfully he wasn't sipping it through a straw so at least he had that going for him.

"Hey, sexy," I felt a pair of hands around my arm. "Wanna buy me a drink?"

The first thing I saw when I turned were a pair of humongous tits. Those things were massive, pulling against her top like her nipples were having a tug-of-war party underneath. Next were her lips, which were proportional to her tits—huge.

And yeah, I'd seen enough. Sure, that while she would've previously been exactly what I was looking for, I wasn't feeling it anymore. My tastes had changed, preferring a subtler, slender figure. And while I had enjoyed porno tits and blowjob lips in the past, the thought of putting my dick close to either made it want to retreat.

I pulled back, shaking my head. "Not tonight, sweetheart, but thanks for the offer."

She sighed, tapping her toe as she moved her attention to Mason. "What about you?"

Unable to stop myself, I barked out a laugh. It was the first real one I'd had for the night and I wasn't sure if it was attributed to the situation or the beer. Either way I was grateful. "You are barking up the wrong tree with that one." I chuckled, slapping Mason on the shoulder. "Trust me, babe. Neither of us are interested."

She flipped the hair off her shoulder and went back to her pack of girlfriends. I assumed she'd call us dicks, which we'd probably earned, me for being rude and Mason for . . . whatever he'd done. It was something because I was sure he was to blame as well; I just hadn't worked out for what yet.

"If the idea was to get laid, why didn't you buy her a drink? I'm not an expert, but I think you'll get a lot closer to your objective doing that than by sending them away."

Man, I was pissed off.

Pissed off, annoyed and hated the sound of the moron's voice.

"Just drink and get me more beer." I put the current bottle to my lips and swallowed until it was empty. It was a talent, and one that served me well when I needed to finish in a hurry or get drunk quick. "I'm going to take a piss." I pulled a fifty and stuck it on the bar.

Didn't even bother looking at women on my way to the john, instead went in, did what I had to do and headed back to my seat. Thankfully, talky-mc-talk hadn't disappointed me and had gotten me another beer.

I'd just gotten the bottle to my lips, about to take a drink when I heard, "Does this have anything to do with the blond that was in the shop today?"

Whatever was supposed to go down my throat retreated, spraying out of my mouth as I put down the bottle. "We are not talking about her, okay. In fact, new rule. No more talking at all."

I wasn't sure what I wanted but conversation wasn't it.

Mason was probably going to tell Josh what an asshole I'd been but I didn't give a fuck. As long as he continued to order me drinks, and then drive my sorry ass home, I didn't care what chewing out I'd get later.

Wisely the new kid took what I'd said to heart, keeping his mouth shut except when he'd pass me a new bottle. And when I was concerned I might not be able to walk, I called it a night and Mason drove me home. He spoke to me in the car, but I didn't listen or answer, his mumbling putting me to sleep before we'd left the parking lot.

I didn't remember getting home, getting out of the car or getting to my bed but by some miracle it had managed to happen. Maybe Mason was a fucking wizard, or had super strength, or maybe I'd woken up at some point and gotten myself there and couldn't remember.

My head felt like it had been hit with a baseball bat as it hung off the edge of the bed face down. It wasn't comfortable, and even less so when I lifted it to reposition myself.

"Jesus Christ," I cursed out loud, thinking it would be a good time to make my peace with him if he had the ability to make me feel better. If he could turn water into wine, surely he'd been drunk a lot. Bet if anyone knew a good hangover cure, it would be that guy.

"You going to spew?" a voice answered back from the dark corner of my room.

"Jesus?" I asked, surprised the man had bothered to answer me back.

There was a pause, followed by a low and slow deep breath.

"Are you serious?"

"Sorry," I cleared my throat, trying again. "Not really good with the protocol, Jesus Christ. But if you want to share your secrets for beating the hangover, I'm all ears. Actually, wait." I wriggled on the bed, reaching into my pocket and pulling out a crumpled bill. I had no idea if it was a single or a fifty. "Something for the collection plate." I held it out, hoping he wouldn't take too long to take it.

"It's Josh, you moron. How fucking drunk are you?" His hands—Josh's I guess, unless Jesus was riding shotgun, and then I had no idea who was touching me—grabbed me and turned me over. My back rolled onto the mattress, the change in direction not doing wonders for my head. At least it was no longer hanging over the side, so that was something.

A shadow loomed over me, the light from the hallway creeping into the room just enough for me to make out his face. "Josh? What the hell are you doing here?"

There was no way to be sure the bed I was in was mine, and to be honest, I hadn't really cared. But the last time I'd seen Josh was when we'd left for the day. He'd gone home to Eve, and Mason had enthusiastically agreed to join me for a few drinks.

Okay, so he hadn't been enthusiastic, who cared, he came.

"Where am I?" I asked, hoping the blinking would make my eyes adjust quicker.

"You're in your house. Mason called me when you guys got home. I helped him get you up here. I drove him home and then came back to check on you." He put a glass of water in my hand. "Drink it."

I was tempted to tell him to fuck off and that I didn't need him to tell me what I needed to do. But I was thirsty and my mouth was dry, so I flipped him off with the hand that wasn't holding the glass and took a drink.

"Dallas, you need to tell me what the hell is going on."

Why the hell did everyone want to talk?

I wish Jesus would come back, at least with him the chatting had been kept to a minimum.

"I had sex with Kitty." I put down the empty glass and hoped there was a way to refill it without having to move. And there was another reason JC's return would have been appreciated.

"I thought you said you guys were *friends*?" Josh didn't sound surprised, but then again he was a pretty smart guy.

"We were, we are. Fucking hell, do you have an Advil?" My fingers squeezed the bridge of my nose, the headache intensifying. "We ended up sleeping together and then it all went bad."

"Give me a minute and I'll get you some out of your medicine cabinet. Then you're going to tell me exactly what happened and we're going to sort it out."

Honestly, I wasn't sure why he bothered.

He had a hot woman in bed waiting for him, in a house that he loved. Why the hell did he drag himself away from all of that at God knows what time to get me Advil and talk out my fucking problems?

"Why?" I turned to look at him, surprised he wasn't yelling. "It's got to be late, surely you are sick of getting calls in the middle of the night and bailing me out of trouble."

He sighed, taking a seat on the edge of the bed and tapping me on the shoulder. "D, you're my best friend. And I know you well enough to know when you're hurting. So, whatever it takes, we're going to fix it."

If I was sure I wouldn't have puked, I'd have shaken my head. The effort to fix what was going on seemed like a task that was even beyond him.

Fuck, I missed Kitty.

I just wanted her with me, even if we weren't having sex. I didn't care what we did or didn't do any more; I just wanted her.

"Then maybe you should tell her."

My eyes snapped to Josh, wondering if he had mind-reading abilities. "Huh?"

"You just said you missed her and that you wanted her with you even if you weren't having sex."

I scrubbed the front of my face. "I thought I was having that conversation in my head."

"Nope. Now let me go get the Advil."

He disappeared out of the room, returning with more water—maybe he could read minds—and something that would hopefully make the throbbing in my head stop.

I swallowed a couple of pills, finished the water and shuffled myself up the bed so my head was at least resting on some pillows. It was going to be touch and go for a few hours.

Josh took a seat on the bed again, and I started talking. Told him how close we'd been, the stupid experiment and then how we'd ended up breaking the agreement and sleeping with each other anyway.

I'd told him how shit had changed for me over the past couple of weeks. How I'd been waking up early, stopped hanging out in bars, stopped chasing women. How I'd realized the morning after and tried to talk it out with Kitty. And then I'd left and shit hadn't been the same.

He didn't talk, not giving me the fucking lecture I was sure I deserved, or tell me all the ways I was a screw up. He just sat there and listened while I spilled my guts out, confused where I'd ended up.

"She told me to go do whatever made me happy. None of this makes me happy anymore, dude."

"D, do you think maybe you're in love with her?"

Maybe I wasn't the only one who'd been drinking.

"We weren't even dating." While I was no Einstein, I was fairly sure you needed to be in a relationship to fall in love. "We *barely* even slept together."

"No, you were getting to know her instead."

I wasn't sure if he was right, but I was positive I'd never been in love before. I'd been in "like" plenty. Find a girl, "like" her, and date her for a while. Then when the break up happened, I'd be bummed for a minute or so, and then move on. But love, that wasn't something I was interested in.

Too much trouble.

So the likelihood of falling in love when I wasn't even attempting to was sort of ridiculous.

"But . . ." I had no words, shaking my head which was dangerous when you were already having an internal battle with the contents of your stomach.

Josh stood up, tapping me on the shoulder. "Let me rephrase that. You *are* in love with Kitty."

Fuck.

Me.

Was I in LOVE with Kitty?

"Jesus," I groaned, closing my eyes as my head spun.

Josh—the bastard—laughed, finding the situation too amusing for my liking. "Yeah, thought we already went through that. It's *Josh*."

"Dude, this isn't funny." The panic rose inside of me. "I don't know *how* to be in love with a girl. I suck at relationships. What the hell am I supposed to do?"

And this wasn't some bullshit where I wanted him to feed my ego. Fuck that, I was serious. I knew nothing about love.

Nothing.

As in, the day they were giving out the instructions on how to do it, I was probably getting a hand job somewhere else.

Fuck.

"You'll figure it out, trust me." He gave me another tap—if he was trying to be reassuring it wasn't helping—on the shoulder. "Kitty is an amazing woman, D, I couldn't think of anyone better."

Oh.

Fucking.

Hell.

"She's on a fucking date with someone else." It tore out of my mouth as my ass lifted off the mattress. Whatever was going on with my stomach would have to wait as my chest tightened so much I could barely breathe.

In slow motion, the last conversation Kitty and I'd had replayed in my mind.

Her mentioning some douchebag, and me telling her to do whatever.

And none of it close to what I'd wanted to say.

Ironic that I'd finally fall in love with someone, and then keel over and die.

"I'm having a heart attack." I clutched my chest, my life flashing before my eyes. "Call 9-1-1."

Josh grabbed the back of my neck and shoved it down toward my knees. He didn't even grab for his phone, telling me to "breathe," while I stared at my floor.

"What the hell are you doing? I'm dying here. Now is not the time to try and give myself a blowjob." I struggled against his hold, wanting to grab my own damn cell if he wasn't going to be proactive. Besides, self blowjobs were impossible, I'd tried it when I was sixteen and there was no way I'd suck my own dick now.

"You're having a panic attack, you're not dying." The pressure on my back didn't ease. "You need to fucking slow down your breathing before you pass the hell out."

"I'm dy—"

It was all I managed to get out, the edges of my sight getting blurry as being awake seemed like an optional extra. He was wrong. I didn't have panic attacks, why the hell wouldn't he call the paramedics?

He no longer seemed interested in keeping my head down, letting go of me as I returned to vertical. "D, you need to stop fighting me and slow the hell down. You are *not* dying."

If I'd thought his fetish for manhandling me was over, I'd been mistaken. Shoving me back on the bed and holding me down. "Breathe."

Not having much choice—and no energy to struggle—I opened my mouth and took as much O2 into my lungs as possible. Then I held it for a second, giving it just enough time to burn before I let it spill out. And after a few more breaths, the heart attack seemed to ease, my chest no longer feeling like an elephant had parked on top of it.

"You good?" he asked, his hands lifting slowly.

Was I?

Not sure that I was, my head nodded all the same assuring him that at least for now I'd beaten the grim reaper.

"Kitty is with another guy." It wheezed out of my throat like a broken squeeze toy. "She told me, gave me an opportunity to stop it and I didn't."

"Ah, fuck, D." Josh sat down. "Well, here is where you're going to have to man up, tell her what you're feeling. Trust me, the longer you let that shit go, the more complicated it will get."

"TELL HER?" My chest tightened again with the possibility of round two. "Did you miss the part when I said I don't know how to do this? I can't just tell her I think—" *No fuck that, there was no thinking about it, I was in love with her.* "I can't just tell her I'm in love with her, what if she says she doesn't feel the same way?"

I wasn't sure which scenario terrified me the most. The fact I'd actually fallen in love with someone, or that I had no idea if the feeling was reciprocated. Add in the complication that we weren't in relationship, and she was probably kissing some other dude, and we had Defcon 1 level issues.

"If she doesn't feel the same way, then at least you know. But you *need* to tell her." Josh leveled me with a stare.

Easy for him to say, he didn't have to put his balls on a chopping block, hand someone else a cleaver and hope they were nice about it. Not to mention the minute I opened my mouth and spilled that kind of confession it would be the end of the world as we knew it.

"Okay, okay." I appeased him; too busy trying to deal with the shitstorm in my own head than to worry about arguing with Captain America.

He was good at that shit, knowing what to say and when to say it. I, on the other hand, was not. So of course he didn't get why the hell I was losing my goddamn mind over the idea of telling her.

"Yeah, I'll tell her. Sure thing. I'll call her." I did more convincing. "I'll tell her everything."

He rose off the bed, satisfied by my act. "Just wait until you sober up. You want me to hang around tonight?"

Yeah, because it wasn't bad enough I was still freaking the fuck out, I wanted to invite an audience to that sideshow too.

"Nah, go home to your woman. I'm fine. Going to go to sleep. Sleep it all off. Sleep," I repeated my plan, positive I'd have a better chance of time traveling than sleeping.

He nodded, giving me one last look over. "Don't freak out, D." *A little late for that, asshole, but thanks.* "If you need anything give me a call, I'll come by in the morning and pick you up."

"Sure, yep, all good," I agreed, not even sure what I was agreeing to. But if it got him out of my apartment then it was a good thing.

He waited like he wasn't convinced but didn't make shit any more uncomfortable by asking me again if I was ok. "I'll show myself out and lock up behind me. See you."

And then as promised he left, the sound of the front door shutting coming soon after.

I was so incredibly screwed.

I was freaking in love with Kitty.

KITTY

DALLAS.

Not only had he not taken my call last night—letting it go to voice mail—but he hadn't returned it either.

And deep down I knew it wasn't an accident.

We hadn't seen each other for two days and when I finally do see him I tell him I'm going to be with someone else. If he was waiting for an excuse so he didn't look like the bad guy, I'd given him one.

He had probably gone out, found someone new and had an amazing night. Why wouldn't he? He had no obligations, no commitment to me—there was no reason for him not to do what he'd been doing before.

And while I had no right to be, the thought of him with someone else made me so incredibly sad.

Not because she—who ever she was—had his body, but because she got to spend time with him, kiss him, hold him, and I wasn't sure I'd get that chance anymore.

Stupid.

Stupid girl.

The reality of everything I'd lost made me want to throw up.

While morning didn't improve my mood, the fast-paced hustle of the day kept me too occupied to give it much thought. It also didn't give me much time for a break either, missing my regular lunch with Lani as I decided to work through.

"You sure you can't take twenty minutes to go get something to eat?" She looked at me with disbelief. "Braxton Hill isn't a sweatshop, you're entitled to a break."

I shook my head knowing the break wouldn't help. "I know I'm entitled to one, I'm choosing to not take it. I'll grab something from the vending machine in the staff room. I would just rather get it all done and go home on time than need to work late tonight."

"But why?" she whined, unable to understand why I had so much to do. "What do you have to do for Garrett that's so important?"

There was no way I could explain the complexities of my relationship with my boss. And how over the course of months, my responsibilities had surpassed what would be expected of an assistant. Besides our agreement—the one between Garrett and I—being confidential, I was positive she'd be annoyed I'd kept it from her all that time. And while I didn't doubt she'd be happy for my success, I didn't want to risk her jealousy. Work was the one place I had my shit together, I didn't want it to unravel, one person at a time.

"He just likes things done a certain way. By the time I've explained it to someone else, I could've done it myself." I shrugged, hoping she'd buy it.

For the most part it was exactly the truth.

Garrett was more than particular, and had a tendency to get annoyed quickly. Most people thought he was a grouch, avoiding him at all costs. But I hadn't been scared of him, which in turn had earned his respect.

"Fine, but I'm bringing you back something decent to eat."

She pointed her finger at me in warning. "There is no way I'm going to let you survive on the offerings of the vending machine."

With my thanks and a very stern, "I need to get back to it," she left to go eat her lunch alone. I hadn't told her about my date last night or my feelings for Dallas and it felt like it was easier to avoid the conversations than lie to her.

I wish I could say that being a hot mess with a boatload of complications wasn't usually my thing, but it was apparent that it was.

That was me.

One. Big. Car Crash.

The kind you see on the side of the road on fire hoping the driver got out of there alive.

It was all I could hope for, that whatever disarray I got myself into, I'd eventually find my way out of.

My cell buzzing pulled me from my thoughts, the number not one I recognized.

"Hello?" I answered it tentatively, not knowing if it was an ex-boyfriend or a telemarketer looking to give me a hard time.

"Kitty, it's Justin. How are you enjoying your day?"

Great.

Just freaking great.

I'd tossed my number at him last night like it was a flaming bag of shit, and he'd somehow remembered it. Not only did he seem to possess a subhuman memory, but he'd called me the next day. Who even did that?

"Hey, Justin." I didn't bother answering his question, rubbing my temple and wondering how many more distractions I was going to need to deal with.

"Wow, just a *hey Justin*, huh? Either your day isn't going great or you're not glad to hear from me. And since we both know it can't be me," he added with a chuckle, "it must be your day to blame."

I'd met men with egos before, but his was bigger than average.

I laughed unable to resist testing how self-assured he was. "You know calling the next day makes you look desperate, right?"

"I disagree. By calling you today and asking you to dinner on Friday, there is a better chance you'll agree. I wait a few days—because some asshole deems it a reasonable time to call—and it's already Friday. Not only do I risk you having already made plans, but I also look presumptuous. And I think we both agree that I'm interested in you, but far from desperate."

He was right about that. Well, about he probably wasn't *desperate* part, his interest in me was likely a novelty. I didn't doubt that he had a phone full of numbers he could call and options he could take. A single, successful, good-looking guy in New York? He probably couldn't go a day without getting hit on. But I'd said no which meant I was a challenge.

"Sorry, but even though you had a pretty solid theory, I already have plans for Friday night." I didn't but he didn't know that. "So, unfortunately, I'm going to have to say no."

"Great, I prefer Saturday nights anyway, don't have to worry about running late from work." He didn't miss a beat, firing back an alternative like he'd expected me to turn him down.

"Saturday night is taken too."

I was curious how far he'd go, whether he'd take the hint or up the ante.

"Well, Kitty, I generally don't like stacking the first few dates so close together but you haven't left me a lot of choice. Thursday. And before you lie to me about the plans you don't have, consider why you just haven't told me you're not interested."

Wow.

It seemed a subhuman memory wasn't the only thing he had going for him. He was able to see right through my bullshit excuses even if I'd thought I'd been convincing.

And what was worse, he had a point.

All I had to do was say thanks, but no thanks and hang up.

There was no gun to my head, or a hostage situation where my agreeing to dinner would save us all. He was pushy, but hadn't handcuffed me, dragged me to a restaurant and force-fed me.

"There is someone else," I admitted, figuring telling a stranger who didn't know me or Dallas was safe. "And things are complicated between us."

It was a relief to say it out loud, wishing there was someone I could talk to. But who was I going to tell?

Katy, who knew him as a guy I'd hooked up with and would immediately assume he was a womanizing whore who'd never commit.

Eve, while being a good friend to me was also marrying the best friend of the man in question. There was no way she could be objective.

Josh—see above but multiple it by a million. There was no doubt where his loyalty would lie, and it wouldn't be with me.

Lani? She just wouldn't understand. She didn't have sex outside relationships and only AFTER an *I love you* had been exchanged.

There was no one.

Which was why I was talking to a man I barely knew about the man I was in love with.

Did it get more screwed up than that?

"Ahhhh, complicated relationship. Hmmm. I see."

There was a pause, probably deciding whether or not to be polite or just hang up the phone without the goodbye. To be honest, it really didn't matter, my feelings wouldn't have been hurt either way.

"Yep, so not sure any night is really going to be a good night," I offered, helping him along and giving him an easy out. "But thank you."

"*Or* you can ignore the guy who doesn't appreciate you and get to know a man who will."

"Wow, you really *are* desperate." I laughed.

Obviously there was something wrong with him, because no one could be that hard up for a date.

"My offer stands. Dinner, Thursday, and you can choose where we go. I'm not going to promise you I'm not going to try and make you forget him, because I'm not that honorable of a man. But I'm not going to take anything from you not given to me willingly."

I closed my eyes wondering, searching my heart for what I wanted to do.

Dallas.

Well, you can't have him, so you need to get over it.

I'd never really given Justin a chance, and while he was probably another bad decision, he might help me forget the one that still hurt.

"Fine, Thursday and there's a place in Queen's that I like. We can meet there."

"Queens? Really?" I could hear the distaste in his voice, the borough I lived in spoken like a dirty word.

I rolled my eyes at the standard response for someone like him. If you couldn't find it on Manhattan, he probably wasn't interested. Well if he was so hardcore on taking me to dinner, he could wear his big boy pants and get the hell out of the city.

"Yes, Queens. You think you can handle it hot shot or do you get scared when you cross the river?"

"No fear here, I just have to see if my shots are up to date," he chuckled. "Send me the details, and don't call me Thursday to cancel. I don't care what lover boy does between now and then, he deserves to suffer."

"Which of course fits your agenda."

"Kitty, *everything* I do is because it fits my agenda."

Well, at least he was honest.

He'd told me up front that he wasn't honorable, and he had an agenda, but at least he wasn't a liar. Freaking ridiculous when that criteria seemed good enough.

"See you, Thursday. And if I do cancel, it won't be because

of him." I hung up the phone before he had a chance to respond.

It was the first smile I'd had all day. A small one, but a smile nonetheless, and I needed to hold onto that.

And just when I was hoping that small smile might last, my phone buzzed again.

Only this time, it was Dallas.

Are.

You.

Fucking.

Kidding.

Me.

And as much as I wanted to ignore it and give him a taste of his own medicine, I was compelled—freaking *compelled*—to answer it like the pathetic lovesick fool I was.

That was why people shouldn't fall in love. Because while I'd slept with questionable people and sometimes ended up in a hot mess, at least I still had some self-respect. Apparently something I no longer had as I swiped my finger across the screen and answered the call. "Hello." I didn't give him any more, trying to hold onto any dignity I had left.

"Hey, Kitty."

That was it.

Surely the universe was testing, giving me what I'd wanted— granted a few hours late—but some watered down version of it.

"Did you need something, Dallas? I'm kind of busy at work." It took everything I had not to sound angry, to not yell or snap. But whether or not I had a right to be, I was feeling hurt.

"Um." He cleared his throat. "I missed your call last night because I got pretty drunk. Then I thought I was seeing Jesus in my room, but it ended up being Josh. Needless to say, I wasn't in any condition to talk to you."

"You thought Josh was Jesus? How drunk were you?" My mouth gaped open, wondering what else he had done when he'd been so drunk he'd mistaken his best friend for the Messiah. He'd probably had two women, three—a whole freaking harem.

"It doesn't matter." Pause. "Look, do you think we could hang out sometime?"

Was he seriously asking me to hang out sometime?

My eyes widened to match my gaping mouth astonished by the whole thing. I didn't even know what he meant, hang out as in fuck? Hang out as friends? Hang out because he was worried Josh might try and convert him to religion?

"What do you mean, Dallas? You want to go to a movie, like that kind of hang out?" Because I swear if he even suggested it was for sex, I'd have made my way to Queens, grabbed that tattoo gun and shoved it right up his ass.

"Yeah, a movie is good. We can do that."

There was something off about him, his voice different. And if it hadn't sounded *exactly* like him—albeit a different version of *him*—I might have suspected it was someone else.

"Did something happen, Dallas?" I held my breath both needing to know and terrified to find out. "Is there something wrong?"

He breathed out deeply, pausing before answering. "No, not wrong *necessarily*." He paused again. "Fuck, I don't know. Kitty, we were freaking tight before and I could talk to you about anything, and now I'm bumbling on the phone like a fucking idiot. Look, whatever the hell happened between us—the freaking experiment, getting to know each other, sleeping together—whatever the hell we did, I don't want things to be like this."

"Yeah, well me either." I breathed out, allowing myself to feel a tiny shred of hope. "Please tell me you didn't avoid my call last night."

"Kitty, I would *never* avoid your call. You think we can do this in person? I have a client coming in soon and I suck at doing this shit over the phone."

"Doing *what* over the phone?" The tiny hope I'd allowed myself to feel retreated into the corner and cowered. Was he going to say that it was no longer worth it? That we'd no longer even pretend we were friends?

"Just please trust me, okay? Come over to my house and meet me tonight or I'll come over to yours, whichever works best."

"Mine," I offered, wanting to be home in case it ended badly. At least then I could throw him out and then not have to call a cab before I could have a cry.

It seemed to be the day for messed up criteria for helping me make decisions.

"Great, but I've got a client until nine. You good with it being a little late?"

What choice did I have? Say no, and then spend the night obsessing. It wasn't like I was going to be able to think straight until he told me whatever he had to anyway. Nine, ten, midnight—we'd already established I'd lost my self-respect; I didn't want to lose what was left of my mind too.

"Yes, Dallas, that's fine. I'll be home." Because that's what pathetic people did apparently, waited at home to be dumped by a man they were never really dating in the first place.

"Great." He said the word again for the second time in as many minutes. "Okay, I'll see you tonight."

I waited, curious to see if he was going to say goodbye or just end the call or add something else that might make sense.

"Kitty?" he asked, not choosing any of the options.

I could barely breathe. "Yeah?"

"Nothing, I just wanted to make sure you were still there. Bye, I'll see you tonight."

"Bye, Dallas."

I heard the call disconnect a second after I'd said his name.

And to think I didn't want to go to lunch with Lani because I was too busy to take a break. Ha! I think I'd have been less distracted if I'd just gone with her and got my damn overpriced salad.

Nine seemed so far away.

So many hours to sit wondering what the hell he was going to say with the only hint that he didn't like the way we'd left things.

Good?

Bad?

Oh God, why couldn't he just tell me on the phone like a regular person?

"Kitty." Garrett stood in my doorway looking like it wasn't the first time he'd said my name.

"Sorry, I'll be there in a minute." A quick check of the time revealed I'd missed our scheduled catch-up by fifteen minutes, and it was unlike me to be late.

Dallas, Justin, and all the drama that went with my personal life were going to have to wait. I had a job to do and I wasn't going to fall in a heap.

DALLAS

I'D GONE OVER IT IN my head a million times on the drive over to her house.

And every single thing I'd said not only sounded lame, but not even close to what I wanted to say.

Josh had been at my house as promised the next morning and I was positive he was going to give me a hard time. But he didn't. He handed me a coffee so big I almost reached across and kissed the big fella, and we drove to the shop in relative silence. Not weird quiet where you know the other person is pissed, like just quiet in that neither of us needed to say anything.

My head was killing me—from the hangover and the revelation—and the last thing I wanted to do was talk. I'd have preferred tattooing a biker's sweaty ballsac before I'd have volunteered for conversation, so the silence was fucking welcomed by me. And Josh knew me well enough to know that if I needed something from him, I'd have asked.

So we got to the shop, set up and ignored the elephant in the room. Mason, on the other hand, looked like he was going to piss his pants. He was so worried I was going to kill him for calling

Josh, he hid in his room for two hours until I'd cornered him in there when we were both in between clients.

And after I explained that I wasn't mad and appreciated him looking out for me, he seemed to calm down. To be honest, not sure what would have happened if Josh hadn't been there, but I was really glad I hadn't needed to find out.

It took the better part of the morning to work up the nerve to finally call Kitty. If it weren't bad enough I'd found her message on my phone when she'd called last night and I'd been too drunk to answer. There was that other issue where I was in love with her and didn't know how I was going to tell her.

Or *if* I was going to tell her.

Maybe there was a way I didn't have to tell her and she'd just work it out.

Unless the new guy had already put the moves on and then I was going to have to kill him.

Damn it.

Nothing worse than a shady, prison tattoo with a homemade machine. Yet, that was going to be my future for the next ten to twenty years if I'd missed my opportunity. Which was probably why I didn't ask her outright on the phone when I'd finally grown a pair and dialed her number.

Better to live in ignorant bliss a few more hours than to know.

Not that she sounded happy to hear from me, but she hadn't sounded unhappy either. At least she'd agreed to let me come over and speak to her. All I had to do was work the hell out what I was going to say.

"You on a break?" Josh walked into my room carrying a sandwich.

Usually before he'd buy lunch he'd ask who was hungry and what everyone wanted, and whoever had free time would go hunt and gather for the rest of us. More recently it was Mason, but I'd done it too.

So it was odd to see Josh with an unsolicited lunch, especially since the man was booked more solidly than either of us and rarely left his room during work hours.

"You're playing lunch boy now?" I couldn't help but smile. "How did you even know what I wanted?"

He rolled his eyes, shutting the door behind us and tossing the paper bag my way. "You have the same thing every day. Roast beef, on white. So I figured it was a safe gamble."

With my mind preoccupied with other shit—all of which included Kitty—I hadn't even realized how hungry I was. I'd skipped breakfast because I wasn't confident it wouldn't come back to haunt me later and then I'd just become distracted.

"Hey, thanks for everything, dude." I held up the bag hoping he knew I was thanking him for more than the sandwich.

He nodded, taking a seat as I unwrapped and took a bite. "You need anything else?" And in case there was any confusion, he wasn't talking about the sandwich either.

While earlier I hadn't wanted to share, the phone conversation with Kitty had made me a new brand of edgy.

"I called Kitty. I'm going to see her tonight. After work," I mumbled in between bites.

He didn't look surprised but was classy enough to keep the *about fucking time* I was positive he was thinking to himself. "I'm glad, Dallas. You tell her what you wanted to talk about?"

Josh was smart, not asking out right if I'd spilled my guts yet but leading me exactly where he wanted the conversation to go.

I swallowed, the roast beef feeling like lead as I tried to get it down my throat. "We didn't say much to each other to be honest. I told her I wanted to hang out."

"Are you fucking shitting me?" Josh looked at me with disbelief. "You told her you wanted to hang out? Jesus, D, I don't mean to be a prick, but you need to lift your game, brother."

"Dude, I'm not you, okay? I can't go in there and just tell her

I love her and hope for the best. I'm working out my play, making sure it doesn't turn into a bigger mess than it already is."

There was a better than average chance she wasn't going to feel the same way. After all, we'd never discussed the idea of us being together. It hadn't even been a possibility. So it wasn't like I could go in there, guns blazing and . . . fuck . . . what was I even supposed to do?

"Oh shit." The tightness in my chest was back. "I can't do this."

I wasn't sure if it was her idea or mine that we date other people, or why the hell it was a suggestion in the first place. But whoever's idea it was, it was a terrible one. I didn't want anyone else. I doubted that I'd even be able to get hard with another girl let alone fuck her.

"I want her to be my girlfriend." It was my voice saying words I'd never heard out of my own mouth. And what's more, I actually freaking meant them. My head shook as I scrubbed my hand down my face. "Josh, I want her to be mine."

Josh shot me a look of sympathy. "I'm not the person you need to tell, D."

It wasn't enough I had admitted it to myself, and said it out loud, I needed to admit it to her.

Shit.

But what the hell were my options?

Pretend I didn't want her? Ignore it?

Not likely.

"I'm going to do this. I am," I said more to myself than to Josh. And that time, I knew I meant it.

elee

NINE TURNED INTO NINE THIRTY with my last tattoo taking longer than I'd expected. As much as I wanted to rush out of there and get over to Kitty's, there wasn't a chance I was giving someone something other than my best. It was there for life, and I didn't want the memory I left to be a shitty one.

So, even though I knew I'd done the right thing, I was still annoyed it was later than I wanted it to be when I knocked on Kitty's door.

"Hey." She opened it, standing in the doorway looking a little unsure. "I was going to call you and see if you'd forgotten."

"I'm sorry, I ran over. Can I come in?" I looked beyond her to the hallway hoping she wasn't going to tell me to leave. It was always a possibility, especially since I hadn't called or texted her to tell her I was going to be late.

She lifted her shoulder in a little half-hearted shrug. "Sure, if you want. Let's go sit down on the couch."

She turned, leaving the door open and walked off toward the living room. I followed, closing the door behind us, freaking terrified of what happened next.

If I'd ever needed proof that things were different between us, then I'd gotten it courtesy of that greeting. No hug, no smile— the indifference something I'd never seen. Not just to me, but in general too.

Kitty wasn't the kind of person who waded through life in neutral; everything she did—good or bad—was always done to the max. She didn't care what people thought, it was one of the things I loved about her.

Love about her.

So, to see her sitting in the wasteland of ordinary made me realize how screwed up it was. And if I had anything to do with it—her being that way—then I was going to do everything in my power to change it.

"Kitty." I grabbed her before she had a chance to sit down. "Please look at me."

She didn't resist, letting me put my hands around her waist and bringing her in closer. But her eyes were all over the place, floating above and below mine so they didn't make direct contact.

"Do you want something to eat or drink? I could make something," she offered, our eyes connecting only for a second.

"I'm not here for any other reason than you. I need to tell you something."

The intention hadn't been to go from zero to a hundred the minute I'd walked through the door. I'd planned to ease into it, ask her about her day, pretend to listen like I wasn't really freaking the hell out, and *then* tell her.

But seeing her, and the change between us, made shit critical. Fuck our day, and small talk, and anything else.

I needed to tell her and I didn't want to wait a second longer.

She lifted her eyes, giving me what I'd been craving since I'd got there and looked at me. God, I wanted her to smile too, but if all went well that wouldn't be too far behind.

She kicked up her chin, the defiant spirit I knew her to have still simmering underneath. "What Dallas? What do you want to tell me?"

And fuck me, if I wasn't already entirely in love with her, I'd be one hundred percent convinced after that.

"Jesus, you're beautiful." My hands lifted to her face, my thumb running along her jaw. "So freaking beautiful."

It wasn't the first time I'd told her, but it might as well have been. Because as pretty as she was on the outside—and trust me when I tell you she was a stunner—it was what was inside that knocked me right on my ass.

"Dallas? Now you are starting to freak me out. You came all this way to tell me I'm beautiful?" The defiance was replaced by concern as she put her hands on me too.

I was so freaking done.

Done.

"No, but you should be told. Every single day. And I want to be the guy who tells you that."

She narrowed her eyes in confusion. "You want to tell me I'm beautiful every day?" She shoved roughly against my chest. "Dallas, I thought this was something important. I've been losing my mind all day and most of the night, what the hell?"

She didn't understand, didn't get what I was trying to tell her. "Baby, this *is* important. We screwed up; this agreement, the stupid plan about getting to know each other, sleeping with each other and then comparing data—it was the dumbest thing ever."

"It was NOT fucking dumb," she shot back, her confusion morphing to anger. "And I actually *liked* spending time with you, getting to know you. How can you say that? You've become my best friend."

"Yeah, well I didn't *like* spending time with you." My voice rose to match hers, her eyes widening in shock as she heard the words. "I fucking *loved* it. I loved it, Kitty. Every second of every freaking day. And the last few days I haven't been with you, I have been miserable as hell."

God, I wanted to kiss her.

To show her with my mouth what I was clearly so terrible at telling her with my words. But I wasn't going to touch her until she'd heard every last thing I needed to say.

"You *loved* it?" She repeated the word, looking at me to see if it was the one I'd meant.

"Yeah, and I love you."

She took a step back and gasped in surprise. Not exactly the response I was looking for, but she hadn't run yet either.

"What the hell are you saying?" She shook her head, her hand clutching at her chest.

"Kitty, I'm in love with you. I've been in love with you, and I was just too dumb to work it out."

"But I thought you wanted to sleep with other people, I thought you missed your old life? I thought—" She stopped, tears she hadn't allowed to come before, filling those beautiful green eyes. "You didn't want this."

"Yeah, well it turns out I didn't know what the hell I wanted. Because I don't give a shit about the other stuff. There is no one else, Kitty. NO ONE. I don't want to screw around anymore, I don't want to go get drunk and party. I'm happier grocery shopping with you on a Sunday morning at ridiculous o'clock than drinking in a bar surrounded by a bunch of women I care nothing about. You told me to go do whatever it is that makes me happy, but *you* are what makes me happy. *This* is what makes me happy."

Too bad if she wasn't feeling it, I'd put all my chips on the table and gone all in. And if for some reason she didn't feel exactly the same way, or I'd lost my chance, I'd still leave her apartment with my head held high. A hole in my heart the size of an ocean, but at least I'd know.

Her hands grabbed me, pulling me toward her mouth. "I love you too," she managed to get out before she kissed me. Her lips so hungry against mine it took everything I had to stop myself from taking her right there.

"Wait, Kitty." I pulled away for a second, hating myself for doing it but knowing it was necessary. "Did you just say you love me too?"

There would be no freaking misunderstanding. No confusion as to what I wanted and being appeased wasn't it. I wanted her in every way.

Her mind.

Her heart.

Her body.

But I wasn't going to take the last option unless I had the other two as well. And wasn't that the freaking shock of the century; that I—a man who screwed like it was an Olympic sport—was giving up sex for a chance at a relationship.

"Dallas, I've been so conflicted because I wanted to tell you how I felt but didn't want to make you feel trapped. I'm in love with you, you're my best friend." She brought her lips to my chin, kissing my jaw.

My hand reached up to her cheek, stopping her again. "Best friend as in, can't see me as a *boyfriend*?"

"As in." She grabbed my hand from her face, lowered it to her chest and grinned. "If you don't kiss me right now, your *girlfriend* is going to kill you."

It was all I needed to hear.

Stopping was no longer an option as I pulled her closer and kissed her like my life depended on it. I wanted her, but not just for gratification. It was deeper than that, needing to be closer to her and feel that she was mine.

"Bedroom," she mumbled against my mouth, wrapping her legs around me as my hands fused to her ass.

And what did I tell you? My girl was so incredibly smart.

Our hands and mouths got reacquainted with each other while I carried us from the living room to her bedroom.

Her body hit the mattress and was instantly covered by mine, my mouth moving to her neck while she writhed underneath me.

I was rock hard, the rod between my legs like freaking steel as I tried to unzip my pants one-handed. Seeing what I was doing, her hands got busy too, yanking at her clothes as we touched and kissed each other between stripping.

She elbowed me in the face twice while attempting to take off her dress but I didn't care, willing to take a black eye if it meant having her naked.

"Sorry," was all she was able to get out, the rest of her apology swallowed by my mouth as I peeled off her bra and panties.

With less to take off, she'd been faster, the rest of my clothes dumped in a pile not long after, leaving us both naked.

I loved the way she felt, her soft, mostly unmarked skin against the mess of colors that was mine.

I could never get enough of her. Never taste or kiss her enough to get my fill, and as I feasted on what she had so generously given me, I needed to make her come.

With my hands on the most perfect tits I'd ever seen, I moved my mouth further south. She fought me, not willing to let my lips go even though I was positive she would like where I was heading. She whimpered, pulled at the longer part of my hair as she tried to force my mouth back to hers, but I wasn't so easily swayed. And instead of giving her what she thought she wanted, I gave her what I knew we both needed.

My tongue hit her pussy with no preamble or foreplay. I hadn't teased or touched it with my hand, my mouth wanting the pleasure first. She moaned, arching her back as I licked her again, skirting the edges before circling her clit. It wasn't too slow or too fast, keeping my tongue moving as her hips rocked against my mouth.

Her juices coated me, letting me taste her sweet gifts as I couldn't resist any longer and fucked her with my tongue.

"Oh God, Dallas." Her hands went to her tits, palming them and playing with her nipples while she bucked against my face. "It feels sooooo good."

She wasn't kidding about that, my dick straining against the mattress as my own hips rocked in time with hers.

I reached down with one hand and gave myself a quick jerk, pumping against my shaft a few times while she watched. I wanted her to see what she was doing to me, how hard she made me and how desperate I was to get off.

"Let me suck you," she begged, her eyes wide like dinner plates. "I want your cock in my mouth while you lick me."

Fuck.

Me.

How I didn't spill my load right then and there was a mystery, but I managed to twist around and angle my dick to her mouth. And while I continued to do exactly what I had been doing, making her wetter with each pass of my tongue, she stuck my cock in her mouth and sucked me hard.

"Fuck," I groaned against her pussy, unable to stop my hips from thrusting forward and fucking her mouth. "Jesus, Kitty."

She mumbled something I wasn't able to hear, the vibrations traveling up my shaft and making my balls ache with need. Damn it felt good—too good—which was why I needed to concentrate on what I was doing rather than think about what she was doing to me.

With sheer will and determination, I blocked out the need to come as I stuck my finger inside of her and sucked her clit. The combination made her moan, lifting off the bed while I continued my mission.

She was so close, the desperate whimpers coming faster against my dick as I picked up speed, my hand and mouth working in tandem. I needed her to come, *needed* to feel her come on my mouth before I'd take her again and have her come on my dick. It was like a sickness, wanting them both before I'd allow my own satisfaction, while loving the sweet burn of self-torture as I deprived myself.

I flicked her clit one last time, pumping into her with two fingers when I felt her tense and then pulse around my hand. She let out a muffled cry, holding my dick in her hand as she pulled it from her swollen lips.

"Dallas," she breathed, saying my name over and over as I continued to tease her, making her body shake.

That was number one.

My tongue savored her one last time, kissing her sweetly before repositioning myself.

"You have to let go of my dick, baby," I laughed, finding some resistance as I tried to swing my body back into position. "As much as I love feeling it in your hand, I need to be inside of you instead."

Her grip loosened, nodding as her eyes slid back open and watched me. "Dallas, that was incredible."

"Not even close, babe. Not even close." I smirked, dropping my mouth to kiss both her tits and swirl my tongue around her nipples.

"I thought . . ." She closed her eyes, not finishing the sentence as I blindly opened the drawer of her nightstand and felt around for a condom.

I knew very well what she *thought*, and I was going to get to that in a minute. But I wasn't going to waste a second of my time not touching her even if it meant I had to multitask while I did it.

Needing two hands to get the rubber on, I kissed her beautiful tits one last time before I ripped open the packet. I stretched it over the piercing in the head, rolling it down the length of my dick as she watched, and then lined myself up with her opening.

I'd intended to be slow, inch in easy and let her adjust. But that thought went out the window as I thrust in all the way, bottoming out the minute the head of my cock had entered her.

Fuck, she felt good. Her core squeezed me as I dragged my dick out and then thrust it back in.

Her eyes flashed to mine and I needed a minute. Needed to be in the moment with her and know what we had was real. I opened my mouth wanting to tell her how much I loved her, but I couldn't find the words to do it justice.

Nothing I said would ever be good enough for her.

So I didn't even try.

Like she'd seen inside my head, she lifted her hand to my cheek and smiled. Not an average smile either, the kind that left freaking doubts on the doorstep and kicked uncertainty to the curb. She was my sure thing when I hadn't a clue.

"Dallas," she purred, moving her hand down my neck and across my chest. Her fingers ran along the bar in my nipple, playing with it as she kept her eyes on me. "Make love to me."

"I'd do anything for you," I answered with no hesitation, not concerned about what that promise entailed, other than I meant it.

And dropping my lips to her neck, I did what my woman had asked. I kissed her, taking my time as I savored her tight, hot core clamping me as I pushed in and out, both fast and slow. I watched her excitement build as she writhed under me, her little breaths coming faster, more erratic with every drag of my hips.

Pushing myself up onto my knees, I lifted her legs and wrapped them around my waist, driving into her deeper and hearing her moan.

She was so close, her body started to shake so I picked up speed, watching her eyelids fighting to stay open as I reached down and thumbed her clit.

Her mouth opened wide and let out a shout. "Dallas, I'm going to come."

Even without the memo, I could tell she was right there. She tensed, wrapping around my cock like a fist and pulsing as she came hard for a second time.

Over and over again she said my name as she unraveled, watching her come undone as I continued to pump into her. Any control I had was gone, my need to come spiking up right from my balls as I exploded into her. Our gazes locked the entire time.

"I love you." I wanted her to hear it almost as much as I wanted to say it. "I love you, Kitty."

She flashed me a smile that made my chest puff out and jack up my spine a little straighter. The pride in knowing I'd been responsible for putting it there made me feel like a million dollars.

"I love you, Dallas."

KITTY

I DIDN'T WANT TO MOVE.

Warm arms wrapped around me as lips pressed gently to my shoulder. And I couldn't have wiped the smile off my face if I'd tried.

We'd only been lying like that for only a few minutes but the world could have stopped turning and I wouldn't have known the difference.

He was mine.

I was his.

And we would work out the rest.

Never in a million years had I expected him to tell me he loved me, it was something I hadn't dared to hope. He cared for me sure, and there wasn't a doubt we'd become close, but he went further than that and opened his heart and let me inside. Which was an amazing coincidence since I'd done the exact same thing.

"I say we both call in sick tomorrow." He tightened his grip, nuzzling against me.

I turned in his arms, facing him as I nibbled on his chin. "We can't do that, but I can send you sexy messages all day and take you to bed the minute you walk in the door?"

It was a compromise because I wasn't pleased with the idea of leaving him either when morning eventually came.

He grinned, bringing me in closer. "I like the way you're thinking."

I had a hunch he would, my lips inching their way toward his when my phone went off spoiling the moment. "I should get that, just in case it's anything important."

He pouted playfully and released his grip, allowing me to be able to shuffle out of bed. "I'm heading to the bathroom, tell whoever is on the phone you're busy." He shot me a smirk as he headed out the door, my hand reaching my phone in the living room just before it hit my voice mail.

Shit.

It was Cameron.

"Cameron," I answered in a rush, panic flooding me thinking something must be wrong. "Is everything okay? Lani?"

"Hey, Kitty, ummm, no she's fine. Look, sorry to call you so late, but I know I promised you the report tomorrow so I've been doing some extra work from home."

My butt lowered to the chair wondering if "doing it from home" meant Lani had found out and he was giving me a heads up that he hadn't been as confidential as he'd promised. "Is there something wrong?" I asked, not wanting to outright accuse him.

"Well, yes and no. Look, I ran the numbers three times and you're right, there is a variance. And not a small one either. It was buried pretty deep so it's not immediately obvious."

I listened as Dallas joined me in the living room, his eyes on me and the phone at my ear. I mouthed, *"work,"* and he nodded slowly, but he didn't leave, taking a seat beside me.

"Okay, so do you know where the variance originated? Is it an accounting error?" I asked, not sure why he couldn't have put it in his report and told me tomorrow.

"Yeah, I do." There was a rustle on the line like he was moving the phone. "I've checked it multiple times just to be sure."

It was clear he was nervous which didn't make sense. "Cameron, whatever it is, I'm sure it's fine." I tried to reason, wondering what the hell it could be.

"Kitty, it's O'Shea."

Shit.

Of all the people it had to be.

"Does Lani know what you found?"

"Kitty, of course not. She thinks I'm freelancing for NYU. Which, I am but obviously not tonight. Anyway, that's not important. There's some other stuff too. Do you know a Matthew Crisp and JD Easton?"

My body tensed at the mention of Justin's name. "Matthew is one of the senior executives on my floor." I kept my eyes glued forward convinced my voice would give something away. "And Mr. Easton is an attorney."

"Yeah, well either O'Shea is the fall guy for these two, or he's in on it. Either way, I need to see you first thing tomorrow."

O'Shea and Crisp being involved was terrible. Other than professionally, I didn't know Matthew all that well, but I'd been to O'Shea's house on more than one occasion. Not to mention he was Lani's boss. But add in Justin, and I felt sick. He seemed like such a nice guy, cocky as hell, but not someone I'd suspect as being shady.

Although, he'd been attracted to me so that should have been the first clue.

"Sure, do you want me to come to you or would it be easier to meet somewhere else?"

"You think you can get me an appointment with Garrett? It's probably easier if I go through it with the both of you at the same time, especially since this screw up will probably affect him."

He was right about that, and while I had a long leash, when

it came to work there were a few things that were above my pay grade. Possible embezzlement was one of those things. "Yeah, I can do that."

"Okay, well let me know what time is good and I'll see you tomorrow. And, Kitty, I'm not sure how this is going to affect Lani, but there is no way she was involved. I know you have some pull with your boss, so if you can, make sure she's okay."

"Of course," I responded, the request not needed. "You know I will do everything I can."

We said our goodbyes and ended the call, the knot tightening in the pit of my stomach.

Dallas asked, wrapping his arms around me, "Who was that?"

There was no accusation in his tone but I could tell he was curious. After all it was late, the call ruining the awesome mood I'd been in minutes ago.

"It was Cameron, Lani's boyfriend. He was doing some work for me." I turned to face him. "And he didn't have good news."

I wasn't sure how much to tell him especially when I didn't know very much myself, but I needed to tell someone.

"Lani's boss, and maybe some other people are involved. I don't know, Dallas. It's just really not good." My head dropped to my hands, Cameron's words playing out in my head.

"Is Lani involved, is that why you're so upset?" he asked, lifting my chin. "Babe, talk to me."

I know I hadn't done anything wrong when I went out with Justin. I had no idea who he was and what he was involved in, and at the time, I was unsure on where I stood with Dallas. But in my gut it had felt wrong, and I should have listened to my instinct. But the last thing I wanted to do—when Dallas and I had *finally* gotten our shit together—was to start that relationship with half-truths.

"Remember the guy from work, who asked me out?"

I felt his body stiffen beside me, his jaw tightening. "Yeah, I remember."

"He's involved. How exactly, I don't know but Cameron mentioned he's been implicated somehow." I wanted that to be the end, to give him enough so I wouldn't feel guilty but I knew that wasn't the end.

"I'm supposed to be seeing him tomorrow, we made plans for a date. I didn't think you . . ." I stopped, refusing to blame someone else for my actions. "He seemed like a nice guy so I agreed."

When Dallas had arrived, everything had happened so quickly. Who cared about plans I'd made earlier in the day, my mind was too preoccupied with Dallas and what he needed to tell me. Of course once I knew what that was, I was even less concerned, so happy to finally be able to tell him how I felt too.

But now . . . well, obviously it wasn't a date I was going to keep, but I needed to tell him all the same.

"Kitty, the idea of you being with another man makes me insane." The words were as clenched as his teeth, but he didn't yell. His lips moved to mine and kissed them—either to reassure me or him—before he continued. "Like honestly, I want to know who the fuck he is, and then feed his own dick to him. And yeah, I know that's irrational, but it doesn't change the fact."

I knew it was wrong, but I liked he'd been jealous. The idea of him wanting to beat up someone else just because they'd been with me was hotter than it should have been. But I wanted to put him out of his misery too, tell him that nothing even remotely romantic had gone on.

"Dallas, I didn't sleep with him. I didn't even kiss him." I smiled as he grinned back.

"Not going to pretend that doesn't make me motherfucking ecstatic, even though you had every right to do whatever you wanted. I was the dumb shit who sent you into his arms in the first place, and there will be a cold day in hell before I ever make that mistake again."

"Dallas."

"Babe, let me finish." He held up his hand, brushing his thumb against my lips. "There's been no one but you. I went out a couple of times looking for someone because I was a dumbass, but I never even got close. I wasn't interested. I need you to know that it went both ways, Kitty. I need you to know there was no one else, so there isn't any doubt. I may not have been with you, but you sure as shit were with me."

Hearing those words made me want to cry; he was incredibly sweet. And like him, I'd been glad there'd been no one else. I'd tried to push it out of my mind, pretending that nothing mattered except what happened in the future, but I would have been faking it. So knowing that he didn't, and that he hadn't wanted to, was the best gift ever. And it was about the only good thing that had come out of Cameron's phone call.

"So unless you tell me you're still keeping the date with the prick, I don't want to hear any more about him."

"Yeah, I'd say the chances of me seeing him again are almost zero." I screwed up my nose, not wanting to see or hear from Justin again.

He stood, holding out his hand and waiting for me to join him on his feet. "Then let me take you to bed, sweetheart. I've got lost time to make up for."

clees

IT WOULD FIGURE THAT ONE of the best mornings of my life would also be one of the worst. I'd woken up with Dallas still in my bed, his body wrapped around mine. We made love slowly, showered together and then ate breakfast. We almost didn't make it out the door, the temptation too great as we had sex up against the wall.

But as much as I wanted to live in the new bubble we'd created, there was a reality that needed to be dealt with.

I'd told Cameron to come in at ten, clearing most of Garrett's schedule for the day and giving me enough time to explain to him we had some serious issues to discuss. I didn't bother calling Justin, texting him a lame message that something had come up and I wouldn't be able to make it. I didn't bother explaining that I'd *never* be able to make it, not really concerned about him or the date.

He'd responded of course, telling me that he would keep the date open just in case, but I was positive he'd soon find out it was never going to happen.

"Hey, Kitty." Cameron nodded, taking a seat in Garrett's office as I showed him in. "Your boss ready?"

"I'm right here." Garrett walked in, straightening his tie and holding out his hand.

Hands were shaken, introductions made and seats were retaken as we got down to business. And my heart pounded nervously the whole entire time.

"So money was embezzled?" Garrett looked over the reports, trying to make sense of it.

Cameron shook his head. "No, that's where it's tricky. The money wasn't actually taken, it was moved. See this account." He pointed to a column that looked like all the others in a sea of numbers. "The money has been taken out of your budget and parked there. There have been some payments made from that account by Matthew Crisp to JD Easton—which from what Kitty tells me is an attorney—but no money has been stolen."

"Which means no crime has been committed. Why would someone move around money and park it elsewhere? And what do Crisp and the lawyer have to do with it? I though you said it was O'Shea?" Garrett leaned back in his chair as he waited for Cameron to explain. I didn't blame him for being confused; I wasn't following either.

"O'Shea moved the cash, he authorized the transactions to the holding account. But Mr. Crisp paid Mr. Easton, which other than O'Shea's deposits, are the only activity on those accounts."

It didn't make sense.

Why would someone hide money within a corporation?

I flicked through the reports, not that I expected to decipher anything from them. "I'd understand if they took the money and dumped it into an offshore account, or just stole it outright. But parking it in plain sight seemed ridiculous. What were they going to do, see if no one noticed and then steal it? And why use the money to pay a lawyer? What was Justin's involvement?"

"Who's Justin?" Garrett asked, looking at me curiously.

Shit.

Considering my track record of men and shady pasts, I figured it was just easier to come clean. Besides, I hadn't done anything wrong. We'd seen each other outside of work and we never spoke business. So technically I didn't break any rules. Not that it made me feel any better, hating there was a connection at all.

"Justin Easton, the lawyer." I bit my lip. "We saw each other socially one time."

"You dated him?" Cameron asked, looking surprised. "Why didn't you tell me last night when I brought up his name?"

"Because my relationship with him isn't relevant, and there isn't much to tell. I ran into him at work twice, the second time he asked me out. He'd assured me his business with the company was done so I didn't think there'd be a conflict." I turned to Garrett to assure him. "It was just drinks at a bar, it wasn't really a date."

"You think he was targeting you?" Garrett asked, which honestly never occurred to me.

I shook my head, convinced it was just a coincidence. Justin had known nothing about me, he barely even knew my name. "No, no I don't think so."

"Well, let's not rule it out." Garrett snapped his fingers. "In any case, while a crime might not have been committed, it stinks of impropriety. I want a meeting with in-house legal counsel, and then we'll go from there."

Cameron handed over all his findings and promised to be available if anyone needed anything else. And after thanking him for a job well done, Garrett got on the phone and started talking to one of our attorneys.

"I'll walk you out." I motioned to the door, Cameron following me out of Garrett's office.

We headed into my office and I closed the door. Other than money playing hide-and-go-seek, we didn't know why. "Thanks, Cameron, I'll get your check. I really appreciate what you've done for us. I know it couldn't have been easy keeping it from Lani."

He rubbed the back of his neck clearly uncomfortable with the situation. "I just want her to be okay. Her boss is a douchebag, but this is the best job she's ever had. I'd hate for something to happen to her."

"I promise you it won't." I reached out and touched his arm to reassure him. "If O'Shea is fired or something like that, I'll get Garrett to reassign her. Maybe we can finally work on the same floor?"

I was just about to go write Cameron his check when my door swung open. Standing in the door way was Lani, looking at me with my hand on Cameron's arm.

"What the hell?" She looked to her boyfriend and then to me. "You guys are sneaking around behind my back?"

I snatched my hand back, taking a step toward her. "No, Lani, that isn't what's going on. I would never do that."

"Never what, Kitty? Screw someone else's man? No, you'd *never* do that," she spat out at me, clearly not willing to listen to reason.

Cameron tried, reaching out for her as she took a step back. "Baby, listen. I'm just here for work. Nothing else."

Lani's nostril's flared, her eyes glassy as they narrowed. "Work?

Please, I'm not an idiot. I checked your phone and I saw your late night call to *her* last night. You expect me to believe you were doing business?"

"Lani, it was. I swear to you." He tried in vain, looking at me for help. "Kitty hired me to go over some numbers, that's all. There's no way I'd cheat on you, especially not with *Kitty*."

WOW.

It was like a slap to my face, my name almost sneered like it was trash. Like *I* was trash. And while I believed he wouldn't cheat on Lani, the added insulting blow was unnecessary.

"Don't lie." Her head shook before turning to me. "You can have any man you want, why did you have to take mine." Her tears began to fall. "What they say about you is right, you're nothing but a whore."

My chest hurt, the air knocked out of me as I watched a person who I thought was a friend think I was capable of sleeping with her boyfriend.

I'd made mistakes.

And yeah, when it came to men, I usually screwed up. But I never would intentionally hurt someone, not someone I thought was my friend.

I wanted to scream at her, to tell her that I wasn't and would never be a whore. That despite me enjoying sex and being open about it, I still had feelings like everyone else.

But I closed my mouth, not willing to show my vulnerability when she clearly didn't care. "Why are you here?" I managed to croak out, not allowing myself to cry.

"O'Shea told me he saw Cameron coming up here, considering the phone call last night, it made me suspicious. I never thought you'd be stupid enough to get caught red handed. But I guess I was wrong."

Of course O'Shea had told her, it was like the man lived to start trouble. He probably didn't even suspect that Cameron had come because of the shady shit he'd been up to with his buddies. No, he was too cocky for that. Instead it had to be me, having sex with one of my friends boyfriends on the company time.

"You need to both leave." I pointed to the door, not willing to waste my time or energy explaining myself.

What was the point? She'd walked in, seen a conversation completely out of context and immediately thought the worst. We hadn't been kissing—we were barely even touching—but of course the only explanation could be that we were having an affair. That she made that leap so fast meant she'd always had such little faith in me.

When they didn't move, I squared my shoulders, cleared my throat and slammed my hands down on my desk. "Get out of my office. NOW."

Lani looked at me stunned, like she couldn't believe I'd had the nerve, while Cameron didn't seem like he knew what to do either. He worked it out though, hooking Lani around the arm and edging her out of my office.

I followed them to the door, slamming it in their face as I breathed a sigh of relief. I didn't care what he told her—it was no longer my problem—but it didn't make what she said hurt any less.

I didn't care that she'd called me a whore, I cared that she'd believed it.

Alone, and no longer needing to be strong, I walked back to my chair and crumbled.

All I wanted to do was go home, but that wasn't an option. I had no idea what Garrett and legal were going to do, or what it all meant for the company. Not that I cared about any of that at that moment.

I reached for the phone, just about to call Dallas when there was a gentle knock at my door.

Great, because dealing with more people was exactly what I needed.

I wiped the corners of my eyes, mopping up any tears that were threatening to fall and cleared my throat. "Come in."

It was Garrett, his large frame filling the now open space. "Kitty, everything okay in here? I thought I heard screaming."

"It was nothing." I tried to smile, not wanting to admit what happened.

He walked into the room closing the door behind him. "It didn't sound like nothing but I'm not going to pry." He took a seat and looked around my office.

It was probably the first time he'd spent any quality time in it, usually summoning me from the doorway and me meeting him in his. But for whatever reason he'd decided to say whatever he was going to say here.

"So, I spoke to legal. We have a meeting in about an hour where both O'Shea and Crisp will be asked to explain. I believe Matthew already called his attorney, with whom you're already familiar with."

"Garrett, if you're worried about me seeing him, don't be. It was *one* date, nothing more." Last thing I needed was for my boss to think I had invested feelings and my judgment was clouded. That was one area I was crystal clear.

He smiled, easing back into his chair. "Good, because I want you to sit in on the meeting."

"What?" My eyes snapped to his, confused on why I—an assistant, granted an extremely good one—would be asked to sit in on the meeting.

"It was your suspicion that started this train rolling in the first place. I'd have probably looked those reports over and signed them and who knows what the repercussions would have been." He sighed, shaking his head. "You've saved my ass more than just a few times, Kitty. Don't think that because I don't say it every day it goes unnoticed."

"Thanks, Garrett, I appreciate that. But I think it's best if I sit out of the meeting."

He laughed, probably assuming I was kidding. "What are you talking about, you love that stuff, you live for it."

On any other day, I would have jumped at the chance. An opportunity to sit in on a high level meeting could only mean good things, and I'd taken those opportunities every single time they'd come my way. It gave me more insight into the company than any other executive assistant had, giving me the ability to do more than just my regular responsibilities. And I'd been paid well, Garrett more than making up for what I did around the office with financial compensation.

But that was it.

I hadn't been promoted. I hadn't been publically acknowledged, or given credit, with other assistants and executives whispering about me behind my back about why I was always so busy.

I was a dirty little secret.

And I wasn't going to be that anymore.

I stood, feeling both empowered and terrified as I grabbed my handbag and my phone and straightened my shoulders. "I'm an assistant, Garrett, yours. And there is no reason for an assistant to be anywhere near that meeting unless it's to take notes. And we both know, I'm not going to do that. I have loved working with you, and I have thrived with the freedom you have given me, but you need to either promote me or let me do my job. *My* job, Garrett, not yours. I'm tired of being less than, and I'm not doing it anymore."

Not entirely sure I hadn't inadvertently gotten myself fired, I strode to the door with as much confidence as I could. "And I'm taking a personal day, but I'll get someone to cover for me."

Garrett was so shocked he didn't even move, watching me leave as he sat in my office, a smile affixed to my face, and walked out.

I didn't even think, knowing exactly where I was heading.

To the one person who'd known me from the start.

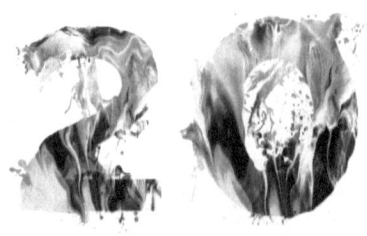

DALLAS

"DALLAS, I SWEAR TO GOD, I didn't put a hex on you." Mason was already off his ass and backing up when I entered the room. "I thought we were good, bro?"

I had to admit, making him jumpy gave me a sick sense of pleasure. I still think he'd had it way too easy, and could use some good old-fashioned toughening up. Which was why I'd demanded he meet me in my room the minute he had a moment.

I'd even gone into Josh's room to make him wait, loving the idea he had to sit and stew for a while until I made my grand entrance.

"Relax, I'm just here to tell you some good news. We've been busy so I haven't had the time. But I've got myself a girlfriend." The smile almost cracked off my face at the thought of Kitty being mine.

Mason relaxed, the tension in his face bleeding out when he saw I wasn't hostile. "Wow, that's great. Congrats, man, I'm sure you'll be happy."

"You bet your ass, I'll be happy." I pointed at him for good measure. "Because if this fucks up in any way, I'll know exactly *who* to blame."

I was fucking with him of course because there was no way *anything* was going wrong. And even if it did, the chances the poor fucker had anything to do with it were slim.

Unless he did put a hex on me, in which case that would not be cool.

"Dallas." He lifted his hands, starting to protest.

"Leave him be, D." Josh walked in and clapped me on the shoulder. "Ignore him, Mason. He's jerking your chain. I was hoping love might make him more agreeable, but I guess a miracle was too big to expect."

I tipped my chin at Josh, he and I had already discussed the change in my relationship status. "Hello? Have you seen the girl I'm dating? Everything about her is a miracle so you can just shut your mouth."

She was more than a miracle, she was perfection, and I still couldn't believe my dumb luck. Not that I gave a shit on how it came about—or whether I'd earned it or not—nope, all that I cared about was that she was mine.

It was a rare time in the shop when the three of us weren't busy but shit didn't usually get situation critical until after eleven. So even if we had bookings before then, they were usually simple stuff we could knock out easily.

I'd already done some scrollwork on a college girl earlier, but it wasn't until later that I broke out my more impressive skills.

"Yeah, I think it's a miracle she's agreed to be with you too." Josh laughed. "Make sure you thank Jesus later. The *real* one this time, and probably don't try and tip him because that's just tacky."

I laughed because it was freaking funny, but poor Mason had no idea what we were talking about.

Too bad, sucker.

But our good time was cut short; the bells on the door jangling to let us know someone's next customer had arrived. It had to be one of the two of theirs, because my next dude wasn't due for another ten minutes.

"Well boys, looks like it's time to go back to work." Josh looked at his watch. "I think that's yours, Mason."

He nodded in agreement. "Yep, I have a consult for an arm piece, I'll go get her."

He'd barely made it to the door when Kitty walked in. She looked surprised, staring at the three of us standing in my room and probably wondering what the hell we were doing.

"Wow. Hi!" Mason popped a grin that was far too enthusiastic as he shot out his hand. "I'm Mason."

"Easy, celibate. She's not here for you." I tapped him on the shoulder as I pushed him aside. "She is most definitely here for me."

I didn't give a shit who was watching, wrapping my arms around her and kissing her right in front of them. Those lips were mine, and I'd been separated from them for too many hours already.

Kitty's body softened in my arms, giving me her mouth as I pulled her closer. "You guys should leave now if you know what's good for you," I managed to mumble out between kisses.

"Don't suffocate her, D." Josh chuckled as he left, Mason following him.

And even though I wasn't paying them any attention—all of mine required elsewhere—I could tell both of those bastards were smiling.

Josh—because he was happy for me.

Mason—because as long as I was preoccupied with Kitty, I couldn't give him shit.

"God, I needed that." Kitty took a breath, hugging me and laying her head on my shoulder. "It felt like forever until I got here."

I'd been so caught up in the excitement of seeing her I hadn't realized she should have been at work. Not that I wasn't thankful for whatever had made it possible for her to materialize in my room, but I assumed it probably wasn't good.

"What happened?" My hand moved down her silky hair and

rubbed her back. "I swear if someone's upset you, I'll tear off their arms."

She chuckled against my chest. "You can't go randomly tearing off people's arms just because they upset me, Dallas."

Ha, she had a lot to learn. I'd do a hell of a lot more than that just to keep her happy. As far as I was concerned, I'd spend my days beating the shit out of people if it meant she continued to smile.

"Sure I can, where's it say I can't?" I tilted her so I could look into those beautiful green eyes.

She smiled but it wasn't the kind I liked. The kind that assured me that everything was fine. "Pretty sure there's a few laws that say you can't."

"Well fuck the law, I still say I can and I will." My thumb traced her chin, just needing to keep touching her. "Tell me, beautiful, tell me what happened."

"Where to even start." She sighed; her shoulders sagged as she shook her head. "I have no idea what I'm even doing anymore. Lani thinks I'm having an affair with Cameron, Justin might have been using me or—and most likely—I am an extremely bad judge of character, I feel like the other woman at work, given money and kept out of the spotlight, and I might have quit my job."

That was a lot to take in, especially with the mention of the dipshit. And no matter how that turd was involved, I knew it had nothing to do with Kitty's judge of character. The woman had a heart three sizes too big and assholes took advantage of that. And as for her friend thinking she was screwing her boyfriend? That was a special kind of messed up. "Babe, you know you need to give it to me again, only slower."

"Do you have time?" She looked at me and then at the door, knowing I probably didn't.

"Give me a minute." I unwrapped my hands from her and gave her a kiss. "Take a seat in my chair, baby. I'll be right back."

I knew I had five minutes, ten tops before my client walked

in and that wasn't going to be long enough for Kitty. And as much as I hated to blow off work, she was more important.

"J, you got a minute?" I knocked on this doorframe, the dude already setting up for his next job.

He looked up and rolled his eyes. "I'm happy for you, Dallas, and you guys are adorable together. But I'm not giving you time off to go have afternoon sex."

While afternoon sex with Kitty was worth blowing off work for, it hadn't even entered my mind. She needed me, so I needed to be there—it was as simple as that. I walked in and shut the door behind me. "Dude, Kitty's upset and she needs to talk. I swear I'll make up the time."

I'm not sure if it was the fact I was asking or the tone of my voice, but Josh dropped his smile and rose to his feet. "Is she okay?"

"She will be, you better believe I'll make sure of it." I didn't know how I would do that but I didn't doubt that I would. Whether it was to tear off arms like I'd suggested earlier, or holding her until it was better. "I need to do this."

He nodded and put out his hand. "I know I give you a lot of shit, but you are a good man and an even better friend. Go do whatever you need to do, we'll take care of things here."

I clapped it with mine, giving him a shake. "Thanks, man. Means a lot."

There was some throat clearing—possibly even done by me—but I didn't have time to get caught up in the sentiment. Kitty was waiting and that's where I needed to be.

I pulled open Josh's door and left the room, heading back into mine. Kitty was sitting on the edge of my large reclining chair, her legs swinging off the side. She looked so small, her tiny body dwarfed by the huge black surface.

"I'm all yours, sweetheart." I closed the door behind me and grabbed my rolling stool. "Now, tell me everything."

My hands rested on her thighs as I parked my butt in front of her, but I wasn't trying to get her naked. It wasn't the first time that sex hadn't been the first thought in my head, but the need to just be with her was definitely more important as time went on.

She took a breath and then told me, starting at the beginning on how she met numbnuts, and then about the report. Then moved on to Cameron's involvement and how Lani had put two and two together and ended up with sixty-nine. I swear, I never liked that girl, but it wasn't my place to say.

Not going to pretend that hearing all of it didn't jack up my shit. I'd mentally created a list of enemies all because they'd made my girl upset. But flying off the handle was probably not that helpful at the minute, which was why I kept my mouth shut and my need for retribution to myself.

"You're quiet." She looked at me from under her lashes. "You're *never* quiet."

"Babe, I'm just new to this and I don't want to say the wrong thing." I gave her honesty, wishing I had more to offer.

"I don't care if you say the wrong thing, I just need to hear something."

There was an edge in her voice and I hated it. Hated that these pieces of shit had somehow gotten inside her head and made her doubt herself.

By the same token, I was out of my mind proud of her for standing up to them and telling them to shove it. Both her friend and her limp-dick boyfriend, and her boss who clearly had no idea what a goldmine she was.

Didn't mean I felt confident being in a room with any of them any time soon. "You want me to say something?" I asked, trying not to raise my voice. "None of these fuckers deserve you. Hell, I'm not even sure *I* deserve you, but we're going to pretend I didn't say that."

She chuckled which was good because I was hoping she would see the comedy.

"You can find another job, you can find better friends, but none of them will find a better you."

I could see her head start to shake, ready to disagree. And yes, she'd told me that she seemed to jump from one fire to the next when it came to her personal life or some other bullshit. But that wasn't a bad thing either. "Kitty, we're not like them."

She stopped, looking at me curiously. "What do you mean?"

"I mean, we buy condoms in bulk, and cook really badly, and chain ourselves to headboards." I laughed. "I mean, we get confused by religious people holding plates of cookies and need to read a page five times before it makes sense. Or maybe that's just me, but you get my point. We're on the fringes, baby, and trust me, it's a better place to be. The only thing you need is to make sure there's someone to share it with, and I'm more than willing to take that spot. Do you know why I fell in love with you, baby?"

I should have probably made it clearer last night but I was crap at explaining. But regardless of how bad I was with my words, I needed her to know why I was willing to give her something I'd never given any other woman.

Not because she was beautiful, even though she was.

Because of the gifts she'd given me.

She raised her eyes and smirked like she thought it was a bogus question. "Ummmm." Her finger tapped at her chin like she was thinking carefully. "I'd say how most people fall in love. Because we're compatible and we have a great time together."

I couldn't help but laugh. Lord, that sounded as boring as dog shit. If that was what other people were doing it then I felt sorry for them.

"Well, yeah, okay smartass." I rolled my eyes, giving her a D for obvious. "But more importantly it was because you didn't once ask me to change. You never told me to do anything differently, or be more this or that. You accepted me, as I am."

If I had a buck for every time I'd been told to be less *this* or more *that*, I'd have a house in the Hamptons. But Kitty just didn't. Even when I was being a dick, and could have done with a clip over the ears and stern talking to—she didn't.

"I could never ask you to change, baby. I love everything about you."

"Times two, Kitty. Times two." I got my ass off my stool and brought my mouth to meet hers. "You don't need to change a damn thing. You be crazy and impulsive and if the situation ends up a dumpster fire, well at least you'll keep warm. I work better in chaos anyway, and since I'll be spending so much time with you then you should take that into consideration too."

"You know the two of us together could end up a disaster. Like a huge, epic level disaster the likes of which neither of us has seen before." Her eyes were wide, and I couldn't tell if she was worried or excited.

"You scared?" I asked, wondering if she was looking for a way out.

Not that I was going to let her walk if she decided to without a fight. And if she thought different then she'd lost her damn mind. Even so I'd continue to love her, crazy without her mind and everything.

She shook her head. "I'm not scared, Dallas. I've turned hot mess into an art form."

"Good, because if you start being ordinary, we're going to have problems." I was only half joking, almost positive neither of us were capable.

She grabbed my shirt and pulled me down to her mouth and kissed me. Not like the sweet kisses I'd been giving her but the kind that probably didn't belong in that chair. Not saying I didn't give them to her, because I wasn't able to deny her mouth if I tried. But if Josh walked in and saw us in action, I would never hear the end of it.

"I love you," she mumbled in between kisses. "You said exactly what I needed to hear."

I laughed, never having heard those words before. "Probably the first and the last time it will happen so let's mark it on the calendar or something."

While I'd finally made her smile, I really hadn't solved anything. And as the relationship thing was new to me, I wasn't sure if I was supposed to.

"Hey, so I've been working on something for you." I figured it was as good a time as any to bring it up, giving her a soft kiss before heading back to my desk.

I still wasn't sure on the design, but I'd drawn and redrawn the same concept at least thirty times so it was definitely where my head was at.

I grabbed the latest version, taking it back to my chair and handing it to Kitty. "So usually with a tattoo, I like to consult the client first. But the more I thought about you, I figured this was the way to go."

Her eyes widened as she looked at my sketch, the color hopefully showing her what it would look like on her skin. I wasn't sure she'd even dig it—her previous piece an art painting done by someone else—but I wanted to give her something no one else would have.

She didn't speak, which didn't tell me much, looking at the picture like she was trying to commit it to memory.

"If you hate it, we can change it." My nerves started to get the better of me, thinking it was probably not her style.

She shook her head and grabbed my arm. "Are you kidding? It's beautiful, Dallas. It looks so real."

"It will look better on your hip, that's where I'd like to put it if you'd let me." My hand touched the spot I'd imagined tattooing at least a thousand times, holding it there and hoping she'd say yes.

"Yes, a million times, yes." She threw her arms around me and kissed me. "I love it, and you so much."

I tilted my head to the chair and got out a couple of towels, and handed them to her. "Take off your skirt and your underwear and lay back on my chair."

She nodded, not bothering to take any more time to think about it and lowered the zipper at her back. The material dropped to the floor, revealing a pair of barely-there panties that I'd preferred to take off with my teeth.

I didn't though, keeping it as professional as I knew how, watching her strip for me. My dick knew it wasn't going to be involved but got hard all the same; the idea of her letting me mark her skin for eternity almost hotter than sex at that moment.

I covered the chair with another towel and directed her to lie down. I wasn't usually around for that part, letting the client get themselves situated, but with Kitty, I wasn't missing a second.

She covered herself with the towel, leaving her right hip exposed as she turned to the side. God, she was beautiful—everything about her so freaking stunning I was almost scared to mess with the perfection. But I made a silent promise to her and to myself that my addition would be worthy of her.

Having been prepped for another tattoo entirely, I dropped a soft kiss on her forehead and walked over to get my machines and colors ready. Kitty watched as I got the design copied onto transfer paper and carried everything back to my station.

I gave myself permission to look at her one last time before I started, knowing that once I'd drawn the first line, all my concentration would have to be there. She smiled, resting her arm above her head as I went to pick up my machine.

"Shit." I stopped the buzzing from my hand and put it down. "I almost forgot."

With a grin, I rolled over to my desk and snagged my *Beats*, rolling back to Kitty in my chair. "I promised you could listened to my play list when I did this, and I'm a man of my word." I covered her ears with my headphones before pulling out my phone from my pocket and hitting play.

Her body eased back into the chair, her grin widening as the music started. I wasn't exactly sure what track was playing, but she closed her eyes as her head rested against the leather.

Ignoring the most beautiful woman I'd ever seen was not going to be easy, so instead I focused on her hip and told myself if I fucked it up I'd never forgive myself. That, and I'd offer to tattoo every tramp stamp and tribal armband that walked through the door for the next three years. There wasn't a chance she wasn't getting my best work.

After taking off the transfer, I started with the outline, the heavy black line staining her skin. I moved with intention and precision, careful not to overwork the skin or blow out a line, wanting every single one of those babies to be rock solid and as flawless as the woman wearing them.

Kitty didn't move, the perfect canvas, not even twitching as the time ticked away.

There was a knock at the door, but I didn't yell to *"come in"* like I usually did, instead I made sure Kitty was properly covered before giving the okay.

Josh walked in, shutting the door behind him as he strode over to where we were. He clearly was expecting something else when he'd opened the door and looked surprised that I was working. But whatever smartass remarks he might have had were kept to himself as he looked down at Kitty's hip and upper thigh.

"Wow, those lines are insane, D. It's going to look crazy good when you add the color."

Kitty noticed Josh but didn't give him more than a quick smile before resting her head back down. She knew the drill, moving as little as possible until it was done. She didn't even cheat and try and snatch a quick look, being the model client I knew she would be as she let me do my thing.

"Thanks, man. I want it to be perfect."

Not big on chatting when I was working, I went back to what I was doing and started filling in with color. Bright pops of reds, greens, blues and yellows started to give it more life.

I didn't even notice when Josh left, too caught up on what I was doing to realize he'd stopped watching and left us alone. As far as I was concerned we were in our own world so it didn't matter who was standing around.

Five and half hours had passed when I finally put my machine down and looked at the final piece. It couldn't have been finished a minute sooner, every last second needed to add every last bit of detail I'd seen in my head. And when I wiped away the excess color and took a step back to look, it was probably one of the best tattoos I'd ever done.

"Are you finished?" Kitty opened her eyes, pulling the headphones from her ears. "I'm dying to see."

I nodded, shooting her a grin. "Just let me finish cleaning it up."

She might have been still while the needle was at her skin but she couldn't stop wriggling as I washed the area and patted it dry. She wasn't the only one who was getting impatient, my hand working as quickly as I could so I could show her.

"Okay, baby, you can look." I rose to my feet and watched as she twisted to see. Her eyes lit up as she saw it, dropping her fingers to touch the freshly inked skin.

Not able to see it in its entirety, she jumped to her feet and walked to my full-length mirror. She'd ditched the towel, oblivious she was half naked as she looked at herself in the mirror.

Hopefully Josh didn't decide to come back and check on my progress, not sure I could be held responsible for my actions if he saw Kitty naked. But lucky for everyone the door stayed closed and no one got to see her but me.

"It's amazing." She turned, checking it out from every angle. "It's just so beautiful."

On her hip and upper thigh were three oriental lilies. They

were bright and vibrant, each of them a different color. I'd shaded them so they looked 3D, the purple dragonfly I'd added above the center looking like he was midflight. I added a string of pearls snaking between each flower, careful to make each circle just right. And instead of a traditional clasp like you'd find on a necklace, I finished the end with a tiny dragonfly trinket.

"I'm glad you like it."

Her finger ghosted above our little purple friend and smiled. "I would have thought you'd have drawn a bird."

"Not special enough, and there wasn't a chance in hell I was giving you a butterfly. You needed something unique, something exactly like you."

I knew I was in love with Kitty, I had already accepted that.

What I didn't know—and I found out at that exact moment—was just how much.

And, man, I was so far gone.

I'd inked her skin.

But she'd stamped my heart.

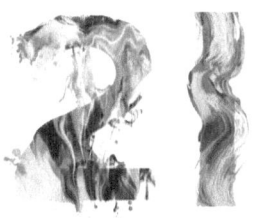

KITTY

WHEN I WENT TO SEE Dallas, I hadn't planned to get a tattoo.

I just needed to be around someone who cared and understood me so I could talk it out. And I'd done that; he'd listened and hadn't done what most guys did and attempt to fix it. I didn't expect anyone to *fix it*, maybe it—and me—were just unfixable.

But he didn't seem to care about the mess I apparently was.

No, he took everything I said and somehow managed to turn it around and tell me how awesome I was. Like a magic trick, he'd pulled an ace of spades out of his sleeve. And right when I thought he couldn't do or say anything else to make me feel better, he showed me the drawing he'd been working on.

It was stunning—so colorful and beautiful, and feminine without being too over the top girlie. It's the right mix of everything that I loved, and that he drew it especially for me, made my heart squeeze.

So when he told me to take off my clothes and get into the chair, that was exactly what I did.

I'd always been impulsive, so why bother to stop?

And most of all, I *trusted* him. Which was saying something since I wasn't exactly sure who else I included in that list.

I couldn't stop staring at his beautiful work. The oriental lilies were so realistic I swear I could almost smell them, and that charming little dragonfly which looked like it was about to fly away.

"Babe, as much as I'm enjoying the view, I think you should probably get dressed." He handed me my skirt and underwear.

It hadn't even occurred to me that I'd been standing there naked, not that I cared, the beautiful flowers and dragonfly worth showing off.

"Probably." I grinned, slipping on my panties but stopping when I got to the skirt. "It's so beautiful, I just want to look at it a little longer."

His hand slid up my leg, resting on my hip. "You're beautiful." He smiled at me in the mirror.

After I insisted he take a million photos for me with his phone, he covered the tattoo and I finally put on my skirt. Even though I could no longer see it, my skin tingled, still sensitive even though it was covered.

"I'm probably going to spend the rest of the day naked, just so I can keep looking at it," I warned, turning to face him.

"And this is a problem how?" he asked, kissing me.

My hands wrapped around his neck and he deepened the kiss, and it was easy to believe that everything was fine. That whatever problems that did exist weren't ours, and all was perfect in our world.

"I've been dying to do that for hours." He chuckled. *"Hours."*

He edged me back to his chair, my ass dropping to the soft surface as he lowered himself and took my mouth like he meant it.

"If this was the plan all along, why did you tell me to get dressed?" I laughed, my hands wandering under his T-shirt and touching his hard abs.

I was positive if my fingers went in the other direction I'd find a different kind of *hard*, and that excited me too. I loved that I drove him just as crazy as he drove me.

"I'm seriously thinking about it." He pulled away, biting my bottom lip and teasing it with his teeth. "But Josh will kill me, and I already owe him for rescheduling the clients I was supposed to be doing today."

"Oh no. Dallas, I'm sorry. " I sat up in a rush, realizing how much he would have had to rearrange just to have spent that time with me. I didn't even think, or offer to come back later.

His finger rested on my lips as he shook his head. "Don't. Don't apologize for any of it. I don't want you to even think about it. You need me, you tell me and I'm there, Kitty. Not only when I have time—*I'll make time*—always."

He was so incredibly sweet, and I was so lucky to have him, and I swore to God that I would do whatever it took to make sure I didn't screw it up.

Not him.

I just couldn't lose him.

"What's wrong?" He tilted my head sensing my change in mood.

"I'm worried I'm going to fuck this up," I answered honestly. "I'm not going to lie to you, Dallas. I'm really in love with you, and I'm worried—"

"Kitty." He said my name and stopped me right there. "I can't promise you that one or both of us isn't going to mess up. Probably more so me, because let's face it, this is probably the first real relationship I've ever been in. I won't remember the date we met, or our first kiss, and I suuuuuuck at putting the toilet seat down. But I can promise you that nothing you do is going to change how I feel. And if you can make me the same promise—that we'll deal with all that other stuff as it happens—then there is honestly nothing to worry about."

I wasn't sure if I wanted to cry or laugh and hug the hell out of him. All I knew was that I'd never let him go. "For someone who hasn't done this before, you're pretty good at it."

"I'm a fast learner."

He was right about that.

"Well, since you already owe Josh for the time, can we sneak out of here and go home?" It was selfish to ask, but I knew if I went home by myself, I'd obsess about things I couldn't change. And I didn't want to think about anything but him.

"Let me get my keys."

✧

HE WAS BOTH HARD AND gentle, screwing me up against the wall of my apartment the minute we got home and then making love to me on the bed later. I loved it both ways, losing my mind with him when he was out of control, but pretty fond of his softness too.

I ignored all calls and we stayed in my apartment the whole night. Making love, having sex, and eating badly cooked food.

It was perfect.

And the next morning when my alarm went off, I didn't immediately want to puke. Sure, I may no longer have a job, but either way I needed to go in and find out. Besides, I could always help Josh and Dallas at the shop, they had *yet* to hire someone to handle their front desk and it was starting to get ridiculous.

"You want me to drive you." Dallas pulled me against him, both of us still wet from the shower. "Josh never expects me there before eleven anyway, I could take you and still be back in time."

"No, but thank you. You have done way too much already." I kissed his lips softly before heading to my wardrobe and trying to pick out a dress. *What does one wear when they stormed out of their office the day before and possibly resigned?* There wasn't a section for that at Bloomingdale's that was for sure.

I settled on a purple dress with black trim that reminded me of my dragonfly, and with a little time on hair and makeup, I was ready sooner than I'd planned.

Dallas dressed in the same clothes he wore the day before, and I made a mental note to clear out some closet space for him later that day. He'd never once complained about not having his things, but I wanted to give him room to leave some things at my place for when he was here. We hadn't really spoken about it but since I didn't see us spending a lot of nights alone, I figured it was a safe bet.

He kissed my hand and walked me to his car, and even though I told him it was unnecessary, he drove me to the subway station. I'm sure he wanted to come with me—the look of hesitation all over his face before he left—but it was something I was going to have to do alone.

I knew I would be okay, especially when I had one hell of a safety net.

There was no hesitation when I got to my building, pressing the button for my floor and heading right to my office. I didn't ask questions, or go see Garrett, taking a seat at my desk and turning on my computer.

Garrett's door was closed and I could hear talking so whatever we needed to discuss would have to wait. The last thing I wanted was to go in there all guns blazing when they—whoever was in there with him—were potentially discussing my exit. That would be awkward. Instead, I'd wait and have our meeting on my terms. When I was ready.

It had been an hour when the first knock came at my door. I was surprised I'd managed to be there that long without everyone noticing. But it seemed I wasn't the only one who had been preoccupied that morning.

"Oh my God!" Linda, one of the PA's on my floor came

bursting in. "Where have you been? Yesterday was an entire shit show! You should have seen it, O'Shea and Crisp were conspiring to get Garrett fired."

Motive was something I hadn't been able to work out. I knew there were people who weren't fond of my boss, but he'd earned his place honestly. And while he'd delegated duties recently, he was still a very smart and shrewd businessman. I didn't think for a second he'd gone soft, maybe bored, but he wasn't the kind of man you should underestimate.

I shrugged, pretending I knew nothing about it. "Really? I should probably go see Garrett and find out what happened. What else do you know?"

Linda glanced around, looking to see if there was anyone else to hear. "They got this hot Wall Street lawyer in on it, and they were going to make it look like Garrett had lost the money. Then when he was gone, they were going to pump the money back in like a profit so they had guaranteed growth for the quarter. How sneaky is that? And since the money wasn't actually taken they're not at risk for any serious crimes. Not that it isn't questionable, but really it was sort of smart."

"I'm sure they'll both be glad to hear that, Linda." Garrett's voice came from behind her. I wasn't sure how long he'd been standing there, but he'd obviously caught enough. "You want to return to your desk? Or would a visit to HR be better?"

"Sorry, Mr. Brown." Her eyes flooded with panic as she quickly waved goodbye and disappeared.

He shook his head but didn't look as annoyed as I'd thought he'd be, shutting the door and taking a seat opposite me for only the second time since I'd started working for him.

"Well that was the condensed version, mine is slightly longer and not as complimentary. I wasn't even sure you'd be joining us this morning to be honest."

"I wasn't going to walk out and leave you hanging, Garrett," I admitted, not wanting my time at the firm to be reduced to office gossip, speculating on my departure under suspicious circumstances.

"Good, then let's set a scenario where you don't leave at all."

"Garrett." I took a breath, about to launch into the thousand reasons why things couldn't stay the same when he cut me off.

"I know, I took advantage of you and your willingness to step up. And I know I should have been doing more than just paying you. I was/am bored, so I figured if you were happy to do it then what was the harm. So let me finish and then you can decide what you want to do. And I can't promise I'm not going to try and make you stay, but whatever choice you do make, I'll respect."

"Okay," I agreed, wanting to at least hear him out.

I'd done a lot of growing in the last couple of weeks and part of that was not to assume I knew what other people wanted. I nodded, urging him to continue.

"Matthew had seniority but O'Shea had the ambition. They figured between the two of them they'd take me out and convince Braxton to appoint Matthew as CEO and O'Shea as COO. They've been sniffing around for a while, but I didn't take the risk seriously so they knew I was vulnerable. They'd assumed I wouldn't check the figures, or if you did, you wouldn't be smart enough to see something was off. Of course they were right about me, but completely wrong about you. I think a lot of people have been wrong about you, including the woman who claimed to be your *friend*."

He didn't need to elaborate. I already knew he meant Lani, probably overhearing her choice words for me yesterday.

"So, they decided to play a fun shell game with some money. Deciding that as long as no one took it and it was returned, there could be no criminal charges, and Mr. Easton was the attorney they employed to ensure that was the case. He specializes in corporate law, knows all the loopholes, but the idiots paid him out of the company funds. Funnily enough, they both decided to hand in their resignations effective immediately."

"Did he . . . was I part of it?" I swallowed, not even sure if he had an answer for me.

I didn't want to believe that I'd been so blind that I couldn't see when someone was using me, but it wouldn't have been the first time. And considering how devious their plan had been it wouldn't have surprised me that they'd intended to use Justin against me. As Lani had so eloquently pointed out, so many people thought I was a whore. Surely I wouldn't be able to resist a man who was smart and successful, throwing himself at me?

Ugh.

"From what we can ascertain, no. He claims to have not known who you worked for until you told him during your first . . ." He waved his hand in the air. "Whatever. So either Mr. Easton is far more intelligent than we're giving him credit for or he honestly didn't know. I do think he wouldn't risk disbarment by involving himself in something as messy as corporate espionage. They weren't paying him enough for that."

Well that was a small comfort; I hadn't *totally* been blind. And I had felt there was something off about him from the start, so my instincts were there even if I didn't always listen to them.

"So what happens now?" I asked, the conspiracy revealed but not the resolution.

"Braxton made it very clear that he wouldn't tolerate anyone who wasn't a team player. My complacency allowed it to happen, and that will stop. I'm taking a week off starting the end of today and when I come back, I'll be ready to be the CEO I haven't been for a long time. He was kind enough to not say it in front of the staff, but they are aware there are big changes happening and any-one not on board can find their own way out the door."

"Is Lani still here?" I asked.

I didn't want to uphold my promise to Cameron that she'd keep her job and part of me felt like I shouldn't care. No one would blame me for defaulting on my word especially when she'd been so cruel with hers. But, being mean with intention wasn't in my make up, and I wouldn't allow myself to sink to her level.

"Lani is still employed and will be reassigned. I figured that would be something you would want to do." He straightened his tie and smiled.

I stared at him blankly. "Me? Why would I do that?"

While I appreciated the gesture, an executive assistant didn't have authority to assign or reassign roles in the company. And as much as I would have loved to do to her what I'd done to Oliver, I thought I'd made it clear that I wasn't doing Garrett's job for him anymore.

Even if I was *really* tempted to do that one last thing. Think of it as severance payment for a job well done.

"Well, Kitty, the reason *you* would do that is because it is one of your duties in your new role as chief operations officer. That is assuming you accept the promotion."

"But I'm not—" *qualified*, I finished in my head. But I stopped myself from saying it out loud. The truth was I *didn't* have a business degree from an Ivy League school, but that was all I didn't have. I'd been with the company since I'd graduated college, working my way up by sheer determination, learning as I went. I was hard working and dedicated, and knew more about the company than most senior level executives. So while it made no sense on paper, it made all kinds of sense in real life. And I wasn't going to sabotage the opportunity because someone else might think I was lacking.

"Yes, I'm accepting the promotion," I said quickly in case he changed his mind. "Does Braxton know?"

Garrett laughed, leaning back in his chair. "Who do you think came up with it? As much as I would like to take the credit, it was his idea. He's rather fond of self-made people, which was why he'd hired *me* in the first place. I had suggested we make you an office executive and he decided to go one better. His name is on the letterhead so I figured I'd let him have that one. And I figured with you working beside me instead of below me, you'd be able to kick my ass when I need it. See if we can't bring Braxton Hill into a new era of greatness."

"No morale building dinners at anyone's house," I warned, glad I'd never have to suffer through another of O'Shea's.

Garrett stood, buttoning up his jacket. "On that we can agree. Take a minute or two and let it all sink in, then come see us in the boardroom. Braxton has HR working on a new contract for you as we speak, and I'm sure he'll want to tell you in his own way too."

"If I've just agreed, how can HR already be working on my new contract?" I joined him on my feet and eyed him suspiciously. "What happened to *it would be my choice and you'd respect it either way?*"

"Kitty, as I told you before, a lot of people underestimate you, but I'm not one of them. You've been doing the job for months and it was time we gave you the title. But . . ." He smirked. "If you don't want it, I can go ahead and tell HR—"

"Nothing, you will tell them nothing." I pointed my finger accusingly at the man who, up until a few minutes ago, had been my boss. "I want this."

"As you should. Now I'm going to head to the boardroom and we'll see you in there in the next few minutes." He tipped his head goodbye and walked out of my office.

Probably wasn't going to be my office for much longer, I might even have an assistant of my own. I knew who it *wasn't* going to be. While I might be willing to forgive Lani, I sure as hell wouldn't be forgetting.

I picked up the phone and scrolled to Dallas's name. I was sure my parents and sister were going to be out-of-their-mind proud, but I had to tell him first.

"Hey baby." He answered immediately like he'd been waiting for my call. "Everything okay? You need anything?"

He didn't say, *"Do you need me to come down there and straighten someone out,"* but I could read between the lines. I loved that he let me do it my way, even if I'd have enjoyed watching him walking into work and starting a fire of his own.

We were quite a pair the two of us.

And I wasn't ever going to forget it.

"Everything is fantastic." I smiled into the phone. "I just wish you were standing in front of me so I could see your face when I tell you, but the phone will have to do."

"Or you can open the door and let me in. Pretty sure the people on your floor have already called security though." He laughed into the phone.

My butt rose off the chair and raced to my door, yanking it open. There on the other side was Dallas with his phone to his ear.

"I'm not here because I didn't think you could do this on your own." He lowered his phone. "But because traffic in Manhattan is a fucking nightmare and if you needed me it would take too long."

"I don't care why, just come in here and hug me." I pulled him into my office and closed the door. "Is Josh going to be pissed you are blowing off work again?" I kissed him only being slightly worried about his job.

"He's the one who told me to get my ass here in the first place. I told you, I'm not that smart." He chuckled against my mouth. "I am going to be pulling some long ass days for about a week or two, so we'll have to work around that."

"Well, I might be pulling some long ass days myself." I laughed back, standing up proudly. "Pretty sure as the new COO, I'm going to be expected to put in a few more hours."

"COO? I'm not great with acronyms, babe."

"It means I'm one of the bosses. Not like the big boss, but pretty fucking important." It was over-simplifying it, but I'm sure I'd have fun later telling Dallas all about it.

"Pretty fucking important sounds about right." He brushed his mouth up against mine. "Means if I fuck you on your desk, you can't get in trouble, right?"

I liked the way he was thinking.

But it would have to wait. "Let's leave that until I get my new desk and office. I have a meeting I need to get to."

He chuckled. "Fine, ruin all the fun, Kitty. But if this promotion turns you into one of *them*, we'll be having words."

"I promise you, I will never be one of them. And desk sex in my new office is at the top of my agenda," I promised, absolutely committed to it as my first order of business.

He kissed me, but he didn't linger, tearing his mouth away too soon as he squeezed my ass. "Good. Go give them hell, babe. I'll be at home waiting for you."

It was the first time any man had said that to me and I'd wanted to hear it.

And I couldn't wait to get home to him.

KITTY

EVEN THOUGH I'D SIGNED MY contract, it was hard to believe I was the new COO at Braxton Hill. I'd heard snickers in the halls, wondering whose cock I'd sucked for the promotion, with others complaining I didn't have the necessary résumé to be put in the position.

It might have bothered me if I'd had the time, but I was going to be too busy proving what a badass I was. So they could take all their innuendo, suspicions and speculation and shove it. They would eventually see exactly why I was promoted, and if they didn't—who the hell cared.

I'd gone back to my office and was disappointed to find it empty. I knew Dallas had to get back to work—as did I—but I missed having him there, able to kiss and hug him as I wanted. It was definitely going to be difficult with both of us so busy, but I didn't doubt for a second we'd make it work.

Between the promotion and Dallas, I didn't think there was anything that could wipe the smile off my face. That was until there was a knock at my door and Lani walked in.

"You have every right to hate me, but please give me a second."

She raised her hands defensively before I'd even had a chance to say a word. "I shouldn't have said that to you, but you have to admit it looked suspicious."

A lot of people felt that as long as you gave an apology, it was all good. Or that if you somehow rationalized your actions that it excused bad behavior.

I'd even done it myself.

But.

I wouldn't accept it anymore.

"It might help me believe you're sorry if you meant it. But the truth is, even now you believe you were justified." I shook my head, no longer wondering why I'd made such shitty relationship choices. "No matter what it looked like, Lani, I never would have slept with Cameron. You were my friend, and I don't do that to friends. And yes, you can go ahead and throw the mistakes I've made in the past in my face if it makes you feel better, but I didn't know at the time. I have never willingly been involved with someone else's infidelity. And maybe I was too trusting, and I chose to see the good in people instead of the bad, but that doesn't make me a bad person."

Her eyes got watery, realizing her apology wasn't going to be as easy as planned. "Kitty, it's just that you look like you do, and all the guys—"

"No." I stopped her, not allowing her to use what I did or looked like to excuse *her* behavior. "It was *you*, it was *your* choice, Lani. And personally, if you think Cameron would cheat on you so easily then there is a whole lot wrong in your relationship that has nothing to do with me."

She sobbed quietly and I hated I didn't know if it was for real. I wanted to believe that she was sorry, but I wasn't sure. Too many times I had played the sucker, and I deserved better. "If Eve was willing to forgive you for actually being with Oliver, surely you can forgive me."

And there it was.

Proof that it was more about her than it would ever be about me.

She wanted absolution, not to make things right. For me to give her the words so she could sleep better at night for trying to tear me down for no reason at all. And as good as my heart was, and as much as I would have liked to, it was something I didn't want to give her.

"Lani, maybe one day I will. And maybe I won't, I honestly don't know. But either way we're going to work together and you are going to realize that regardless of my personal feelings I will support you. Why? Because you are good at what you do. And that's all that matters between these four walls. Not who you sleep with, how you dress or what you look like. I hope you'll pay me the same respect."

It felt good to say it out loud and to mean it, and to believe it myself.

"Honestly, I'm sorry."

This time her apology didn't come with a "but," and I felt that was progress.

"Thank you." I nodded my head and gave her a small smile. "You'll be reassigned next week but for today you can help out Martha."

She'd been hoping for more, but she knew she wasn't going to get it. "Okay, thanks. Talk to you later." She left, leaving me in my office alone.

I turned around and looked at the space and felt a sense of warmth wash over my body. I couldn't remember a time when everything had been so right in my world or when I'd been so incredibly happy.

I used to think it wasn't possible for me to have it all. And then

I found out the only obstacle in my way was me.

eleep

DALLAS

"YOU KNOW, ALL THIS BEING nice to me is making me a little nervous." I handed Josh his beer. "Giving me time off, closing the shop early—how do I know aliens didn't take over your body and this is some alternate Josh?"

Josh took a sip from his bottle. "Guess you'll just have to wonder."

Eve didn't seem to have the same concerns, his girlfriend putting her arms around him like he couldn't be an imposter and shooting me a grin. "When's the guest of honor getting here? I can't wait to congratulate her."

While I'd promised Kitty to be waiting at home, I decided she needed more than just a lame celebration at home. Nothing huge because I sucked at organizing, but a few drinks with our friends was definitely in the cards.

I'd messaged her to let her know, but all I'd gotten was a thumbs up emoji followed by an *I love you*. So, she was either totally fine with it and busy or she was willing to humor me. I guess we'd find out which when she finally got here.

"Not sure, soon I hope." I checked the time, noticing it was close to nine.

I should have gone into the city and given her a ride. I didn't care how much she liked taking that goddamn subway; I hated the idea of her riding it at night. Loving someone wasn't all orgasms and cooking shitty dinners, worrying about them came as a package deal. And at the moment, that was the feeling that was edging up my neck.

"I see her." Eve gave my arm a shake. "She's at the door."

Even without being told, I knew when Kitty entered a room. Something inside me changed, like I could breathe a little easier and the world made more sense.

And seeing her smile, that took me into a whole new level of happiness.

Her face was beaming as she strode through the front door and found us congregated around the bar. I could tell just from looking at her, her day had been awesome, and if I had anything to do with it, her night was going to be pretty spectacular too.

"Hi." She waved and smiled to everyone, saving her best for me. "Hope you haven't been waiting long, there was a ton of stuff I needed to go through with my old boss before he took off for vacation."

"You are worth the wait," I answered for everyone, not giving a shit whether or not they had a problem with it. Then I did what I'd been dying to do for hours and kissed her.

"Let your woman breathe, Dallas," Josh called from behind us.

And just to show him how awesome I was at multitasking, I flipped him off while I continued to kiss her.

Maybe the bar had been a bad idea, my hands grabbing her ass and pulling her closer. God, I loved how she felt in my hands, every single inch of her perfect—like she'd been made just for me. And if by some miracle she couldn't *feel* the rod in my pants, she was going to see it very soon as the bastard got bigger.

"Uh-hmm." Mason cleared his throat, totally raining on my parade.

Kitty pulled away, her lips leaving mine to give the bastard attention he didn't deserve, smiling as he introduced himself.

"I'm Mason, remember? We met briefly at the shop." He stuck out his hand with a grin I did like.

"Of course I remember. It's nice to see you again, how are you settling in?" She returned his shake but stayed close by me, her other hand snaked around my waist. I liked it there and was already thinking up strategies to keep it there most of the night. Not sure where she'd put those handcuffs, but they'd be useful if I had them.

Eve got Kitty a drink and we moved to a booth. While I wasn't a fan—preferring to sit at the bar—it was hard to have a conversation with the four others in the group without constantly getting whiplash.

So, as I sat back with my woman tucked up beside me, Kitty told the rest of them all about her new job.

I could listen to her talk for hours; I didn't even care what she said. I just wanted to know everything, never getting sick of hearing her voice.

OOOOOOOOOOOOOHHHHHHHHHHH.

The big freaking smile spread across my face as the realization hit me; *that* was what Mason had been talking about.

I hadn't even needed the goddamn list, the *getting to know her* happening all by itself. That was lucky actually because I was almost positive I'd washed the jeans I'd stuffed the stupid list into.

"Kitty, I need you for a minute." I shuffled out of the fucking booth and wrapped my hand around hers. "Be right back, guys, this is kind of an emergency."

"Dallas, what's wrong." Kitty laughed as I pulled her to her feet. "Are you okay?"

"Yep, just come with me." I tipped my chin to Josh who rolled his eyes but knew better than to ask questions. Mason and Eve looked like they didn't have a clue, which was fine by me.

Without bothering to explain, I pulled Kitty down the hall. She was giggling, asking me where we were going but followed me all the same. Man, I loved that about her, she always seemed up for anything and I guess I was going to find out how far she was willing to go.

Bricks and Mortar was one of my favorite bars in Queens, but there was no way I was taking her into the bathroom. I barely liked to take a piss in that place and even then I made sure I made no contact with the walls. But I knew they had a supply room toward the back, all I had to do was hope it was unlocked.

Lucky for us management was trusting—or stupid, I didn't care which—and all it took was a twist of my wrist and we were in.

"Is there a reason why we're in a closet?" She looked around the walls, as I hit the light and closed the door. Closet was a more accurate description. The walls were tiled floor to roof, with a big padlock securing a metal locker up near a sink. But other than that, the place looked pretty good, cleaner than the bathroom for sure.

"We need to have sex." I pushed her up against the wall and kissed her mouth, my hand skating underneath her hem.

She moaned in my mouth and grabbed my cock. "Thank God, I thought I was going to have to wait until we got home."

Her fingers got busy on my zipper, pulling out my dick and giving it a stroke while I bunched up the bottom of her dress and pushed aside her panties. She was already wet, coating my finger as I plunged first one and then two in, while my thumb played with her clit.

I was a man who prided himself on foreplay, liking the first orgasm I got from Kitty to be courtesy of my mouth or my hand, but it was one time I couldn't wait. My lips moved south as my other hand palmed her tit, and if there was ever a time I could have used an extra set of arms, that would have been it.

Her hands were magic, jerking me off with a steady rhythm that was about a minute or two from making me come. I gritted my teeth, dropping my hand to hers and stopping her.

"Slow or fast?" I asked her, reaching into my pocket and pulling out a condom. "You'll still be getting both when I eventually get you home, but for right now, it's the lady's choice."

There was no way I wasn't going to take her home and spend hours worshiping her body. Slow, fast, and everything in between, but as I stood there—rolling on a rubber with my dick in my hand—I didn't care which, as long as I got to be inside of her.

"Fast." She grabbed my shaft and pulled me toward her.

"Fast it is."

I slammed into her, filling her with one thrust as she cried out my name, gripping my shoulders as I pushed her against the wall. Her pussy was vise-like tight, needing a minute to adjust as I pulled out and slammed back in.

"Jesus," she screamed out, pushing up my T-shirt to play with the bars in my nipples. "That feels so good."

"Yeah, it feels pretty fucking awesome for me too." I thrust in again, hooking her leg against my hip to get in deeper.

Man, I liked fucking her. I loved watching her come unhinged as I banged her against the wall. I loved that we could do slow against a mattress too and neither of them felt like a compromise.

Most of all, I loved her.

She reached down between us and fingered her clit, letting me pound her as I felt her core tighten.

It was good, my balls aching with the need to come as she came apart while I was inside of her. I wanted to hold on, but I couldn't, exploding with a shout as each one of her contractions milked my dick.

"Kitty." I leant down and kissed her, holding her against me as both of us rode out the wave. "I love you."

"Love you too," she panted, kissing me back just as fiercely.

I groaned, looking around at the shitty closet. "I hate we have to go back and be social."

"You're such a beast." She pushed lightly against my chest. "They're our friends."

She was right about that, they were and while I was perfectly okay with being rude, I knew that wasn't her style. I pulled out of her, making sure she was steady before letting go. She righted her dress and adjusted her panties while I took care of the condom.

The janitor was going to get a nice surprise when he checked the trash, but other than that no harm done.

Kitty was grinning when I turned back around, her hands on her hips like she knew something I didn't.

"What?" I asked, wanting to know the secret too.

She waved her finger at me, giggling as she spoke. "Did you want to have sex with me because you couldn't wait a second longer? *Or* did you suddenly realize how much better we know each other and wanted to continue to test out Mason's theory?"

"Yes." I nodded, not bothering to lie. What would be the point, she was way smarter than me anyway and would totally figure it out.

She popped an eyebrow, the grin still there *"Yes* to which?"

"To both." I grinned back, pulling her into a hug. "Yes, I needed to have sex with you because I'd wanted to all day, and yeah, I wanted to see if his theory held water."

"And?" She tilted her head waiting for an answer.

I laughed, and gave her the only reply I could. "And, I was too busy having the best sex of my life to worry about collecting data. We're going to have to do it a few more times just to be sure."

"I like this plan."

"Jesus, Dallas!" The door swung open, Ken the dude who owned the bar looking at us both. "You better not be fucking in here!"

"Come on, man," I scoffed, waving my hands between us and showing him we were both still clothed. "We're not freaking animals. I just needed somewhere private for a minute to have a conversation with my girl."

He looked at us suspiciously but bought it hook, line and sinker. "Yeah, yeah. Sorry." He tipped his head to Kitty. "But this is for staff only, you can't be in here, even to talk."

Kitty turned on the charm apologizing for any inconvenience before dragging me out. "You are going right to hell." She threw her head back and laughed.

"No I'm not, Holly from the drycleaner says she's gonna save me. And if it all goes shit, well at least you'll have company." I puffed out my chest proudly.

She grabbed my hand and held it to her heart. "Very true."

We walked back to the table and re-took our seats, listening in as Eve told Mason all about her gallery.

Josh had probably guessed what I'd been up to but was too classy to say anything, hiding the grin behind his beer as Kitty and I joined in the conversation.

I waited until Kitty was talking to Eve about something when I yanked on Mason's arm and whispered in his ear.

"Hey, if I didn't say so before, thanks for the advice."

He turned, whipping around so fast you'd think I'd told him I wanted to lick his balls. "What did you say?"

"Relax," I laughed, keeping my voice low. "I can admit when I'm wrong, celibate. Getting to know a woman is by far the best thing ever."

He nodded, lowering his voice too. "Hey thanks, Dallas. I'm glad it worked out for you. But I told you, I'm not celibate."

"Whatever, dude, it's your dick, your business." I held out my fist for a bump. He shook his head, but bumped it, and tuned back into the conversation.

And as I looked at my friends and Kitty, something else occurred to me. Thankfully not the kind of realization that needed me to go have sex with Kitty again because even I knew that would be pushing my luck. But what I came to figure was I'd actively been avoiding relationships my whole freaking life.

Never had a proper girlfriend and never wanted one.

And I didn't for a second regret it.

Because it meant what I had with Kitty was brand new, as fucking hilarious as it was, I was a virgin. And it had been a very long time since I'd been one of those. Hell, I was almost giddy with the excitement of it all, about doing it with her and never having shared it with anyone else.

Sometimes it's good to play the field, to screw around, to be the "whore."

Because when you find that one person you want to do forever with, you *know* with one hundred percent certainty.

Zero doubts.

She was my one.

And I was all in.

EPILOGUE

DALLAS

IT WAS LATE AND I was still at the shop.

But with Josh on his honeymoon, we were down one, and I was trying to pick up the slack. I didn't want the first time he trusted me to keep the business running, for it to fall into a pile of shit.

"Hey Dallas, I'm done. You want me to stick around?" Bec rapped at my door, folding her arms across her chest. "Mason is cleaning up his room and then he's done too."

Pretty sure they built the Empire State Building in less time than it took us to get a front desk person, but it had eventually happened. Bec had dropped out of NYU but could organize the shop like no other. Even got us on a full computer system, retiring Josh's appointment book of death. She wasn't only efficient and funny, but could tell a massive biker to sit his ass down and wait his turn when needed to. They never expected it either, considering she was barely five-foot and looked like a goth princess.

"Nah, I'm just finishing up here and then heading home. Tell Mason I'll see him tomorrow too. No need for him to stay either."

"Thanks D, you're the best." She gave me a smile-wave combo and then disappeared down the hall. I had no doubt she'd be heading to Mason's room whether or not I'd given her a message.

Those two had been doing a lot of talking lately, and we all knew how that ended up.

Sneaky fuckers.

Just as long as they didn't screw in the rooms, because if I wasn't allowed to do that shit, neither was anyone else. Health inspectors had zero sense of humor, and there was no way I'd let those bastards risk my best friend's business.

Not on my watch.

I heard the two of them shuffle down the hall, laughing and *talking*, and I rolled my eyes. There'd been no noise from the front door lock engaging as they pulled it closed.

Goddamn it.

They'd both been so caught up in their freaking "conversation" they couldn't even remember to lock the fucking door. I swear they had no sense of responsibility at all, cursing under my breath as I got out of my chair to do the thing my fucking self.

Shit.

When did I turn into the most responsible person in the shop? Thank God Josh was coming back soon, not sure I'd survive under the pressure.

"Kitty!" I grabbed my chest almost having a heart attack when I rounded the corner and saw her in the hall. Not only had I thought I was alone but I'd assumed she still had a few hours left of work herself which was why I wasn't in any hurry to get home. "You scared the shit out of me. What are you doing here?"

"I missed you." She put her arms around me and lifted her head to kiss me. "We've both been working such crazy hours, I just need to tell you how much I love you."

"Well, you can go ahead and tell me as much as you want." I scooped her into my arms, forgetting all about the door, the lock or the irresponsible fuckers I worked with. None of it mattered.

I was just about to kiss her again when she stopped me, putting her hand to my chest and biting her lip like she was nervous. "Actually, there's another reason I'm here."

"Babe, whatever it is, tell me." I wrapped my fingers around her hand and brought it to my lips. "You know you can tell me anything."

"Okay." She nodded and took a deep breath, and then lowered herself to her knees.

"Wow, baby! You're going to give me a blowjob? You're the best girlfriend ever." My hand dropped to my fly, and unzipped. I'd been a little stressed so a hummer was more than a little welcomed. And man, did my woman know me.

Her hands reached up to mine, stopping me from pulling my dick out. "I'm trying to propose to you, Dallas." She huffed out a breath of frustration, her tone lacking any of the joy that usually accompanied sex. "I'm asking you to marry me."

"What the fuck?" My eyes got wide as I looked at her on her knees.

Jesus.

Freaking.

Christ.

The blowjob was a proposal?

"Kitty." I joined her on the floor, kneeling in front of her. "Baby, you cannot propose to me."

Her body stiffened, looking up at me from under her lashes. God, she was beautiful, so perfect in every single way, and even though I'd completely ruined what was probably supposed to be a special moment, she still wasn't mad. "Are you not ready? I know we haven't really spoken about it, but I love you and I want to be with you forever and—"

I held my hand up to her lips, shaking my head as the rest of her sentence got lost in my fingers. "I'm plenty ready. I love you, and I want to be with you forever too. I want you to be my wife." I took my hand away slowly and dug into my pocket. "And you can't propose to me because I want to propose to you."

I had the ring designed and had been carrying it around for the past two weeks, but could never find the right time. I wanted for the proposal to be something she'd be proud of, like those morons on Instagram with their fancy engagement videos that went viral. Not because I gave a shit, but because she deserved only the best. But as creative as I was on skin, I couldn't think of a way to ask that would be meaningful enough to do her justice. But seeing her on her knees wanting to ask me was the wakeup call I'd needed.

She never was and never would be about any of that shit.

Just me, and her, and our forever.

I pulled out the ring, the most perfect diamond I'd been able to find and set in an art deco platinum band. My girl was all about the classics, and I was going to give it to her.

"Kitty, will you marry me?" I slid on the ring and hoped to God I was putting it on the right finger.

She looked down at the ring, her beautiful green eyes brimming with tears. "Yes, yes. YES," she screamed, throwing her arms around me.

"Well, thank God for that." I laughed, kissing my fiancée for the first time.

She wiggled her finger and smiled. "I can't believe you had a ring, I had literally no idea you were going to propose. It's perfect by the way, I love it so much."

"Well, I had no idea *you* were going to propose," I laughed back. "I almost missed my chance." I pushed the hair out of her face and grinned. "So . . . um . . . I guess that blowjob is out of the question now, huh?"

She threw back her head and laughed before leveling me with a look. "Are you kidding? I'm going to give you the best blowjob you've ever had."

I was the luckiest man in the whole fucking world.

Fuck Instagram and a fancy engagement story.

I'd take my life without the filter every day of the week and twice on Sundays.

"Kitty." I hissed out her name as her hand went to my pants.

"Yeah, baby?"

I took a breath and blew it out. "I love you."

"I love you too, now go lock the door so we can defile the hall. It's out of the rooms so there's no violation to the health code."

I didn't know if she was right or not, but I didn't care.

I'd take whatever repercussions that followed. Just as long as I got to spend the rest of my life—and anything that happened after it—with the most amazing woman I'd ever known.

And it wasn't the ring that I'd put on her finger that guaranteed that.

It was what was in my heart.

THE END

To keep up to date with all T Gephart's news, appearances and releases, please subscribe to her mailing list. Link available on her website: *www. tgephart.com*

ACKNOWLEDGEMENTS

SPECIAL THANKS TO MY FAMILY—GEP, Jenna, Liam and Woodley. You are my safe place always, and accept me how I am.

Thank you to all my family (brothers, sister-in-laws and everyone else) AND the extended group of misfits whom I've chosen to be my family. I love you guys, thanks for being there and loving me and supporting me even if I am three buckets of crazy.

Thank you so much to the team at Brower Literary and Management—Kimberly, Aimee and Caroline.

Thank you to Nichole Strauss, from Insight Editing. This book was different from the last (and thank God for that) and it was good for it not to be as crazy. I'm so glad you get me, it's a pleasure to work with you.

MK and Dani! Thanks so much for your added insight. Lord knows I need extra eyes so I don't have someone in the wrong place LOL.

Thank you to Christine Borgford from Type A Formatting. Your work is brilliant as always, love working with you!

Thank you to the amazing Hang Le for another ridiculously good cover. Man, I know I shouldn't choose favorites but the ones you've done for this series are pretty freaking gorgeous. It was great seeing you in Kentucky and spending time with you.

Thank you to my amazing proofreaders Lisa B, Jackie R and Rosa! SO glad to have extra eyes picking up pesky typos and missed words.

Thank you to my author brethren. I have so much mad respect

for you guys—love you and all your work. Thank you so much for your friendship, support, love, and of course, your awesomeness. I was a reader first, and continue to be, and sometimes I need to pinch myself when I think about being able to call you friends.

A MASSIVE thanks to the bloggers, reviewers and promoters who read my insanity, promote it, review it, and share it with the world. I appreciate all the work you tirelessly do for every single release. Some of you have been with me from the start, some just new to the crazy but I am continually humbled by all of your support.

Thanks to KP, Jessica and everyone on the InkSlinger Team. Thank you for your continued support and promotion, and helping to make my releases be all they can be!

To Liz, MJ and Jillian at 1001 Dark Nights. Thank you for the love and support and all that you do. It's been amazing to be part of the family, and I have loved every single minute of it.

THANK YOU to the T Gephart Review Crew and Entourage. Thank you so much for all the love, support and sharing that you do. I love spending time with you guys and need to be in there more often. But I honestly appreciate everything you do for me. Review Crew—those shares and reviews are so awesome and really make a difference. Special thanks to Michelle Clay and Annette Brignac who have been rock stars!!

And lastly, a huge and heartfelt thank you goes to my readers. Thank you so very much for continuing to read and love my books. Some of you have been with me since Lexi, others have joined in either through Power Station or #1 Crush, but it doesn't matter how you got here other than you're here now. Thank you for reading, reviewing, sharing, and loving my stories. Your support means I get to continue doing what I love to do. SO thank you!

ABOUT THE AUTHOR

T GEPHART IS A USA Today and International bestselling author from Melbourne, Australia.

With an approach to life that is somewhat unconventional, she prefers to fly by the seat of her pants rather than adhere to some rigid roadmap. Her lack of "plan" has resulted in a rather interesting and eclectic resume, which reads more like the fiction she writes than an actual employment history. She'd tell you all about it, but the statute of limitations hasn't expired yet. But all those crazy twists and turns have led her to a career she loves—writing romantic comedy.

When she isn't filling pages with sassy and sexy characters with attitude, she's living her own reality show in the 'burbs of Melbourne with her American husband, two teenage children, and her fur child—Woodley.

She loves adventure, to laugh, travel, and strives to live her life to the fullest.

CONNECT WITH T

www.tgephart.com
Facebook
Goodreads
Twitter

BOOKS BY
THIS AUTHOR

The Lexi Series

Lexi

A Twist of Fate

Twisted Views: Fate's Companion

A Leap of Faith

A Time for Hope

The Power Station Series

High Strung

Crash Ride

Back Stage

The Black Addiction Series

Slide

Sticks

Stand

#1 Series

#1 Crush

#1 Player

#1 Rival

#1 Lie

#1 Muse

#1 Love (coming 2019)

Collision Series

Train Wreck

Car Crash

Standalones

The Fall

One-Night Stand-In (rereleasing soon)